A QUESTION
OF GHOSTS

What Reviewers Say About Lambda Literary Award Winner Cate Culpepper's Work

"Culpepper's writing style can only be described as fluid and soothing. This is a multi-faceted book that will fascinate even the staunchest non-believer. Culpepper is a born story teller, and the reader can imagine her spinning this yarn of ghosts and evil spirits to friends around a campfire."—*Lambda Literary Review*

"There's a lovely ebb and flow to their courtship, a dance that is refreshingly healthy and mature. Of itself, River Walker is a fine romance. …But wait, there's more. Throw in the cyclic killings of abusive men and you have a tight little mystery. …As if a sweet romance and intriguing murder mystery aren't enough, Culpepper throws in a good, old-fashioned ghost story. Romance, mystery, and ghost story—Culpepper does it all."—*Kissed by Venus*

"*The Clinic* sets the tone for what promises to be a terrific series. Culpepper's writing style is spare and evocative, her plotting precise. You can't help but feel strongly for the Amazon warrior women and their plight, and this book is a must-read for all those who enjoy light fantasy coupled with a powerful story of survival and adventure. Highly recommended."—*Midwest Book Review*

"Culpepper's writing is crisp and refreshing, even in the midst of the difficult subject matter she has chosen for this story. Her turns of phrases are unique and resonate like harp strings plucked to create a beautiful tune."—*Just About Write*

"[*The Clinic*] is engaging and thought-provoking, and we are left pondering its lessons long after we read the last pages. …Culpepper is an exceptional storyteller who has taken on a very difficult subject, the subjugation of one people over another, and turned it into a spellbinding novel. As an author, she understands well that fiction can teach us our own history without the force and harshness of nonfiction. Yet *The Clinic* is just as powerful in its telling."—*L-Word.com*

Visit us at www.boldstrokesbooks.com

By the Author

A QUESTION OF GHOSTS

by
Cate Culpepper

2012

CREDITS

EDITOR: CINDY CRESAP
PRODUCTION DESIGN: SUSAN RAMUNDO
COVER DESIGN BY SHERI (GRAPHICARTIST2020@HOTMAIL.COM)
COVER PHOTO BY JAY CSOKMAY

Acknowledgments

As always, warm appreciation to my Bold Strokes Books editor, Cindy Cresap. I also thank Cindy for forbidding my use of the term *chobos* in the *Tristaine* novels, because *chobos* do not exist outside of a certain television series.

My faithful long-time betas, Connie Ward and Gill McKnight, gave me their usual insightful feedback and personal support, and crucial kick-ass reminders to just cowboy up and type.

A smack to the bicep of my beta and sister scribe, Jove Belle, who nailed Jo's diagnosis at first reading of Chapter One. I'm also grateful for the keen legal advice of that talented writer and attorney, Carsen Taite. Sheri did a wonderful job realizing the ghostly themes of this story in her cover design. Warm thanks to Julie Lundquist at Lakeview Cemetery, and to Lynn Brawley-Birkwist and her kin for allowing an image of the statue that graces their family plot to appear on this cover.

Disclaimer: I freely acknowledge that in the writing of this story, I took liberties with the nature of Electronic Voice Phenomenon, the function of the Spiricom, the geography of Seattle, the topography of Lake View Cemetery, the layouts of Swedish Hospital Hospice and Western State Hospital, and the exact position of entire mountain ranges. Please cowboy up and read.

Dedication

For John William Voakes, with thanks for lending me
a name worthy of a serial killer, and for our good amiga
Terri Mervenne, who would fit in beautifully in Tristaine.

Also for William Spillsbury Hayes, who still owes
me a dance I'll collect someday.

"Psychoanalysis has taught that the dead—a dead parent, for example—can be more alive for us, more powerful, more scary, than the living. It is the question of ghosts."

—Jacques Derrida

PROLOGUE

1989

"*Becca.*" The voice from the radio's small speaker was tinny and faint.

Becca's finger stilled on the circular dial. Bette Midler warbled briefly about the wind beneath her wings and the music faded again into static. Becca nudged the dial one notch, and "The Living Years" trickled from the speaker. She turned the dial back to the static.

"*Becca.*"

A damp chill worked up Becca's back and she hunched closer over the small blue box. "Is this a birthday present?" she whispered. "Hello?"

She turned sixteen today, and she hadn't heard this voice in eleven years.

"*Not true,*" the voice whispered and fell silent.

Becca closed her eyes and listened. Nothing but soft, crackling static for a full minute, two.

After five minutes, she sat up and looked around, dazed. Her bedroom hadn't changed. Weak light still played through the butt-ugly frilly curtains she would never have picked out. A faint aroma of chocolate reached her from the birthday cake her aunt was baking downstairs. Becca realized she was trembling.

She crossed her legs on the worn bedspread and clawed her fingers through her hair. Her belly bulged a bit between the waist of her denim shorts and her cutoff T-shirt. Only one piece of cake tonight, she resolved, a small one. A faint yelp of laughter escaped her, but it sounded like a sob. Her dead mother had just spoken to her, and she was thinking of her *diet*.

The voice was unmistakable. Becca had last heard it when she was five years old, a knobby-kneed, doll-clutching kindergartener, but it could be no one else. There was a faint, familiar bell of music in a mother's voice when she spoke her child's name, and Becca had recognized that private chime in those few words.

It occurred to her that no emotion had really hit her yet, unless astonishment was an emotion. Which was probably odd. She should be feeling something. She realized the walls of her room looked fuzzy because of the tears in her eyes.

Her mother had died the night Becca turned five. This loss had for so long been the dominant historical fact of her life, its resonance had begun to fade. She didn't really remember her mother's face anymore. She no longer prayed to her as if she were an angel, as she had for years. No one forced her into counseling these days, as her uncle and aunt had for months after it happened.

"Becca?" her aunt called her from the foot of the stairs. "I'm going to need your help cleaning this place up. The board meeting's at eight, but I'll get as much done as I can before I take off. That was Marty on the phone. She and Khadijah will be here in half an hour, so you…"

Becca tuned her out. She listened to the static still issuing from the small radio's speaker, as empty and meaningless now as the winter fog over Puget Sound. She bent down and wormed her hand under the mattress, then drew out the small baggie holding the syringe.

"Happy birthday to me," she said. "I guess."

Not true.

CHAPTER ONE

Twenty-three years later

"Jeezis God, the Hill has changed." Marty crammed more gum in her mouth and weaved around another black-jacketed teenager with multiple face piercings. "Doesn't anyone smile around here anymore? Zero eye contact from anyone, zero, in the last six blocks."

Becca nudged her friend. "You're perimenopausal, pal. The Hill doesn't change."

With her usual theatrical timing, Marty stepped onto a small mound of dog poop. She rested her elbow on Khadijah's plump shoulder and scraped the heel of her sandal against the sidewalk. "Damn mutts."

"Damn mutt owners," Khadijah corrected her, steadying her. "And the girl's right. The Hill doesn't change."

"How can you say that?" Marty stared at her partner of fifteen years with umbrage. "Are neither of you seeing the same Broadway I'm seeing? Have you not noticed the new condos crowding out the gay bookstores, the chain outlets swallowing the little independent businesses, the—"

"This street saw twenty years of Gay Pride marches, darlin'." Khadijah nudged them on down the narrow sidewalk. "Hot auras don't go away after that long. They sink in."

"Well, they get harsher, then," Marty said.

Becca saw her point. Broadway thronged with people this balmy June evening. The storied avenue on Capitol Hill, Mecca for Seattle's gay community, had always skewed fairly young. Becca, Marty, and Khadijah had strolled often among these charged crowds in their own high school and college years. It was true that the energy in the neighborhood was different now—edgier, a bit darker. There were more hard-core homeless kids on the street. Since the cops clamped down on the University District, more of the city's young addicts and mentally ill sought refuge on the Hill.

But for Becca, Broadway was still and always the sculpture of Jimi Hendrix kneeling on the sidewalk with his guitar, one arm outflung, often with a cigarette or even a joint stuck between his fingers by affectionate passersby. It was the bronze art footprints embedded in the sidewalk below their feet, marking out the steps to a tango. Her queer kindred walked hand-in-hand all around them on this street. Becca hadn't lived on Capitol Hill since she was five years old, but Broadway was still her spiritual home.

They moved on toward the north end of the avenue, and Khadijah rested her hand on Becca's shoulder as they walked. Touch came to Khadijah as naturally as breathing, and Becca appreciated her familiar support. Her stomach was beginning to tighten again. She shouldn't have had the flautas for dinner. Given her anxiety level, she would probably spend her meeting with this crazy scientist constantly trying to suppress some real insistent flatulence.

"I'm still not sure why we're doing this." Becca knew very well why they were doing this, but she needed to hear it again.

"Okay, no prob. One more time." Marty tweaked a folded newspaper article out of the hip pocket of her frayed shorts and flapped it open. She handed it to Becca and tapped one photo on the creased page. "That's Joanne Call. She's the leading national expert in ghost voices. Leading national expert, Becca, says so right there. In our own little Seattle. Who knew."

"And her office is just about two blocks yonder," Khadijah added. "We're doing this so you can talk to Joanne Call about the voice you heard on your birthday when you were sixteen. The one you heard again on your birthday, two nights ago."

Becca frowned down at the face she had memorized from previous viewings. This woman scientist looked pretty buggy. Her eyes were too big, too piercing. "But come on, you guys, being a national expert in ghost voices. Isn't that like being queen of a tribe of lentils, or something? And who says what I heard on my birthday was the voice of a ghost?"

"You know it was." Khadijah slid her arm through Becca's and her tone gentled. "And you know *who* it was. This has you seriously spooked, Rebecca Healy. We're spooked for you. We need to learn more about this."

Becca sighed. Marty chucked her gently on the chin with one callused knuckle, her comfort, as always, gruffer and briefer than Khadijah's. Marty folded the article and they moved on. They were coming up on the Quest, a mystical fruit salad of a bookshop owned by the local branch of the Theosophical Society. All of Becca's friends loved the place, but of course she had never been inside.

"Damn." Khadijah's hold on Becca's arm tightened. "Window."

"All eyes ahead." Marty moved closer to Becca.

"Thank you, Ebony and Ivory," Becca muttered. She trudged on, the center of this protective sandwich. "I know not to look in the Quest's window, for heaven's sake. I've got a passing familiarity with Capitol Hill. I know what windows to avoid."

"True, but you've been really sensitive the last few days, Bec." Khadijah peered at her through her small spectacles. "It's never been this rough on you before, not in my long memory. I'm afraid just a glimpse might set you off."

"Thanks, but I have no intention of *glimpsing*. And I don't really 'go off,' Khadijah. No one but you two would even notice if I was triggered."

Becca had to chastise herself for her flautas-induced crabbiness. The loyalty of her friends was appreciated. Looking out for her was automatic now, for Khadijah and Marty, after years of practice. But all this warm solicitation was starting to feel distinctly maternal, and Becca had never needed mothering.

She pulled herself out of her sulk. Khadijah was right. She was more shaken over that eerie voice now than the first time she heard it, the day she turned sixteen.

Marty pulled them to a stop a few doors down from the Quest. "This is it. At least the queen of the lentil tribe set up shop in a nice funky neighborhood."

Becca stared up at the barred entrance of the tall building. As with all the structures on the north end of the street, this one was tasteful and neatly landscaped, but it gave no indication at all of its purpose. The heavy door behind the bars featured no sign indicating a public space, only a small plaque bearing the street number. Marty waited a courteous ten seconds for Becca to act before stepping forward and pressing the doorbell herself.

Becca was about to try the bell a second time when the door opened. A tall woman with dark hair regarded them silently. The barred gate separating them cast striped shadows across her impassive face. Becca had a distinct impression of a dangerous captive gazing down from a prison cell. She put her hand on her waist and tried to quell the more lurid offerings of her imagination.

The woman studied them from her elevated position. "Something?" Her voice was low and terse.

"Something," Becca repeated inanely. Khadijah scratched a small circle on her back. "You're Joanne Call. Right? I'm Becca? I'm Becca. I left the message on your voice mail, about tonight."

"I'm Dr. Call. And yes, you did. You didn't mention there would be three of you." The woman stepped down the two stairs and unlatched the gate. "My space is quite limited. Your friends will have to wait out here."

Becca felt Marty and Khadijah lock eyes over her head. She slid her arms around their waists before she could think too much. "It's okay. I'm fine. Get a booth at Charlie's and order me a hot fudge sundae. The big one."

Marty frowned. "Are you sure?"

"Definitely the big one."

"But are you sure you—"

"The girl's good." Khadijah slid out of Becca's arm and patted Marty's face. "We'll be right up the street, Bec."

Marty let Khadijah take her hand and tug her away. "We've got our cells," she called back, ostensibly to Becca, but she was glaring at Joanne Call.

Dr. Call swung open the barred door, and Becca had to banish an image of a sexier, female version of Virgil opening the gates of hell for Dante. She hesitated a beat too long before walking up the two steps and following Dr. Call into the darkness of her inner sanctum.

The small entry opened onto a compact, high-ceilinged space. A polished wooden floor and cream-white walls helped soften the starkness of the room. Joanne Call's work area was scrupulously clean, which Becca could have predicted, but she wouldn't have guessed such an eminent scientist's lab would so closely resemble a discount store.

Shelf after shelf was neatly stocked with old radios, small televisions, tape recorders—reel-to-reel and cassette—even two eight-track players that probably came out a decade before Becca was born. She lingered at one wall, fascinated by a series of compact, alien devices preserved within a locked glass case. There was something clinically pristine in the precise, symmetrical placement of each object.

"We're back here." Dr. Call slid into an expensive ergonomic chair before a large oak desk in one corner. "You can put your purse beneath your seat."

"Okay." It's not a *purse.* Becca sat obediently in the markedly less comfortable armchair and dropped her bag under it.

"I started your file when I got your message. We'll start with some background information." Dr. Call slipped a laptop from some recessed space and tapped rapidly at the keyboard. "It's Rebecca Hawkins, correct?"

Becca hesitated. Lying didn't come naturally to her. "That's right."

"Occupation?"

"I'm a social worker with the state. I work with kids in foster care."

"Then you have graduate-level education?"

"Yes, I have an MSW."

"Your age?"

"I'm thirty-nine."

The blunt fingernail hit two keys. "And where have you lived, in your life?"

"I've always lived in Seattle. I have an apartment off Lake City Way now, but I grew up on Capitol Hill. I've read a little about your work, Dr.—"

"Do you have any chronic health conditions?"

"I'm allergic to peanuts." Another lie, but Becca was getting annoyed.

"Do you have a religious affiliation?"

"No, I forgot to affiliate. Can you tell me—"

"Are you currently partnered?"

"Look, the story is that my mother killed herself when I was five years old. Two nights ago, my mother told me, through a radio, for the second time since she died, that the story isn't true. That's why I'm here."

Dr. Call's fingers slowed on the keyboard, then stopped. She pulled her drill bit gaze from the monitor and focused on Becca fully. An awkward few seconds passed. "I'm sorry, Ms. Hawkins. Sometimes I forget that manners are a part of this work, if I'm to deal with the public. I tend to move too fast."

Becca, the public, was startled by this confession. "Okay," she said. "No harm done."

Dr. Call rested her hands in her lap and sat still for a moment. "Can I get you something to drink?"

"No, thanks. I'm good."

"I'm sure I have some chips or something upstairs, if you're hungry."

"I'm really fine."

Dr. Call nodded, as if relieved to have successfully negotiated some kind of social checklist. She relaxed in her chair. "All right. How much do you know about Electronic Voice Phenomenon?"

"Not a lot." Becca must be growing accustomed to dissembling. She might be skeptical, but she'd read a great deal about EVP in the last few days. "Just that some people believe the voices of the dead can be heard in the static of old electronic devices."

"That's correct." Dr. Call lifted a pen and turned it in her fingers. "A major portion of my work involves studying EVP. Recording voices, tracking sources of messages." The corner of her mouth lifted. "You should know that this phenomenon is not considered particularly credible by the science community at large."

"Yes, I can imagine." Becca might share that wariness, were it not for the periodic talkativeness of her decades-dead mother. Her notion of the afterlife was vague in the extreme; more a wistful hope than a belief grounded in faith.

Dr. Call was observing her as if she were a specimen in a Petri dish. "Do you believe the voice you heard two days ago was the voice of your mother?"

"It sounded very much like her...but I was so little when she..." Becca studied her hands, clenched in her lap. "Yes. I believe it was my mother."

"And you said that this is the second time she spoke to you."

"That's right. I heard her for the first time on my sixteenth birthday. It was my birthday two days ago, too."

Dr. Call's fingers drummed softly on the desk, as if itching for the keyboard. "And the message was the same?"

"Both times, yes. She said my name. And the words 'not true.'" To her astonishment and dismay, Becca felt tears fill her eyes. She stared at the wall, praying this unexpected display of emotion would pass without comment.

"I see." Dr. Call seemed as disconcerted as Becca. The silence grew, and Becca feared she might be offered chips again. To her relief, Dr. Call resumed her clipped and professional tone. "Does this message have meaning for you?"

Becca's shoulder twitched, a parody of a casual shrug. "I guess a lot of things about my mother could turn out not to be true." *Maybe she did love my father. Maybe she did love me too much to leave me.* "I've never believed she killed herself."

"And she died when you were five years old." Dr. Call cleared her throat. "Can I ask how it happened?"

She handed me a doll. Then she went into the kitchen. "She shot herself in the head in the kitchen of our house."

"You were present at the time?"

"I was in the living room. I didn't see it happen." The detached tone this interview had taken was helping. Becca was able to relate these distant horrors without dredging them too painfully from the past.

"Explain your doubts about your mother's suicide." Dr. Call winced. "Please," she added.

"I'm not sure I can." Becca released a long breath. Her belief that Madelyn Healy had not deliberately put a gun to her head was like her faith in any god, fleeting and sporadic. She had no memory of the night itself, beyond her father's voice, her mother's delicate hands placing the doll in her arms. But police reports and years of therapy hadn't banished the small, ambivalent doubt that the world was wrong about her mother's death. Becca shrugged, defeated. "Just a little kid's insistence that her mom wouldn't do such a thing, I guess."

"Perhaps an insistence your mother endorses. 'Not true.'"

"Perhaps."

"Do you have any theories, any alternate explanations for her death? Accident? Homicide?"

"No, I have no idea." Becca shifted in her seat. The woman should really conduct her interviews wearing perma-dark sunglasses. She could cut glass etchings with those eyes. "So. Where do we go from here?"

"That's up to you, actually. I can simply note the specifics of this report and close the file. Or I have time in my schedule for a more thorough investigation, if you wish."

"An investigation. What would that entail?"

"I would invade your life, basically." Dr. Call dipped her head, as if acknowledging what a pleasant prospect that must be. "I'd want to examine the radio that transmitted this message. If possible, to see the room in which you heard it, to run sound tests. And together we would try to establish the conditions most receptive to a third transmission."

"You'd try to get her to speak again." Becca stared at this strange woman. First she was queen of the lentils, then Virgil, now she was Merlin. "Is that really possible?"

"Frankly, it's unlikely. In the research, authentic messages are capricious and unpredictable at best. We've had very little success evoking new information from a single credible voice. Either the given message is repeated, or the voice falls silent. But I feel there are enough anecdotal successes, enough promising attempts, to make the effort worthwhile."

"Uh huh." Becca's flautas were coming back on her with a vengeance. She didn't know what she'd expected from this meeting—a one-stop cure, a fast and soothing interpretation. She hadn't planned to bare her life to this odd duck, though, and that would be inevitable if she continued.

Her mother's voice had held such grief, both times she'd spoken. Not outrage or anger, as would be natural from a woman protesting a lie. Sadness. A faint note of pleading, as if she were begging Becca to believe her.

"All right," Becca said. "I want to do this."

"Fine." Dr. Call swiveled back to her laptop and began typing, a jarring transition that pulled Becca out of her pensive thoughts.

"Wait...I'd better be sure I can pay for this."

"I don't charge subjects for my studies." Dr. Call didn't turn from the monitor. "My work is privately funded. I'd like to meet you tomorrow at two o'clock, at the site of the transmission. Address?"

Yes, tomorrow works for me too, thanks. Becca recited the address of the house on Fifteenth Avenue.

Dr. Call frowned, which didn't change her usual expression all that much. "I recall your saying you live off Lake City? This is a Capitol Hill address, five blocks from here."

"I didn't hear the voice in my apartment. I heard it in the house I lived in as a child, where my mother died."

"I see." This time Becca rather enjoyed the doctor's discomfort. "Meet me here tomorrow, then, and we'll walk there together."

"At two o'clock." Becca waited, but Dr. Call just stared at her. It seemed Becca's audience was concluded. She pushed back her chair.

Dr. Call stood quickly and extended her hand across the desk. "It's been a pleasure meeting you, Ms. Hawkins. Good night."

Becca accepted the formal clasp with a small flare of sympathy for this woman's social clumsiness, her studied but stilted attempts at human interaction. Asperger's, perhaps? Doubtful. People with Asperger's were usually uncomfortable with eye contact, and that was not this chica's problem.

Dr. Call escorted her out of her shadowed office and into the darkening street. She closed the barred gate behind Becca promptly, without further comment.

Which Becca would not have waited to hear anyway. She filled her lungs with fresh air and shook off the intensity of the last thirty minutes with every step she took away from the spooky scientist's lair. Walking faster, toward Charlie's and her friends, Becca pictured the immense hot fudge sundae awaiting her, and she homed in on it like a bat on a convention of grasshoppers.

❖

Jo turned the bolt of the heavy inner door. She watched out the beveled glass pane as the blond woman hurried up the street. The bars between them were a tangible and welcome shield. Shivering with relief, she turned back to the solitude of her refuge.

She'd seen the pity in Becca Hawkins's eyes as they shook hands. With long and hard study, Jo had learned to read facial expressions as well or better than anyone. Often, the emotions that prompted them still mystified her, but pity was never hard to grasp.

She moved silently across the dim room. The glass case containing her prized collection of Spiricoms reflected her image in the meager light. Jo recognized a muted excitement lingering in her features. The intellectual thrill of this new study intrigued her. The chronology was unusual—the birthdays. This mother died on her daughter's fifth birthday, then spoke to her on her sixteenth, then again on her thirty-ninth. This implied a meaningful pattern of contact, a consistent sequence that was generally absent in EVP.

Jo lived for it, the wonder of these voices. That a soul could be so connected to the world they were able to reach through death to speak to the living. To be so bonded to humanity, they were compelled to break the ancient command of silence after death. Human connection was Jo's alien frontier, her life's mystery.

The familiar contours of her chair and the burnished wood of her desk comforted her. She smoothed her hands lightly over the keyboard of her notebook. The Hawkins woman presented a more mundane puzzle.

She tapped up one of her programs on microexpressions, checking her conclusion with expert results. Jo would never be a great font of insight into human behavior, but the woman's minute, fleeting facial expressions during this initial interview all told the same story.

Becca Hawkins was lying.

CHAPTER TWO

B ran muffins. Joanne Call was a bran woman; Becca was sure of it. If she wasn't, she desperately needed to be. Becca bit deeply into her huge chocolate cupcake as she walked, juggling the extra muffin and two cups of coffee.

Broadway was relatively quiet this afternoon, bright and hot. Becca wended around the parking kiosks, missing Khadijah's friendly hand on her shoulder. Marty had offered to hide in the closet of Becca's old house as backup today, should things get too bizarre. Becca nearly took her up on it. She wasn't looking forward to entering the house again. Before her birthday two days ago, she hadn't set foot in the place in more than thirty years.

Had not the illustrious Dr. Call gruffly cleared her throat, Becca would have walked straight into her. She came to an abrupt halt and blinked up into twin reflections of her own face. Dr. Call wore aviator sunglasses that mirrored Becca's startled eyes while completely concealing her own. She tried to say something civil, but her mouth was still full of chocolate cupcake. She strived for a dignified expression, chewed furiously, and swallowed hard.

"Breakfast, Ms. Hawkins?" The aviator sunglasses nodded at the burdens Becca carried. "You sleep in rather late."

Ignoring this insinuation of sloth, Becca handed over one cup of coffee and the muffin. "I thought we were meeting at your office."

"We're standing in front of my office."

Becca glanced at the barred gate, three feet to her left. Ach. So they were.

Dr. Call examined the bran muffin, which was the size of a cannonball. A curious transformation came over the part of her face that Becca could see, a slight softening around the mouth. A dimple actually appeared in her cheek.

"Was I that rough on you last night?"

Becca liked her getting the joke. "Eh, I'm not the easiest interview. I guess we both did all right."

Dr. Call nodded, turned, and walked up the street. Becca sighed and appealed to the heavens. All right, there were signs of humor and humility in the lentil queen, but small talk was not her forte. She trotted to catch up.

❖

Jo walked the shaded avenues of Capitol Hill often, but always at dawn, before Broadway fully awoke. There were few other pedestrians blocking the sidewalks now, which suited her. Her mind had charted an efficient path to the address Hawkins had provided and they could be there in ten minutes. The muffin was actually quite tasty, and the coffee an excellent chaser. She tried to remember if she had thanked Hawkins for them.

"Hey, *Batman.* You're giving me bunions."

Jo turned, surprised. Hawkins was far behind her, limping. She waited. "I'm sorry, Ms. Hawkins. I didn't mean to race."

"You have very long legs and I have very cheap Target sneakers." Becca braced herself on a splintered wooden pole, which was stapled with a hundred flyers advertising local bands, and adjusted her laces. She pointed at the small satchel Jo carried over her shoulder. "Can I ask what's in there?"

"Oh. I've brought some instruments to measure the acoustics of your house. Some recording devices. Is it occupied right now?"

"No." A shadow passed over Becca's features. "It's not my house. My uncle owns it. A family friend shows it to prospective renters for him. She's going to meet us there. It's between tenants."

Jo wondered at the shadow, then wondered why a family would hold on to a house with such painful memories for so many years.

She clasped her hands behind her and walked on, shortening her stride so Hawkins could keep up.

She noted an attractive flush coloring Hawkins's high cheeks. Her propensities for chocolate, sleeping in, and bad sneakers aside, Becca Hawkins seemed healthy enough, even vigorous. She couldn't be called trim, but her full curves were aesthetically pleasing. She was dressed in a light blue T-shirt and cotton shorts, and Jo looked down at her own pristine white shirt and black slacks. She envied this woman's easy informality.

"How did you get into this work, Dr. Call? You can call me Becca, by the way."

Damn. Jo considered simply walking faster to evade that most onerous of social conventions, the personal conversation. Why did people always begin with that insipid question? As if she could explain her belief system in a sound bite. She summoned the stock answer she used in interviews. "My doctorates are in organic chemistry and transpersonal psychology. The latter involves the self-transcendent or spiritual aspects of the human experience. I suppose exploring EVP was a natural offshoot of my earlier studies."

"Okay. A little Wikipedish, but fascinating." There was no mockery in Becca's eyes, just a benevolent teasing. "Transpersonal psych. That has to be the coolest degree on the books. Does it still excite you, exploring these ghostly realms?"

Usually a brief summation of Jo's career satisfied the casual inquiry. If it didn't, she was asked about the technical aspects of her research, not her feelings for it. Becca's expression was friendly and open, and to her surprise, Jo found herself answering in kind. "Yes, it does still excite me. Every single day."

"I can tell. When you talk about your work, your face changes. Something in you lights up."

"I see." Jo was unaware of ever lighting up, but she didn't particularly mind this perception. She realized she was walking alone again, and turned back. "Ms. Hawkins?"

Becca was looking into a store window. She seemed only momentarily distracted; one inexpensive sneaker was lifted to take the next step. But her foot was frozen in midair, and an odd, rigid stillness held her body. She looked like a photograph, flat and lifeless. Jo walked back.

She followed Becca's gaze into the large window of a new vintage clothing store, one of several such trendy triflings dotting Capitol Hill. This shop was not of the classier variety. Lifelike mannequins wore glittered, spaghetti-strapped halter tops, net shawls, and artfully tattered denim skirts. Not to Jo's taste, but she claimed no real discernment when it came to fashion. She looked at Becca's still face, at her eyes.

They were rolled back, exposing only the whites.

"Ms. Hawkins!" Jo took her arms and turned her from the window. She spoke her name again, with no reaction. Becca's features were slack and shining with sweat, and her breath came in swift, shallow pants. Seizure? A severe allergic reaction. She was allergic to peanuts. Had there been nuts in her cupcake? "Becca, talk to me."

Becca's eyes fluttered, and Jo glimpsed slivers of green irises. She stood stiffly in Jo's grip, apparently dazed, and then turned back toward the window.

Becca punched Jo in the chest, hard, knocking her aside, and bolted past her. Air woofed out of Jo's lungs. She clutched her sternum in one hand and gaped for only a moment before taking off in pursuit.

"Becca! Ms. Hawkins!" Jo pounded down the sidewalk, ducking under the low-hanging eaves shading it. Becca was running full-out, but at least she had the presence of mind to weave through the few pedestrians she encountered rather than plow them down.

Jo was intensely aware of the spectacle they were creating on a public street. To her relief, Becca's cheap Target sneakers proved, literally, her downfall. She scuffed a toe over a raised edge of asphalt and went airborne, sailing, thankfully, onto a wide patch of grass bordering the walk. She landed with a frightening crash and sprawled gracelessly on her belly.

❖

Becca scrambled mindlessly to her feet, still driven by the horror of the corpses.

"Hey! Hold on!"

It was Joanne Call. For a moment, Becca's disorientation was so extreme she couldn't remember where she was or why Dr. Call was with her, clenching her arms so fiercely. Saliva flooded her dry mouth, and she swallowed convulsively. It had never been this bad before.

"Becca, you look terrible. What's the matter with you?"

Becca wanted to offer a coherent reply, but she looked up into those mirrored sunglasses and saw the distorted reflections of her own face, inches away. She felt the strength drain out of her legs in a rush and her head filled with static. She had a fleeting impression of Dr. Call lunging to catch her as her knees buckled.

Becca had never fainted in her life, so she didn't realize she had until she came to. She was lying in the grass, cradled in a pair of strong arms, one supporting her back, the other clasped across her waist. She could see the lower legs of a few people standing around them. She heard a voice ask if they should call 911.

She rested her head on Dr. Call's crisp white sleeve. Dr. Call had removed her sunglasses, and Becca stared up into those blazing dark eyes.

"I think," Dr. Call said, "you should call me Jo."

"Okay," Becca said. She turned her head and threw up.

❖

"It's called pediophobia." Becca pulled deeply on the straw immersed in her thick milkshake.

Jo watched her in amazement. A half-hour after regurgitation, Becca's yearning for chocolate was fully restored. The woman required regular chocolate infusions like others needed water to live. "Pediophobia? A fear of children?"

"No. Pedi*a*phobia is a fear of children. Pedi*o*phobia is a fear of dolls." Becca looked at her watch. She sighed and slipped a cell phone out of the pocket of her shorts. "Excuse me just a minute."

Jo sipped her green tea and suppressed a flood of questions as Becca clicked keys. They were sitting in wrought iron chairs before a very small wrought iron table, typical of the never-quite-comfortable outdoor furnishings fronting Capitol Hill cafes. But the fresh air seemed to be helping Becca. Her face was losing that unnerving, distant cast, and she was no longer as pale.

"Hi. We're not coming. I'm so sorry I made you drive over for nothing." Becca kept her voice low, cupping her hand over her cell. Her tone was warm. "A hard trigger, a bad one. I'll fill you in later."

Becca smiled at the table as she listened. "Yes, I'm okay now. No, I'm not alone. I'll be fine." She darted a shy glance at Jo. "I'll call you tonight, I promise. Love you, too." She folded her phone and returned it to her pocket. "That was Rachel, the friend with keys to my uncle's house. She's been waiting there for us." She touched the table. "I'm sorry, Jo. I just can't go there today. I don't think my nerves could take it."

Jo was mightily tempted to offer Becca a box of Hershey bars if she'd change her mind. She was chafing to get inside that house. She managed to mask her disappointment. "We can go another time. A fear of dolls?"

Becca stirred her milkshake, her eyes downcast. "Yeah. It's more common than you might think. It's not just dolls. Pediophobia is a fear of any false representation of a human being. Anything that looks like it should be human, alive, but isn't." She smiled wryly. "Which covers a lot of territory. I can't go into the Quest Bookstore because they have these little lifelike figures in the window, carvings of various gods. I can't go into toy stores, of course, or clothing stores, because of the—"

"Mannequins." Jo remembered the posed figures in the shop window.

Becca nodded. "To me, those mannequins looked like living corpses." Her lip trembled, and Jo steeled herself, afraid tears would follow. "It wouldn't have been as bad if they were stylized, with half-arms or faceless. They were pretty realistic."

"Do you see these false representations as physical threats?" Jo's chest still ached with the power of Becca's blow, her desperation to run from the window. "That the dolls or the mannequins might come to life and hurt you in some way?"

"I don't even get that far." Becca sat back in her chair, a weary wonder in her voice. "They don't have to come to life, they don't have to chase me, they just have to *exist*. I can't explain it. But I'm sorry you had to witness it. I'm embarrassed. I've never, ever been triggered so hard as today."

"Well, that's good." Jo couldn't imagine enduring fear like that on a regular basis.

"Normally, all I have to do is turn my head and walk away. I've done that in the middle of a sentence before, which can be awkward, but it's always worked."

"And you say this isn't a rare phobia?"

"It's common enough." Becca rested one sneaker on the table and brushed grass from her lightly skinned knee. "The makers of the Shrek films had to change the Fiona character, the princess, because she was drawn too well. Too lifelike. They actually had to make her more cartoonish, because she made so many people uneasy."

Jo had never seen the Shrek films. What an interesting morass of contradictions Becca Hawkins was. Obviously intelligent, warm, prickly, funny, confident. And haunted by this bizarre terror. She felt the silence grow between them and struggled to think of something to say. "Have you never looked into the origin of this fear? Hypnosis, therapy?"

Becca's face changed subtly, and Jo knew she was going to lie before she spoke. "Rachel Perry, the friend I just called, was my therapist a long time ago. We worked on this for years. I still have no idea why I freak out so badly."

"I see." Jo pondered this for a moment. This study held little promise if she kept running into these random deceits. If learning the truth meant picking delicately through Becca's psyche with sensitivity and restraint, Jo didn't know how to do that. She slid out her wallet and laid a few bills on the table. "Are you sure you're all right physically, now?"

"Yes, I am." Becca looked disconcerted as Jo pushed back her chair, the metal grating over the concrete. "You're leaving?"

"Yes. Please call me when you're prepared to enter the house again. And when you're prepared to be honest with me about what happened there." Jo extended her hand, and after a moment Becca accepted it. Jo shook her hand twice, firmly, and turned to go. The Broadway Market Video was a few blocks away. She would rent the Shrek films on her way home.

"Joanne? Jo?"

There was a pleading note in Becca's voice, and she turned back reluctantly. Becca came to her, and studied her so closely Jo wished for her sunglasses.

"My name isn't Hawkins," Becca said finally. "It's Healy. I'm the daughter of Scott and Madelyn Healy."

Jo waited. Becca seemed to want to say more. She struggled for words and then lifted her hand helplessly.

"You're the scientist." Becca walked away. "Google us."

CHAPTER THREE

Becca phoned Joanne Call three nights later. She could tell Jo wasn't crazy about the proposed location of their meeting, but she agreed to join her at the Wildrose. She could tell she was even less crazed about seeing Marty and Khadijah waiting at their table.

"Becca, I'm not particularly interested in a coffee klatch tonight."

"I know. I should have told you." Becca wanted to touch Jo's arm, but didn't. She realized she was subjecting her to considerable discomfort, and she didn't do so lightly. "I just need to have my friends with me if we have to talk about this."

At least the Rose was dark enough that Jo couldn't wear her damned mirrored shades, and her eyes reflected her internal struggle. She finally nodded brusquely and allowed Becca to lead her to the long table in the back.

The Rose was Capitol Hill's iconic lesbian bar, but business had yet to kick up for the night. It had been two years or more since Becca had been here, and the place seemed smaller every time she saw it. The wood plank floors were still scuffed and uneven, the ceiling still strung with limp strings of electric stars. But shabby nostalgia aside, to Becca the Rose was well-loved faces and laughter—good times here with friends, over many years.

Becca had tipped the barkeep to let her slide a couple of tables together for her small group, to allow Jo as much physical space as possible. She saved a spindly chair with its back to the wall for her, allowing her to survey the blood-red walls of the room.

"Hello. We're the chicks you didn't meet the other night." Unsmiling, Marty extended her hand across the table, and Jo shook it briefly.

Becca threw Marty a chiding look. "Marty Coleman, Khadijah Berry, this is Joanne Call. I've known these strange girls since middle school."

"It's nice to meet you." Khadijah's smile was warm. The many bracelets encircling her wrist clicked pleasantly as she clasped Jo's fingers. "Thanks for trying to help our friend."

Jo seemed as uncomfortable with Khadijah's friendliness as Marty's hostility. "I haven't helped her much, yet."

"Through no fault of your own. Sit, sit." Becca knew her voice was overly bright. She needed food, now. She may not have slept much the last few nights, she might be distracted and irritable, but her appetite, as always, sailed along full titty to the wind. She waved down a server with multiple lip rings.

"I'll have your four cheese hero." Becca pointed to Marty and Khadijah. "They'll have the turkey rueben and the pasta asiago. Oh, and a side of your roasted potato wedges, please. And a hummus plate." She turned to Jo, who was staring at her. "How about you?"

"Tea. Earl Grey. I ate earlier."

Becca hoped Jo would survive this unwelcome socializing without bursting into flame. She also hoped Marty would be able to contain her natural pitbullish protectiveness and stop glaring at the poor woman. Khadijah's fingers brushed lightly over Marty's wrist, attuned as always to her partner's bristling energy. Even through her daze, Becca noted the effortless, nurturing connection between them, and for the hundredth time she blessed and envied them for it.

Jo would be miserable with small talk, so she girded her loins and began. "So. Do you know the truth about my parents?"

"I know what autopsy reports and the *Seattle Times* considered the truth in nineteen seventy-eight, yes."

Becca blinked. "You sound skeptical."

"Not necessarily." Jo clasped her hands on the table. "All sources state clearly that your mother committed homicide as well as suicide. That she shot your father, and then herself, the night of your fifth birthday. But I'm keeping an open mind."

"Okay." Becca absorbed Jo's bluntness. "I guess that's good."

"I'm considering two factors." Jo's shoulders were relaxing as she warmed to her topic. "If you're right about your mother's message, Becca, she could be denying the official verdict on her death. I happen to consider that a credible report. Interestingly, EVP speakers rarely lie when they make factual statements."

"What's your second factor?" Marty asked.

"The autopsy report. The police believe Madelyn Healy shot her husband in the chest, and then herself in the head. But it strikes me odd that the bullet entered her eye. That's a highly unusual way for a woman to kill herself, all but unheard of. That also lends credence to the possibility that things didn't happen as—"

Becca stopped listening and went away in her mind. "Jo, you'll want to understand this." Khadijah's voice was faint in Becca's ears, but she sounded kind. "Becca's in pretty rocky shape, emotionally. She has been, ever since she heard that voice last week. It would be best if we didn't bring up real graphic images of her mom's death."

There was a pause. "But…it happened so long ago." Jo sounded honestly puzzled, and Becca opened her eyes. "And surely, Becca, you've always known how she—"

"Of course she knows." Marty growled. She was turning a fork rapidly in her fingers. She caught a look from Khadijah and set it down. "She just doesn't like to remember that shit. Jesus, who would?"

"That's why we're here, though." Braced by her friends, Becca could play brave as the image of her mother's dead face faded. "What else do you need to know, Jo?"

Jo stared at the table. After a moment she looked up. "All right. What about your phobia, Becca? I know you were ly—you weren't very honest with me, about its origins."

"But how do you know that?" Becca was intrigued in spite of herself. Or maybe she just wanted to delay talking about the doll.

Jo was right. She had lied, but she was amazed Jo had caught her at it. She seemed an unlikely interpreter of the nuances of human interaction. "You just met me, Jo. How could you tell I was—"

"Oh, girl, you suck at lying." Khadijah shook a napkin onto her lap as their food arrived. "You're terrible at it. Always have been."

"The worst." Marty spun the hummus plate on the table. "I tried to teach you to lie in the eighth grade, Bec, when guys started asking you out. You were hopeless."

"Becca, I'm not prying into highly personal areas without good reason." Jo frowned. "I know this is difficult for you. But if this phobia is connected to your parents' deaths, it might shed some light on your mother's message."

"Okay. I get it." Becca picked up her sandwich and dug in. The ensuing chewing took up thirty seconds, allowing time to whitewash her mind. She could only talk about this if she didn't picture it. "The night it happened, my parents were arguing. Again. We were in the living room. My mother handed me a doll and went into the kitchen. My father went after her. There were two shots. I was still holding the doll when the police broke in."

"So your pediophobia is rooted in the trauma of that night." Jo slipped a small device from her pocket and began tapping its keys rapidly. "Thank you. Getting to know the receiver is a vital part of this process."

"You want to know Becca Healy?" Marty eyed Jo over the rim of her glass. "She works with kids in foster care. She remembers every one of their birthdays, and she brings them cakes she makes herself. She's kept every friend she's ever made, and kept Kaddy and me close for twenty-five years. She knows our favorite orders in every restaurant on the Hill."

Jo's fingers stilled on the small keyboard. "I'm sure Becca is—"

"I was out of town when Kaddy found a lump in her breast last year. Becca stayed with her every night until the biopsy came back clean." Marty swirled the soda in her glass and downed it. "If you need to 'get to know your receiver,' Doc, you could focus in a little smarter."

"She went with us when we had to put our Angel to sleep, too. Our sweet little beagle. This girl is the kindest, most thoughtful creature I know." Khadijah's brown eyes were warm behind her small granny glasses. "Go ahead and blush. It's all true."

Becca cursed her feeble tears. Lord, she had no more emotional stamina than a Pop-Tart these days. "Well, that was nice. Thanks. I just don't know if Jo needs sterling character references right now."

She smiled weakly at Jo, who was watching them with an odd combination of muted wonder and sadness. Jo's eyes lingered on Khadijah's hand clasping Becca's, and for a moment she looked as vulnerable as a child.

"Of course, all information about a receiver is useful." Jo slid the screen of her device shut slowly. "It would be helpful to learn something about your mother as well, Becca. Her personality, her habits. I'd like to see how closely she fits the profile of the typical EVP reporter."

"Ooh, there's a typical reporter?" Khadijah brightened. "This stuff fascinates the hell out of me, by the way. You mean all the dead folks able to send messages have things in common?"

"Well, no, that's a little misleading." Jo nodded stiffly at the young pink-coiffed woman in a fedora offering to replenish her tea. "Messages have been recorded from voices that could hail from any demographic. We hear more often from men than from women. From older voices rather than young, which stands to reason, as the dead tend to skew older."

"And what do they say, all these noisy dead people?" Khadijah asked.

"Gibberish mostly." Jo lifted one shoulder, as if apologizing for a child's clumsy performance. "Snatches of words. Coherent, the best of them, but odd tangles of meaning. One recording is of an older man shouting, 'Tab the bathroot!' over and over. Another is a woman saying quite clearly, 'Scallops, my best gender. Steal tomatoes.'"

"So no one tells where the family treasure is buried?" Marty looked faintly disappointed. "Or says anything personal, that makes sense?"

"Some do make sense."

Becca was studying the dynamics of the women around her; an automatic inner shift to safer ground. She noted Jo's body was changing, softening as she leaned into the table. Her transformation was subtle but striking. That guarded glaze was lifting from Jo's eyes as the warmth of Khadijah's interest drew her in. She glanced at Becca. "I have some recordings with me. Would you like to hear?"

"Are you serious?" Khadijah scraped her chair closer over the rugged floor. "Bring it on, girlfriend."

Jo smiled with a note of shyness that touched Becca. She flipped open her device again, swept her finger across several screens, tapped keys. She rested it on the table and turned the small screen so they could see it. "This has strong little speakers."

The screen was an oblong of eerie green light, vivid in the dim lamps of the bar. Its glassy smoothness was featureless for a moment, then a multi-digit number appeared in the upper left of the screen, along with the notation *07.14.76/1400hrs.*

Becca heard a soft hiss from the speakers, and a faint white line darted across the green rectangle. The hiss deepened and more lines followed, tracing the electric contours of the sound in jagged spikes and valleys. The voice spoke abruptly and quite clearly.

"And the merriest of Christmases to you all!"

Becca sat back hard in her seat, astonished at the bright cheerfulness of the woman's voice, its distinct southern accent. Marty's eyebrows shot up, and Khadijah laughed in delight.

"So who *is* that?" Khadijah asked. "She sounded so normal!"

"No one knows." Jo stroked the screen with one finger. "These are all unidentified, or unclaimed messages, collected during lab experiments over the years."

Becca saw more numbers on the screen, and she leaned forward. *02.05.84/0815 hrs.* The low hiss sounded again, and the white lines danced.

"Two hours it took me to haul in that fish." A man's voice, his tone mellow and relaxed, and unmistakably proud.

Becca, Marty, and Khadijah all grinned, caught up in these surreal post-mortem pronouncements. Becca felt a tingling at the base of her spine, and goose bumps rose along her forearms. She wasn't ready to believe with certainty that she was hearing the voices of the dead, but these messages carried an odd flavor of the distant, a kind of remote, antique cadence. The sounds of the Rose faded around the table as they leaned closer again, their food forgotten.

"Jenny, I know you borrowed my sweater!" A woman, sounding irritated, from 1992.

"I fought in Patton's army." An elderly man, in 1984.

"Why are you all here? Please go away!"

That one, from a woman in 1980, gave Becca chills. She sounded resigned and hardly threatening, but Becca could imagine that voice echoing through a haunted house.

"We've recorded many voices demanding that intruders leave their house," Jo said as the screen flickered again. "It's a common message. And we've captured over a hundred varieties of the word 'hello' or simple greetings, in almost every modern language."

"That tool chest is for Tom!" A man, commanding from 1993.

The hissing rose, subsided briefly. A woman spoke next, and a shudder went through Becca.

"I will see you no more."

"Good my Lord." Khadijah sounded wounded. "Can you play that again, Jo?"

Becca didn't want to hear that message again. When Jo tapped the keys and the hiss issued from the speakers, she was swept with despair before she heard the woman's bleak voice.

"I will see you no more."

An older woman, perhaps very old. The screen reflected a recording date of 1959. There was such cheated hopelessness in her words, spoken softly but with terrible grief. This was a woman who had believed her entire life that death would end in reunion, and it had not. She was lost to those she loved who still lived, lost to those who had gone before her, and utterly alone. Becca heard it all in those six words, the pathetic surprise and bitterness of that discovery, that fate. A tear splashed down on her clenched hands.

"Becca, I should have realized that one hit you hard." Khadijah stroked Becca's hair.

Becca managed to raise her head. Marty and Khadijah were studying her with concern. Jo's expression held a mixture of regret and self-disgust, as if she were castigating herself again. "I'm all right. She was just…" Becca gestured helplessly. "She sounded so lost."

"She sure did." Khadijah folded her napkin and handed it to her. "I'm sorry the last one upset you, but I'm not sorry we heard these messages. They're amazing, Jo."

"Shit fire." This meant Marty was impressed. "Are you thinking you can catch a recording of Becca's mom, Doc, if she ever speaks again? Is that what you're going to try to do?"

"That depends on many things." Jo slid her device into her shoulder pack. She looked at Becca evenly, and now her gaze was piercing again, and held only challenge.

"What do you mean?" Khadijah asked.

"She means…" Becca drew in a deep, slow breath. "We have to go back to the house where my parents died."

CHAPTER FOUR

There was nothing distinctive about the two-story red brick house on Fifteenth Avenue, unless sitting directly across the street from one of Seattle's oldest and largest cemeteries was a distinction.

Jo loved Lake View Cemetery. She strolled its grounds often enough to be thought an oddity by the staff, but she had no patience with those who found her affection for cemeteries macabre. To walk into Lake View was to enter a different world. It was a beautiful setting, with views of Lake Washington and both the Cascade and Olympic mountain ranges. It featured rolling hills shaded with dark greenery and extraordinary memorial statuary.

The Lady of the Rock was Jo's easy favorite. The Lady was a tall, cast-iron statue of a seated, cloaked woman holding a book, a young girl kneeling at her feet, her head in her lap. The girl's hair streamed over the woman's knees, her face mostly hidden. The Lady's right hand pointed into the distance, toward some enticing mystery. Her gaze was unfathomable, but whispered of loss.

Becca must have noticed Jo's lingering attention on the gravestones as they stepped onto the front porch of the house. "That cemetery is a map of all the major Seattle city street names, by the way. All our traffic-choked big ones. The Borens are there and the Dennys and the Mercers." Becca fumbled with the keys, and even Jo could pick up on her anxiety level. "Bruce Lee and his son Brandon are buried there."

Jo wondered why Becca was telling her factoids all Seattle natives knew by heart. "Did you go to the cemetery often? I can't imagine it being much of a playground for a five-year-old." Lake View had been a favorite outing for Jo when she was five, but she kept that to herself.

"No, I never hung out there. I was scared of the place when I was a kid." Becca dropped her keys, picked them up, and fit one into the front door. She sighed and slid it free. "First, this is the key to my apartment. Second, Rachel's waiting to let us in." She puffed her hair out of her eyes and pressed the doorbell, a discreet glowing circle in a metal frame. Jo heard a faint bong.

"Rachel's shown a few renters around, but there are no takers yet." Becca resumed her polite chatter. "We're renting it furnished, that's probably one problem. It's a plain house, but this neighborhood's too pricey for most."

Jo could imagine. Like many of Seattle's quirky neighborhoods, Capitol Hill was becoming both a haven for the wealthy and a shabby, subsidized housing refuge for the poor. Middle class families stood little chance of affording its market rate rents. They waited together on the porch for what seemed an unnecessarily long time to answer a doorbell.

"Jo, I'm sorry for ambushing you at the Rose the other night." Becca's tone lost its brightness and she looked up at Jo directly, a first for that afternoon. "I know social gatherings aren't your thing."

"It's all right. I managed to avoid public disgrace." Jo wasn't being flip. She had only wanted to get away from that table when she first sat down, but the evening at the Rose had taken a strange twist. She had almost enjoyed it. Becca and the two other women were so openly fascinated by her work. Khadijah and Marty. Jo remembered the palpable, easy warmth between them. She cleared her throat. "Your friends care about you very much."

"Yes, I'm lucky." Becca's features softened, losing some of their tension. "I'm good at friendship, and I like that about myself. It's work, you know? Friends should have just as much of your attention and time as your job, your family, the other important things in your life. You have to work at it, make sacrifices sometimes. Friends like Khadijah and Marty are worth it."

Jo was lost in the fondness in Becca's eyes as she spoke their names. "I've never had that kind of friend. Not even close."

Becca looked startled, but the ornate handle of the door rattled and the door swung slowly open.

"I am *sorry* it took me so long. A glacier could have let you in faster." A small woman stood in the doorway, about Becca's height. She wore a green silk blouse and expensive-looking slacks. Jo placed her in her early seventies. She was panting lightly, but her shadowed face was wreathed in a smile. "I've put some brownies in to bake. Just for you, Becca, of course. I'll eat half of them only in solidarity with you."

Becca didn't answer right away, her pleased smile matching the woman's. "Hello, you." She stepped over the threshold and wrapped her in her arms, a brief but tender embrace, then stepped back. "Dr. Joanne Call, this is Dr. Rachel Perry. My psychiatrist when I was a kid, and my good friend ever since."

"Hello, Dr. Call." Rachel offered Jo her hand, and her grip was tighter and longer than Jo expected, as the woman seemed frail. "I've spoken to Becca on the phone about the work you want to do together. It's nice to meet you."

"Nice to meet you," Jo parroted. She shifted the strap of the pack on her shoulder, trying to see past Rachel into the house. She was eager to set up the Spiricom.

"Come in, please." Rachel draped her arm across Becca's shoulders and led them into a small entry. "Your aunt is after me for another sit-down dinner, Becca. Can you stomach that, tomorrow night?"

"Any chance my uncle will be out of town tomorrow night?" Becca's tone was light. "Eh, if you're there, I'll be able to choke down a plate or three, whether he's around or not."

"I'll be there. Patricia does make a dynamite manicotti. Just sit close enough to kick my ankle if I bring up Michelle Obama again."

They stepped down into a high-ceilinged living room, furnished simply with an overstuffed couch and matching armchairs. Jo spied a colorful Pendleton rug beneath an antique coffee table. The white walls held tall windows, necessary to catch the meager light of cloud-choked Seattle winters.

Becca folded her arms, and the tension had returned to her shoulders. Jo realized where they were. Five-year-old Becca had been sitting in this innocuous living room when the shootings had happened in the kitchen. Jo stepped closer to her and tried to make her tone gentle. "You heard the voice from a radio in this room the other day, correct?"

Becca nodded. "My aunt asked me to come by here to check out a broken washer. I hadn't been in the house for many years. I was sitting here, in the living room..." Becca was watching Rachel, who was standing in a beam of sunlight that fell across the hardwood floor, and she frowned. She took Rachel's arm and turned her toward the light. "Hey. What's going on with you?"

"Well, I'm having a very bad hair day. Something about my new pillowcases make me wake up looking like a demented woodchuck."

"Rachel." Becca drew the older woman closer to the window. "I'm serious. You don't look well."

"I'm not, of course, you know that." Rachel patted Becca's hand. "Diabetes isn't for the timid, friend."

"I do know that." Becca's forehead was creased with worry, and Jo tried to think of anyone in her own life who would care as much if she were ill. "But you had your blood sugars pretty well under control for so long. Is the insulin not working? What does your doctor say?"

"My doctor says it's time to try dialysis. My kidneys are simply working too hard these days, and it's making me feel rotten. But I have my first treatment next week, and that's going to help my energy considerably."

"Dialysis." Becca swallowed visibly. "Are you in kidney failure?"

"No, I'm just kidney-challenged, at this point. We're adjusting my meds too, so I'll feel much better soon."

"Can I take you to your appointment? I can get off work easily. I have a lot of comp time—"

"Becca, the dialysis center is half a mile from my house." Rachel patted Becca's fingers again, more firmly. "I promise if I ever need someone to hold my hand at an appointment, you'll be the first one I call. But I'll be fine. Now, can we concentrate on you for a moment? You're looking a little peaked yourself."

"Eh, I'm not sleeping well." Becca glanced at Jo. "I was thrown a bit by that trigger the other day."

"Yes, that sounded very unpleasant." Rachel studied Becca. "You know I can't be your therapist now. We've been friends for too many years, and you know all my torrid secrets. But it might not be a bad idea for you to meet with someone short-term, just to see you through this hard patch."

"Rachel, I get by with a little help from my amigas." Becca slid her hand through Rachel's arm. "Always have, always will. But thank you. Do you think we should show Jo the house now, before she starts foaming at the mouth?"

Jo hadn't realized her impatience was so evident, but if foaming at the mouth would get things started, she would foam.

Rachel laughed. "Right this way, Dr. Call." She turned and walked slowly toward the staircase.

Jo followed them, wanting to see the rest of the house but already itching to be back in the living room. The acoustics there were good, as they often were in older houses. The Spiricom would have excellent reception.

Rachel paused at the foot of the stairs. "Why don't you two tour the second floor, Becca, and I'll check on our brownies?"

"That would be fine." Jo stepped between them and started up the stairs. After a moment, she heard Becca follow her, her footfalls muted on the carpeted tread.

The stairway was narrow and somewhat claustrophobic. The walls held framed photos of Puget Sound, a generic but scenic means of pleasing the eye of prospective renters. The hallway led to four closed doors, and Jo went to the first. It opened to a small bedroom, painted in bright colors and furnished for a child, with a single twin bed and a chest of drawers. "This was your room, Becca?"

There was no answer, and Jo turned to see Becca scowling at the stairs.

"You know why she wouldn't come up with us, right?" Becca brushed her hand across her eyes. "She's too weak to climb the stairs. Jesus, Jo. I had no idea."

Jo shifted uncomfortably. "Dr. Perry isn't a young woman, Becca. Many older people have a hard time with stairs."

"She just turned sixty," Becca snapped. "She and my mother were the same age. She just looks ten years older because she's sick. Rachel doesn't have any family now. Who's been taking care of her?"

"She strikes me as the independent and resourceful sort." Jo tried to think of something rational but comforting. "Perhaps you're overestimating how much she needs you."

"For heaven's sake, Joanne, everyone needs friends!" Becca sighed and turned to Jo. "I'm sorry, I don't mean to bark at you. Come on, I'll show you these rooms and you can set up your equipment, or whatever. I'd like to get out of here as soon as possible."

Jo bit her lip. That would pose a problem. Becca hadn't yet grasped the commitment necessary for this project.

The upstairs rooms struck Jo as generic and unpromising, at least compared to the rich acoustic potential of the lower level. She looked them over swiftly, then followed Becca to the stairs. For once, Becca was moving faster than she was, and a moment later Jo realized why.

"Chocolate," Becca murmured, trotting down the stairs. The savory aroma was filling the house, and Jo's mouth watered. Rachel backed her way out of the swinging kitchen door carrying a tin pan.

"In truth, I may not be able to eat these," Rachel said, "but I can sit with you two and drool while you do." She set the pan on a small table, straightened stiffly, and frowned at the brownies. "Oops, Rachel's bad. I've forgotten the frosting."

"No frosting on my brownies. That's another sin to add to your torrid past." Becca had regained her good spirits, or at least she was making a convincing show of it. She lifted the pan and headed for the kitchen. "Allow me."

Rachel straightened, frowning. "Are you sure, Becca?"

"I'm sure I require frosting." Becca hesitated a bare moment before she swung open the door to the kitchen, the room where her parents died. Then she walked through it.

Jo surveyed the space for the best placement of the Spiricom. She slid her pack off her shoulder and opened it.

"Becca tells me you have a degree in transpersonal psychology, Dr. Call." Rachel lowered herself in stages into an armchair.

"That's correct." Jo freed the Spiricom from its protective foam casing and cradled it in her hands. It was a silver beauty from 1976, one of the first made. She had paid an exorbitant amount of money for it. Its design was rudimentary, given the tonal complexity of later models, but still her favorite. She'd had good luck with it.

"Did your studies include working with people with a history of trauma?"

"Most lives involve trauma, Dr. Perry, just as most death involves loss." Jo positioned the Spiricom on a side table, switched it on, and adjusted its settings. "But if you're asking if I have clinical counseling experience, the answer is no. My degree centered on research."

"Then it's possible you don't realize the vulnerability of your current subject." Rachel spoke politely, but her diction had grown more precise. "I don't like Becca's color, Dr. Call. She seems fragile to me. This focus on mysterious ghost messages has called up some very painful memories from her earliest childhood."

"Yes, Becca has no end of defenders, warning me to handle her gently." Jo wondered why she was being so peevish. The woman was only expressing concerns she shared herself. "Where is the radio in this room?"

"That's the only radio I see." Rachel gestured shortly. "I'm just asking you to proceed with caution. There's no need to rush Becca through these experiments, or whatever you're planning here. I'd like to see her have a few days of rest before you—"

"Time might be of the essence, actually." Jo looked around, not seeing whatever radio Rachel had flapped her hand at. "Becca's mother may never speak again, or not for another twenty years. But if voices do manifest more than once, it's likely the messages will be sent in close succession. Oh, my. Seriously?"

She felt a broad smile cross her face. Sitting on an end table was a small radio the size and shape of a tennis ball on steroids. It was one of the globe radios popular with adolescents in the seventies, a bombastic shade of yellow. Terrible frequency range in these models, but surprisingly good amplitude modulation. Jo picked it up.

"I'd appreciate some indication that you're hearing me." Rachel was standing by her elbow. "You're right about Becca having many defenders, and woe betide the scientist who crosses us." A slight smile took the sting from her words.

Jo studied Rachel's face and read the genuine concern in her worn features. "You can relax, Dr. Perry. It's true that this voice might speak again soon, but this process can't be rushed. We might have to listen for days, even weeks, before we hear the faintest whisper. If we catch anything at all." She turned the little ball radio on, and was relieved to hear the strong crackle of good batteries.

"All right, you guys can stop talking about me behind my back now." Becca shouldered open the door from the kitchen and brought in a plate of lavishly frosted brownies. "Were you telling Rach about me throwing up in your lap after I saw that mannequin, Jo? That was my favorite part of the day."

"I was telling Dr. Perry that we may have to be patient moving forward, Becca." Jo fiddled with the ridged circular dial of the radio. "These voices can be subtle and quite elusive, and it might be a long time before we hear—"

An ear-splitting crack of static erupted from the globe in her hand, and Jo almost dropped it. An equally piercing shriek followed.

"BECCA, RUN!"

Becca dropped the plate and it shattered, brownies scattering across the floor. Her face drained of color and her eyes were enormous. She bolted, racing for the entry and through it, and slammed out the front door.

The radio went silent in Jo's shaking hands, not even whispering the dead air space that lay between stations.

"What are you waiting for?" Rachel said sharply, her hand pressed to her heart. "I can hardly run after her. Go!"

Jo went.

And so it was that Joanne Call chased madly after a fleeing Becca Healy for the second time in one week, she thought grimly as she ran down the steep driveway. She skittered to a halt, spying the briefest flash of Becca's blue blouse in the distance. Across the street. Becca had run directly into Lake View Cemetery.

Jo followed her through the ornate wrought iron gates, hoping for sparse attendance among the day's visitors. There were several people wending their way over the sunny paths or lingering by gravestones, so she relied on speed over yelling Becca's name. She ran hard past the stately memorial to AIDs victims and beyond the red rock scattering of stones honoring Civil War dead. She slid around a corner and stopped abruptly on the graveled path. Becca was leaning against the Lady of the Rock.

Jo walked to her slowly, fearing she'd find the same eerie trance that took Becca when she was triggered by the mannequin. She was bent at the waist, one hand on the base of the statue, one braced on her knee, her drifting blond hair obscuring her face. She was panting, pulling hard for air.

"Hello?" Jo tapped her thighs. She had no earthly idea what to do at this point, except try to catch Becca if she fainted again. Her brain was exploding with the ramifications of that extraordinary transmission back at the house, the shriek that still rang in her ears, and she had to work hard to focus on Becca. "Are you all right?"

Becca lifted one hand in reassurance, put it back on her knee, and went on panting. Jo moved closer cautiously.

"Well." Becca's voice was muffled. "At least we learned one thing from this. I'm an obedient daughter. Sheesh."

Becca straightened, and her face was blotched with red where it wasn't cheesy pale, but her eyes were clear and sharp. Jo huffed out a breath of relief.

"If she'd screamed 'Becca, cook,' I'd have a four-course dinner on the table right now." Becca slid bonelessly into the grass at the base of the statue and sat leaning against it. "Good Lord, Jo. Have you ever heard anything like that?"

"Actually, I have, yes. Warnings are a fairly common theme in transmissions." Jo wondered if a scholarly approach would be more helpful to Becca now or a nurturing one, and hoped for the former. "I admit I'm astonished by the volume and clarity of the message. That small radio should be utterly incapable of producing such a blast."

"Yeah, it was impressive." It was taking Becca too long to catch her breath after a relatively short sprint, and Jo realized how shaken she was. "Is Rachel all right?"

"She was fine enough to pitch me out the door after you. Are you…yourself again?"

"I'm getting there." Becca squinted up at her and shaded her eyes. "Would you please sit down before my neck goes into spasm?"

Jo would have sat on the ground where she was, but Becca patted the grass next to her. She glanced up at the Lady's implacable face as if asking for guidance, then lowered herself carefully beside Becca. "You did take that command rather literally. It was your mother's voice?"

Becca shrugged. "It was a shriek. It's hard to hear a voice in a shriek, especially a voice you hardly remember." She hesitated. "But yes, it was her."

Jo nodded. "Your mother is proving to be remarkably reticent. 'Not true.' 'Becca, run.' It seems we can't count on her for more than two words at a time."

"I sure didn't inherit that tendency." Becca sighed and ran her hands through her hair. "I'm sorry, Jo. Normally, I'm not a big fan of drama, but I seem to keep drawing you into some very theatrical scenes."

"Well." Jo sat back on her hands and crossed her legs in the grass. "What's listening for the voices of the dead if not high drama? A chase scene or two probably goes with the territory. But I'm a little surprised that you ran here."

"The cemetery?"

"Yes. Didn't you say this place scared you?"

"When I was a kid, sure." She nodded at the serene statue above them. "But my mom brought me here sometimes, to visit the Lady. I was never scared when she was with me."

"Really? Are you referring to some kind of psychic summons?"

Becca laughed. "No, I mean she brought me here when I was little, for picnics. It's green and quiet and peaceful here, like a park. It's one of the few clear memories I have of my mom—sitting under the Lady, eating peanut butter sandwiches." She glanced up at the cloaked woman. "I've always loved her, Jo. She's one of the few lifelike images that doesn't trigger me now. I'm not sure why. Maybe because she was familiar to me before the…trauma happened. She's obviously a mother, the way she comforts the girl kneeling beside her. I've always felt safe here."

"The Lady means a lot to me, too," Jo found herself saying. "This is my favorite spot in the cemetery, maybe in all of Seattle."

"You're kidding." Becca sounded both surprised and pleased. "I love that you and the Lady are friends. It's a good character reference. For you." She leaned so her shoulder bumped Jo's lightly. "I'm glad she's able to bring both of us a little peace."

Jo felt a warm pulsing on her shoulder where Becca touched her. She realized how very little space separated them. Jo was swept with a distinct, tactile memory of the feel of Becca in her arms days ago, holding her after she'd fainted, looking down into her face. She thought fast. "Are you concerned about the content of your mother's message?"

Becca sobered and leaned back against the Lady. She still looked wan, and her expression reminded Jo of the young girl above them, resting her head in the Lady's lap. "Well, I wish she could have been more specific. She could have mentioned a destination I should run *to*, or at least a direction I should run *in*."

"Becca, you need to take this seriously now." Jo was surprised by a flare of impatience that felt strangely protective. "I've told you that messages received through EVP are rarely factually false. We need to be aware that your mother perceives some danger to you. She's warned you to run."

"But from what?" Becca's brow furrowed. "Gaining two pounds from Rachel's brownies? That's the only threat I know of."

"If your mother didn't pull the trigger that night, someone else did." Surely Jo was pointing out the obvious; Becca must have considered this. "Forensics indicates it wasn't your father. So it's possible there's still a murderer out there who the police didn't have the wit to consider."

"Oh. There's a cheerful idea." Becca closed her eyes. "My mother is warning me to run from a murderer who is still out there. Okay. You and Rachel were the only ones in the room when she yelled. One of you did it."

"I was eight years old in nineteen seventy-eight."

"Joanne. I was kidding. Rachel?" Becca leaned away from her. "You're more likely to have shot my parents than Rachel Perry, eight years old or not. You have no idea what that woman's been through, but she's one of the strongest and most loving people I know. "

"I'm not implying Dr. Perry shot your parents." Jo felt the slight physical distance between them and was unsettled by a sense of loss. "I'm just saying your mother's warning should be taken seriously, is all. You might be in some kind of danger."

A bleakness passed over Becca's expressive features that aged her in seconds. "I'm tired of this," she said quietly. "All these questions, not an answer in sight. I've been asking these questions since I was sixteen, Jo."

Becca's gaze became uncertain, and Jo felt the air between them prickle oddly. Becca shifted closer to her, and lowered her head until it rested on Jo's shoulder. A long breath escaped them both. Becca settled against her, her body relaxing in stages. Her cold fingers sought Jo's in the thick grass and entwined in them.

Jo stared pop-eyed into the distance, her jaw clenched. Words ran through her head in rapid succession, punctuated by exclamation points. Words that rarely occurred to her, like "right" and "need."

Becca's touch was purely platonic. Jo had witnessed this phenomenon the other night, her easy physical affection with her friends. Becca was tired and afraid and she needed comfort. She apparently found something comforting in resting her head on Jo's shoulder and holding her hand. Jo felt the firm swell of Becca's breast against her arm, smelled the light vanilla scent of her hair, soft against her throat. Becca lifted her head and looked into Jo's eyes, and her lips parted. They stared at each other in silence beneath the Lady's kind gaze.

"I set up a Spiricom in the living room," Jo said quickly. "It was active when the radio's transmission came through."

Becca sat up and blinked at her. "A spiri-what, now?"

"All signs look very promising for a repeat sending, Becca. You'll need to take some time off work, and Dr. Perry needs to be informed not to show the house for several days."

"Jo, what are you talking about?"

Jo braced herself. "In order to create the most favorable conditions for an additional message, you're going to have to be physically present at the site of the last two transmissions. Namely, the house."

Becca was looking at her with dawning horror, so Jo got the worst of it over with fast.

"I have to be there, too, to catch the transmission. You and I are going to move into your childhood home, and we'll have to stay there until we hear from your mother again."

Chapter Five

Y ou and Dr. Call are moving into the house tonight," Becca's Uncle Mitchell said slowly, "and you plan to stay there until your mother does *what* again?"

"Until she speaks to us again from beyond the grave." Becca helped herself to another sauce-drenched manicotti shell. "And hopefully, tells us something relevant for once, such as 'Here's how I really died.' You want more of this, Jo?"

Jo shook her head, not bothering to lift her baleful gaze from her plate. Apparently, if Becca's new BFF didn't like what was served, she didn't eat. Well, she had briefed Jo about the menu at this dinner and warned her thoroughly about her uncle's capacity to infuriate. Jo still insisted on coming, and Becca had only the foggiest notion of why. Given her love of socializing, this family dinner should have held all the appeal for Jo as dawn for a vampire. But Becca figured she was a big girl, she could deal.

"Rebecca, you're serious?" Patricia looked to her husband for guidance. "For one thing, the house on Fifteenth isn't really available, is it?"

Becca grimaced with the old mixture of irritation and fondness for her aunt. Trust Patricia to zero in on the crux of the matter. "It's vacant right now, and Rachel sees no problem holding off on renting it for a while." She nudged Rachel's ankle gently with her shoe.

"Yes, that's right." Rachel patted her lips with a linen napkin. "The market's abysmal anyway, Mitch. We'll have a better shot at finding good tenants in the fall, when the universities are back in—"

"Becca, I don't understand the purpose of all this." Mitchell Healy had a mellifluous voice that served him well in charming white-collar juries in a courtroom. Around his own cherry wood dining room table, his tone tended toward the prosecutorial. "Since when did someone with your intellect suddenly start believing in séances and ghost stories?"

"Since my dead mother started yelling at me out of a radio." Becca bit deeply into her third slice of garlic bread and tried to bank her impatience. It was expecting a lot, asking these two to take all this seriously. She still struggled with it herself, and she was less hide-bound than her aunt and uncle. She spoke with her mouth full largely because she knew it drove Mitchell crazy. "We're trying to find out if Mom really committed suicide."

"Becca, Maddie's death—and my brother's—were tragedies." Mitchell's patrician features grew less stern. He nodded to his wife, who refilled his coffee cup. "And no one can blame you for wanting a different ending to that grim story. But honestly. Electronic Voice Phenomenon? No offense intended, Dr. Call."

"As I said, I heard that voice yesterday myself, Mitch," Rachel said. "It was truly astonishing."

Becca appreciated Rachel's support, but Jo was frowning at her uncle with open dislike. Becca hoped she would never be the target of those spooky eyes when they lasered anger. She nudged Jo's foot with her own. If the evening continued like this, Becca would be tap-dancing beneath the table, stepping on Jo and Rachel by turn. Jo ignored her, in any case.

"Sometimes tragedies can be explained by unconventional means, Mitch." Jo had been introduced to Becca's uncle as Mitchell. He was Mitch to no one but his wife and Rachel. "But only if we're open to asking the right questions."

"'The question of ghosts,' to quote Derrida." Mitchell's tone was polite. "I'm afraid I can't follow you there, Joanne. Nothing in my philosophy or my life experience has ever given me reason to invest in the supernatural."

"I appreciate the thought, but my work is quite well funded." Jo was stone-faced.

"Patricia, you've outdone yourself, as usual," Rachel said, and Becca slumped in relief. "I don't see how you put in full days running that shelter and still manage to turn out such delectable din—"

"I'd like to know more about the scientific basis of your work, Joanne." Mitchell steepled his fingers on the table. "In the research, has anyone ever actually produced empirical evidence of an afterlife?"

"All the research has produced empirical evidence," Jo said blandly. "'Empirical' simply means information gathered by observation and experiment, Mitch. If you intended to say proof, it depends on what standard you're referencing. But yes, EVP has provided ample proof of some form of afterlife existence to meet my professional standards."

Becca stirred cream into her coffee hard, her spoon ringing inside the stoneware cup. She caught Patricia's eye and saw her weary smile. Affection for her won over irritation, at least for now. She could remember a hundred times during her adolescence in this house when Patricia's apologetic looks tried to ease Mitchell's interrogations.

"I'd say the question of standards is a relevant one." Mitchell sipped his coffee with a light slurp. "You have a PhD in transpersonal psychology, Doctor?"

"That's one of my doctorates."

"Wait, pull up." Becca set her cup down with a clatter. "Mitchell, how did you know what degree Jo has? I didn't say anything about her degree on the phone this morning. I just told you her name."

Mitchell shrugged, an almost boyish gesture of modesty. "Pardon me, Becca, but that's why God invented search engines. I think you can understand why Pat and I would be curious about the mysterious dinner guest you invited to join us tonight. Apparently, this isn't a romantic relationship?"

"*No.*" Becca tried to control her voice. "And curiosity doesn't give you the right to treat—"

Mitchell cut in again. "I'm just pointing out that it seems a rather idiosyncratic doctorate for a scientist who—"

"Mitch, dear." Rachel's tone was mild, but Mitchell quieted at once. "You know I'm your oldest friend. That's why I can get away with asking you to please stop interrupting your guests. You've done it three times tonight, twice to *me*, heaven forefend, and we haven't even made it to dessert yet."

"Devil's food cake." Patricia sighed. "Ironically, as it turns out."

Becca had to smile at her.

Mitchell stared at Rachel for a long moment, one thin eyebrow arched, and that rare flicker passed over his face that made Becca remember, reluctantly, that a decent enough man resided beneath his often grating exterior. He smiled at Rachel, not a courtroom smile but a genuine one, and offered an amused nod of contrition. Mitchell and Rachel had known each other since elementary school, and they shared a bond of real affection. Not even Patricia could coax out his humanity as reliably as Rachel.

"I do apologize if I was rude, Dr. Perry. To both doctors. You too, Joanne."

Becca was the one he had interrupted, but she could be gracious about this if it meant restoring peace. Jo looked less mollified than bored, but at least she took a crunching bite of her garlic bread.

"I guess reminders of Scott tend to bring out my confrontational side." Mitchell dropped his napkin on the table. "Not pleasant memories for any of us."

"Well, remembering his death is certainly painful." Patricia rested her manicured hand on Mitchell's forearm. "But we both have good memories of Scottie too, dear. You didn't always get along, but what brothers do? The two of you were a lot alike, I always thought. I was very fond of him, and Maddie as well. She was a fine artist, and such a lovely woman, Becca."

Becca knew Patricia was right. Several pictures of her mother survived, and a framed photo of her parents still stood on her dresser at home. Madelyn Healy had the kind of shy blond beauty one associated with reticence and reserve, an understated delicacy that was unthreatening to other women and aroused protectiveness in men. From her own memory, Becca could picture her hands most clearly, her long, tapered fingers the incarnation of gentleness. Then she remembered the harrowing scream from the radio and shuddered. She felt Rachel watching her.

"Are you all right with this, friend?" Rachel leaned closer and lowered her voice. "We don't have to discuss anything that upsets you. I can always bring up Michelle Obama."

Becca suppressed a bubble of laughter. "How can I be upset? There's devil's food cake in the kitchen."

Rachel winked at her, but sobered as Jo spoke.

"Actually, your insights into the dynamics between Becca's parents might be helpful to us." Jo reached into the breast pocket of her white shirt. She withdrew the small silver device she'd had at the Rose and laid it on the table. "Does anyone object if I record this?"

"It's not really my habit to allow—" Mitchell broke off and looked at Becca.

"Good," Jo said shortly. "Becca, I can promise you I'm not going to make any direct references to the death scene."

"Good," Becca repeated. She couldn't tell yet if she'd have to plunge her fork into Jo's jugular before she made this charming dinner any worse.

"Becca and I are working from the theory that the accepted explanation of her parents' deaths isn't true." Jo studied Mitchell and Patricia. "Have either of you ever had any suspicions along those lines?"

"There's never been any reason to question what the police told us," Mitchell answered. "Becca, are you sure you want us to delve into all this personal business?"

"Well, this family doesn't have a big history of delving." Becca was not loving this conversation, but she'd told Jo she would cooperate in learning more about her parents. She looked at Rachel for reassurance and found it in her kind eyes. "You guys have never told me that much about my mom and dad."

"Oh, Rebecca. I'm not sure that's fair." Patricia sounded pained. "It seems to me we've spoken about them quite often over the years. At least when you were younger."

"I don't mean you didn't mention them. You just never really answered my questions. Some of my questions, when I was younger." Becca hesitated. That fogginess was tickling the back of her brainpan again, the mild disorientation that was becoming her natural state these days.

"Before we're all too much older, Becca." Jo drummed her blunt nails on the tablecloth. "What questions would you like to ask?"

Becca threw Jo an exasperated glance while she tried to gather her thoughts, aware the other three were exchanging looks. This gathering had brought out the worst in Jo, the near failure of her meager social skills. At least the other night, with Marty and Khadijah, some actual warmth had developed around that table. The sharp edges of Jo's brusqueness had softened eventually, in the company of her friends. Becca saw none of that gentling in her now. She felt an unexpected pang of wistfulness, missing the friendlier bond she'd shared with Jo in the cemetery, at the feet of the Lady.

A friendliness that had begun to change, Becca remembered. She had tried hard to hold back from touching Jo in that moment; she wasn't given to throwing herself in the arms of people who avoided physical contact. But Becca's sudden weariness had been so complete, her loneliness so stark, she desperately needed some kind of human connection. Leaning into Jo had felt surprisingly natural, even welcome. And the sensation of touching her had deepened, become richer and undeniably sensual. Becca shook her head and tried to clear her mind.

"I guess I've only heard the good stories about my parents. I remember those." Becca granted Patricia that much. "But I know they didn't have a perfect marriage, and neither of you have said much about that."

Patricia started to speak, but Mitchell beat her to it, which was not technically interrupting, it was just Mitchell. "I'd say you've summed it up plainly enough, Becca, and I'm not sure what more we can add. Pat and I weren't privy to the intimate details of Scott's marriage. You're right. It wasn't a perfect union. I haven't known many of those, however, except my own." He lifted his coffee cup to Patricia. Becca noted Mitchell's definition of a perfect union involved Patricia's lifelong willingness to overlook his roving eye, but he was right; their marriage had always been solid.

"But there was no abuse in their relationship, Becca." Patricia spoke with the authority of the director of a women's shelter. "We would have been aware of that, certainly. Scott and Maddie may have argued, but we would have stepped in if we thought there was violence."

"You did step in, though, didn't you?" Becca smiled at Rachel. "You were worried enough that you got them into counseling with the best psychiatrist in Seattle."

Jo had been checking the device to see if it was recording, but now she set it down. "Dr. Perry? You saw Becca's parents in counseling? I wasn't aware of this."

"I told you Rachel was my therapist when I was a kid, Jo, after my parents died." Becca tried not to sound snappish, but she didn't try hard. "That's how I knew her. Mitchell referred my folks to her for marriage counseling."

"I couldn't imagine better hands to entrust them to." Mitchell inclined his head at Rachel. "Pat and I had heard enough to know there was a lot of tension under that roof. And it's true we were concerned enough to ask Rachel to meet with them."

"But it wasn't a referral you should have taken, was it?" Jo turned to Rachel. She didn't sound accusatory, just curious.

Rachel lifted her head. "Because?"

"You mentioned that Mitchell is one of your oldest friends, correct? Doesn't that mean you had at least some personal contact with his younger brother, as well? I'm wondering if it was wise, or ethical, to agree to see a family friend in a clinical setting."

Becca bit back a knee-jerk defense of Rachel, trusting her to speak for herself. The planes of Rachel's elegant face held the same pallor that had worried Becca the day before and she sat stiffly, as if she were in pain, but she answered Jo easily.

"Under any other circumstances you'd be right, Joanne. I really intended just to do a preliminary assessment and then refer Scott and Maddie on to a colleague who would be a good fit for them. It began as a simple evaluation for marital counseling, but it quickly became focused on Maddie."

Rachel paused and took Becca's hand in her own. "Becca, your mother was my patient. You know her death doesn't release me from the promise I make to all my patients, that I'll honor their privacy. You're my friend now, but there are things I can't and won't tell you about Maddie's journey. Do you still understand that?"

Becca ignored Jo's sliding the recorder closer to them. She didn't answer Rachel right away, letting the room mellow until it was just the two of them again, comfortable and familiar. "You've told me that so many times, Rach. I do understand. Or I do whenever I'm not feeling this raw. But I really need your help with all this tonight, okay? Tell us what you can."

Rachel sighed and straightened in her chair. "All right. Most of this is fairly common knowledge anyway. Becca's mother suffered from bipolar disorder, Joanne. She only had one manic episode to my knowledge, before her child was born. But she struggled hard with some devastating depressions when Becca was quite young."

Rachel spoke gently, but Becca saw no need to cushion these words. Not only was her head too dim to host much feeling right now, she remembered her mother's emotional cataclysms as the natural order of things. As far as her small self had known, everyone's mother stayed in bed for days at a time. Everyone's father came racing home in the middle of the day to feed their kid.

"Becca, she fought so hard to get well." Patricia seemed to think Becca needed comfort, too. "Maddie really tried, dear. I can't say I knew her terribly well. I wanted to be closer to her, but I felt she and Scottie resisted spending time with Mitch and me. But those depressions scared her enough to agree to see Rachel privately. And I know Maddie did everything she could to help herself. She made all her appointments, she stayed on her meds. I wish half the homeless women I work with had her courage."

A small, hard kernel in Becca wondered at Patricia's unusual wordiness on this topic. She had probably just said more about her mother than Becca had heard throughout puberty. And there was a note of professional detachment in her aunt's tone, some nuance that made her sympathy sound rehearsed. Lord, Becca thought, I'm getting as scratchy as Jo.

Rachel rubbed her eyes. "In Maddie's case, Becca, more than any I've ever seen, it came down to chemistry. The chemical imbalance in your mother's brain was just too complex to be helped by medication for long, at least the ones we had back then, in the mid-seventies. It's a lifetime curse for many of my patients, even today—to be born with minds that are simply too inscrutable for modern psychiatry to offer any real, lasting healing."

Becca started to speak, but closed her mouth, confused. Jo was staring at Rachel with an odd mixture of foreboding and distaste. Her hands were folded neatly on the table, but Becca could see her fingers were so tightly clenched that her knuckles were white.

"Help me understand this, people." Jo loosened her hands and traced a pattern on the tablecloth with one finger. "We're talking about a young mother, by all accounts a loving one, highly motivated to control her behavior. A troubled marriage, but a husband supportive enough to send his wife to a competent psychiatrist. Madelyn Healy was fully compliant with her treatment. How long was she in therapy with you, Dr. Perry? Before the shootings?"

"Eight months," Rachel said quietly.

"Eight months of private sessions. And she had a husband, concerned in-laws, and a good therapist as her support system. I'm trying to understand why none of you saw the crisis coming. If things happened that night the way all of you say they did, if Becca's mother suddenly flew into a psychotic rage and took two lives. How is it that none of you were alerted to—"

"I believe Rachel has explained all that, Joanne." Mitchell was every inch the prosecutor again. "Tragedies happen in families afflicted with mental illness. It's a fact of life. Pat and I see it every day in our work, and we both deal with the carnage that kind of sickness leaves in its wake. The best treatment in the world can't save some people."

"And on that happy note, I'm afraid I must take my leave." Rachel smiled at them and pushed back carefully from the table. "Patricia, dinner was wonderful, but I have early sessions in the morning."

"Rachel, please. No need to rush off." Mitchell got to his feet. "Sit for a while longer. You don't look well tonight. I'm sure Joanne didn't intend to imply any criticism."

"I'm not offended, Mitch, honestly." Rachel laid her hand on Becca's shoulder before she could rise, and spoke to her alone. "I promise to help you in this investigation in any way I can, Becca. I've just had enough for tonight, and I need to take care of myself."

"Of course, honey," Becca whispered.

Jo looked uneasy for the first time. "Dr. Perry, I'm not necessarily talking about any professional failing on your part."

"We're talking about the first and saddest professional failure of my career, Joanne. Perhaps of my life." Rachel bent stiffly, lifted her purse from the floor, and opened it. "Becca, here are the keys to the house. Remember that damn washer is still on the blink. I haven't had a chance to get it fixed."

Becca accepted the keys numbly. "I'm sorry, Rach."

"No harm done." Rachel kissed Becca's cheek. "Night, friends."

"I'm walking you to your car," Becca decided. Then she decided the night was over for her, too. "Patricia, Mitchell, thank you for having us. Great manicotti. Jo, you can ride back with me now, or you can jump into Lake Washington and swim to Capitol Hill. Your pick."

CHAPTER SIX

The lights across the I-90 floating bridge burned an eerie fairy path across the dark water, and Jo sat back in Becca's rattling Toyota and tried to enjoy the ride. She drove this bridge often enough in her own Bentley, but always alone; she seldom got to take in the scenery that was Seattle's inherent blessing. Not that the palpable tension in this car allowed for such innocuous pleasure.

Jo's stomach rumbled, and she considered asking Becca to stop at a Dick's Drive-In en route to Capitol Hill. She didn't know what Patricia Healy considered decent manicotti, but it was not whatever had inhabited Jo's plate tonight. Dick's offered an excellent cheeseburger. She glanced at Becca's still profile and decided against it.

"I didn't like the way he spoke to you." Jo hadn't intended to say this aloud, but it was the truth.

"What?" They were the first words that had passed between them since Becca pulled away fast from the stately house in Kirkland. "What are you talking about?"

"The way he made you feel. I didn't like it." Jo struggled to shut up. Her voice revealed too much emotion, too much of the protectiveness that was still so new to her. "Your uncle talked to you as if you're simple, as if your opinions don't matter. It was so different the other night, with your friends. They respect you, Becca. I could hear it in their voices. They treated you the way people who love you should. But your face changed tonight when your uncle spoke to you. You got smaller in your chair. It made me angry."

"Jo." Becca's hands still clenched the wheel, but at least she wasn't "Joanne" anymore. "Mitchell and Patricia took me in when I was five years old. They never expected to be parents, never even wanted kids of their own. But they raised me kindly. They did the very best they could, bringing me up. And I didn't always make it easy on them, I promise you."

"I find that hard to believe." Jo looked at Becca's features, lit softly in the light of the dashboard, and realized she found them lovely. "Except for your phobia, and perhaps your too-hardy appetite, I'd think you'd be easy enough to raise—"

"Jo, you have to listen to me." Becca's voice was less chilly, but still firm. "I'm telling you that you don't have my permission to be rude to the people in my life. However you might feel about my uncle and aunt, Rachel, my friends, you've got to be courteous to them. If we're going to spend a lot of time together, you have to understand that. You have to do better."

Jo stared miserably out the window, flecked now by slanted dots of rain. "I'll try, Becca." It was the best she could promise. She had been trying for courtesy all her life and falling short of the mark.

"Thank you." Becca glanced at her, and her eyes warmed before she returned her attention to the road. Jo understood she was on her way to being forgiven. She realized she didn't need to consult her files on microexpressions to know the truth about Becca anymore. This was puzzling, as they'd met only eight days ago. Jo didn't trust herself to interpret the motivations of many people in her life, even after years of acquaintance. Becca's face seemed familiar to her now, open and expressive and honest.

They chugged up the steep rises of Capitol Hill, but the silence inside the car was more comfortable. Another welcome oddity in Jo's sparse social life, not having to struggle to fill perfectly good quiet with empty talk. She watched Becca's fine-boned hands on the wheel, her wrists delicate in spite of the strength in her arms. She imagined Maddie Healy's hands had been much like her daughter's.

Becca pulled up in front of the house on Fifteenth Avenue with a squealing of brakes, and the engine harrumphed several times before dying.

"Doesn't the state pay their social workers enough to buy decent transportation?" Jo hoped Becca would hear the teasing in her voice.

Becca chuckled and tapped the steering wheel. "Well, the state pays me more than the staff makes at my aunt's shelter. Basically, I'm too cheap to buy a decent car. Or decent sneakers. I love to get out of the city on weekends, so I save all my dinars for trips."

"Where do you trip?"

"Cannon Beach. Lake Crescent. I seem to run for pretty water whenever I get a chance." Becca was still tapping the wheel. "I'm stalling. You can tell, right?"

Jo nodded. "It's hard for you, going back into this house."

Becca gazed out her window, to the dark cemetery across the street. "It's going to be hard for me to sleep in this house again. We don't know how long we'll have to stay here?"

"There's no telling, Becca." Jo was sympathetic but resolute. "If it's any comfort...I'm not sure why it would be, but if it's any comfort, you won't be alone in there. I'll be with you every minute." She smiled. "You won't hurt my feelings if you scream in dismay now and run away again."

A brief laugh escaped Becca. "Both of us are pretty private people, Dr. Call. If we're alone together every minute, for days on end, I can imagine we..."

Jo wasn't sure what Becca was imagining until she started to imagine it, too. Becca's gaze changed, deepened, as she studied Jo more intently. They stared at each other, and the warm confines of the car seemed suddenly close and confining.

"Pop the trunk," Jo said. "I'll get our bags."

Becca reached beneath the dash and popped the trunk.

❖

"We should plan to sleep in this room, and spend most of our time here." Jo was tinkering with a silver radio on the coffee table in the living room, so she didn't see Becca's look of dismay. "It's best if we consolidate all of our resources in one area."

"We're going to sleep in here?" Becca said faintly. "Not in the bedrooms upstairs? I don't think I can do that."

"Why can't you? We'll be perfectly comfortable."

There were a vast number of things Becca felt incapable of at the moment, but she decided to focus on dealing with this one, this thing with Jo. She didn't want to keep ignoring what was happening between them. She continued her slow circle of the living room. "Listen, maybe we should talk. I don't want to make you uncomfortable, but it's my way to be direct about things like this."

"What is it, Becca?" Jo sat back on her heels, turning a tiny screwdriver to tighten a recessed screw in the radio.

"There's a funny energy between us." Becca hoped she wasn't making a mistake. Khadijah said Becca's willingness to confront elephants in the room was admirable, but this elephant was Joanne Call. "We've had a couple of moments, lately. In the cemetery, and just now, in the car. I think I'm starting to feel some attraction to you, Jo."

Jo kept working, her long fingers nimble and sure on the machine. "It doesn't matter."

"What?"

"Your attraction to me doesn't matter." Jo positioned the radio carefully on the tabletop and adjusted its many dials. "It's nothing we'll act on."

"Okay." Becca felt a flare of embarrassment, which didn't surprise her, followed by a pang of disappointment, which did. "We won't act on this attraction because we're working together? Or because I'm alone in feeling it?"

"Becca, what difference does it make?" Jo switched on a small screen in the box, which cast her austere features in a ghostly amber glow. It was an unfortunate effect that rendered her almost alien. "I don't sleep with the subjects in my studies. That's a basic tenet of ethics in any credible research."

"Joanne, I wasn't suggesting we ravish each other tonight on the Pendleton rug." Becca felt her cheeks flush with heat. Even knowing Jo's limitations, it hurt, putting herself out there honestly and meeting such brusque rejection. "I just don't believe in ignoring my feelings when they're this strong. Not when I believe you might share them." Good Lord, had Patricia spiked her manicotti? What in the world was she doing?

Jo's back straightened slowly and she pivoted to face her, moving with the feline grace Becca couldn't stop noticing. "You're the most transparent person I've ever met, Becca, so I'll respond in kind. I'm not capable of the kind of emotion you're talking about. I never have been. I don't do people. I can be your guide in this project, and your ally, even your protector. But I can't be your friend or your lover. I'll never be those things."

Jo turned back to the radio.

Becca lowered herself carefully into the deep sofa, that strange fog surging through her again. What kind of linguistic warp was wandering through this conversation? Becca had been talking about sexual attraction. Hadn't she? Good old red-blooded lesbian lust. They had both felt it in the cemetery, in the car, she was pretty sure of this. But Jo was telling her she was incapable of love—emotional connection, devotion, etcetera. A miscommunication of the highest order. There wasn't the faintest possibility on the planet that Becca was falling in love with Jo. She was almost certain of this.

They were quiet for a long while. Jo moved methodically to each of the small radios she had set up around the room, including the yellow ball that had blasted her dead mother's voice the day before. She adjusted them until they all hissed softly with low-key, empty static, much like Becca's brain.

Becca waited until the grandfather clock in the corner chimed ten and her mind had settled a little. She wanted to be sure that pang of hurt had faded. There were things she needed to know now, for all kinds of reasons, but she wanted to be sure she would speak from kindness alone. "Do you know anything about Nonverbal Learning Disorder, Jo?"

Jo's hands stilled on the silver machine, and the corner of her mouth lifted. She smiled rarely, and Becca had never seen this particular smile. She remembered her first impression of this woman—a tall, dark wraith who seemed quite capable of cruelty.

"Most people guess autism. You're closer."

Becca nodded. "I don't know if you give much credence to labels like that."

"I don't fit forty percent of the diagnostic criteria for Nonverbal Learning Disorder." Jo lifted a white cloth from her satchel and rubbed her hands in it. "I have no problem with eye contact or spatial awareness. I'm not physically clumsy. I've worked hard to compensate for my inability to read facial expressions."

Becca suppressed an urge to apologize, and a stronger one to offer comfort. The anger was draining from Jo's voice.

"I guess I give credence to the label Rachel Perry used tonight. She said some minds are too inscrutable for modern psychiatry to help. That's the diagnosis the best of those useless doctors gave me. That's what they told my parents."

"Inscrutable?" Becca remembered the stark change in Jo's expression when Rachel used that term. "A psychiatrist told your parents you were inscrutable?"

"Yes, when I was ten years old."

"And what did he mean by that?"

"That no one would ever really know me, basically. They didn't have your fancier diagnoses back then, all these disorders. I decided being inscrutable is preferable to being an emotional cretin, which is how another doctor described me."

"Jo." Becca closed her eyes in pain. "Please tell me no doctor laid that idiocy on a ten-year-old kid."

"No, I was eight when we heard that one. My parents took me to lots of doctors. Luckily, my mother and father were smart enough to let me be, for the most part. They hired competent au pairs." Jo rested her hand on the silver radio. "May I show you this? It's something special."

Becca blinked, trying to shift mental and emotional gears. Jo was doubtless only capable of a given amount of personal disclosure in one night, and she may have reached her limit. She pushed her way out of the sofa and stood next to Jo at the coffee table. "There's something special about this radio?"

"It's not a radio, it's a Spiricom. Spiritually speaking, a Spiricom is to a radio what a computer is to a hand calculator." Jo shrugged with that note of shyness that humanized her completely. "Sorry. I'll try not to wax too rhapsodic. But this little device successfully established afterlife communication in nineteen seventy-six, and several times since. It detects signals and broadcasts them, like a radio. But it can also send signals back."

Becca stared at the innocuous box and its small, glowing screen. "We can send messages back? Back where, exactly?"

"Back to the source. Wherever they came from. I'm simplifying all this terribly, Becca. But theoretically, if your mother contacts us again, if she speaks to you…"

"Then I can speak to her." Becca had shot heroin exactly six times in her life and not for more than twenty years, but the craving came back on her strong and sweet and hard. She clenched her teeth on an expletive and her knees went weak.

"Becca? Maybe you should sit down." Jo gripped her elbow and steered her back to the sofa, and Becca sat. "Your lips have gone that alarming limburger shade again. Are you all right?"

"Limburger lips," Becca murmured. "Sounds lovely." The fog was roaring through her, scraping her nerves raw. She swore if her mother bellowed out of any of these infernal radios right now, the top of her head would blow off.

"Jo, I'd only rage at her." She looked up at Jo helplessly. "That's all I could feel just now, when you said she might hear me. If I could talk to my mother tonight, I'd just scream at her. I didn't know I'm still so *angry*. After all these years, my work with Rachel, all the insight I have into mental illness…" Becca trailed off as her throat closed, and she felt tears threaten. Again. She knew Jo was uncomfortable with such overt emotion, but she wasn't sure she could hold them back.

"Slow down a moment." Jo lowered herself beside her on the sofa. She sat in stiff silence, her expression intensely thoughtful.

When she spoke, she measured her words as carefully as Becca would if she were trying to describe a mathematical theorem. "It makes sense to me that a small child would rage at a parent who chose to leave her. But I'm sure you have other feelings for your mother as well, Becca. Gentler feelings. They're just not accessible right now, given your emotional state these days." Jo cleared her throat. "But I hope you'll continue with this, no matter how hard it gets. The child has a right to rage, but the adult daughter has a right to know the truth about what happened that night."

The dizziness was receding, but Becca still gazed at Jo in confusion. This was the same scientist who described her mother's dead, bullet-pierced face without a qualm. Now she was discussing human emotion with a calm logic that Becca found soothing beyond all reason. The tears that had filled her eyes subsided easily.

Becca sighed and rested her head against the back of the couch. "You define our relationship any way you see fit, Jo. I'm going to think of you as a friend."

Jo looked at Becca as if she were a queen granting her an honorable but distinctly dangerous knighthood. "Well," she said finally. "Do as you feel you must."

Becca grinned and took mercy on her. "You're really expecting us to bunk down here, for the immediate millennium?"

"Yes, I think we can make ourselves comfortable enough." Jo looked around the spacious room. "You take this sofa. I sleep at my desk half the time anyway. I'll be fine in one of those armchairs."

"Not for nights on end you won't, but we'll take it one stiff neck at a time." Becca levered herself out of the deep cushion and went to the duffel bag she had dropped in one corner. "We might be able to find a blanket or two in some drawer upstairs."

A muffled clank emerged from the bag as she lifted it, and Jo frowned. "What do you have in that thing, if I may ask? Bowling pins?"

Becca opened the duffel and drew out two smooth, rounded sticks just over two feet long. They were slightly thicker than broom handles, and fit in her palms with practiced ease. "These are my *chobos*. Mock not my *chobos*." She lifted a warning hand to Jo.

"They travel with me everywhere. To the beach, sometimes to the grocery store. I'm sure not sleeping here without them. I don't think I'd have the guts to shoot anyone, but I'd happily wale the merry hell out of any burglar with these."

She caught Jo's suddenly intense gaze, and her smile faltered. "Jo? What's the matter?"

"You referred to money as *dinars* earlier. And now you use the term *chobos*." Jo walked to Becca slowly. "Chobos were a weapon utilized by an ancient Amazon clan. But only an Amazon clan portrayed by a late nineties television series. The term chobos does not exist outside this particular television series."

Jo had reached her, and her eyes still held that strange light. Becca realized why the light seemed strange to her. Jo looked happy. She reached out and clasped the chobos gently, her hands between Becca's.

"Becca," Jo said softly. "You're a *Xena* fan."

CHAPTER SEVEN

S in Trade.' We could be watching 'Adventures in the Sin Trade' instead of this." Marty pelted another handful of popcorn at the curved glass screen of the old television. "'Bitter Suite,' we could be watching. Or 'Destiny'!"

Khadijah made a rude buzzer noise, emitting a genteel spray of popcorn, never taking her eyes from the flickering screen. "No way, baby, we're not watching 'Destiny.' No episodes where Xena dies, uh-uh."

"That limits our choices. A lot." Becca was curled beside Khadijah on the living room floor. "Xena died at least once a season. So we can't watch 'The Quest.' Or 'Greater Good.' Or 'Friends in Need.' Or 'Ides of—"

"No 'Ides of March.'" Jo laid down the law. "Gabrielle also dies in 'Ides of March.' Absolutely not."

She had never been able to abide watching Xena's young blond sidekick suffer so much as a parchment cut. They could kill off the Warrior Princess weekly without ruffling Jo's feathers, but Gabrielle could not be touched. Music trickled from the ancient TV, and she straightened. "Ah. This is why we're watching this one."

A few moments later, Khadijah sat back on a deep pillow and sighed happily. "Oh, my. Would you looky here at lil' Miss O'Connor."

Jo assumed O'Connor was the name of the actress who played Gabrielle, but the people behind the series had never held much interest for her. It was the characters who were compelling to her, the relationship. She watched Gabrielle dance slowly among a throng of painted revelers, brushing her hand lightly across her bare waist. A sweeter portrayal of a young woman's sensual awakening didn't exist in popular culture, elitism be damned.

"Gabrielle's not so little, from here on in." Marty got it at once, which pleased Jo. "This is the first episode where she stops coming on like a pesky girl brat, and starts moving like a woo-man."

"Martha darlin', you know I cherish you." Khadijah smiled dreamily at the screen. "But if that buxom little bard ever wants to dance into my bed, you're sleeping in the yard."

"Okay."

"Will you two shut up and let the cute little woo-man dance?" Becca crammed more popcorn in her mouth, her eyes sparkling.

It was their second night in the house, and Becca seemed more relaxed than she had in days. That faint line between her brows was fading, despite the location and the lateness of the hour. Time with her friends was helping.

Unless she counted the nights she had worked sleepless in laboratories with colleagues, Jo had never attended a slumber party. Tonight was taking on the tone of one. Apparently, Marty and Khadijah had brought over the entirety of the *Xena* series, and they were on their third episode. No one showed any evidence of tiring, either of the stories they loved or the company. Including Jo, which surprised her.

Jo had indulged in one pop culture celebration in her life, and it was this series. She had never shared her affection for it with anyone. There were national gatherings of *Xena* fans, but conferences were not Jo's thing, unless she was presenting at science or paranormal symposiums. But the way Becca's face had lit up as they stood together last night, holding those sticks between them, this party was all but inevitable.

Tonight, for the first time, Jo could see this living room as a place a family would gather, rather than a room adjacent to a murder scene. Lit only by the colorful light of the old TV left by previous tenants, there was no sense of gloominess in the large space. They were lounging on the floor before the TV, Becca and her friends laughing frequently, decades vanishing from their faces as they watched. It was a cozy scene, but as the dance music faded, Jo felt the beginnings of restlessness at last.

She got to her feet quietly and stepped around Marty's long legs, not wanting to interrupt their friendly but rather incessant chatter. The readings on the Spiricom needed regular monitoring, and she wanted to check the tuning of the radios in the room.

"I apologize for my earlier scorn, Doc. I'm ready to salute your taste in *Xena* eps." Marty lifted her bottle of pop to Jo. "Your taste in *Xena* episodes is now your most redeeming feature."

"My only one so far, I'm sure." Jo considered even partial redemption with these friends a positive development. She hadn't failed miserably at the Rose, but she hadn't made the best first impression, either. She wanted to keep her promise to Becca to do better.

"All right, what's next?" Khadijah squirmed closer to the box of disks. "Are we wanting blood and guts? Comedy? Jo, prove you're on a roll now. You pick."

"Anything that focuses on the bond." Jo bent over the Spiricom, adjusting its frequency minutely.

"Heavy on the subtext between X and G?" Marty brushed her palms together. "Hot dog. More rated-PG erotica for little Marty. I'll take it."

"No, not the sexual subtext, necessarily, the friendship. Their love for each other." Jo was satisfied the Spiricom was scanning well. She glanced up and caught Becca's gaze, unexpectedly still and searching. With that new and strange familiarity, Jo could read her thoughts, the question in her mind. She spoke to Becca as if they were alone in the room. "I may not be very good at such things, that depth of friendship. I may not be able to paint a masterpiece, either. But I can still stand in front of one and appreciate its beauty."

Becca smiled at her, and Khadijah looked at them both and raised a sculpted eyebrow. Luckily, Marty was distracted by something she found on the coffee table.

"Hey, don't forget to check this one, Jo." She picked up the sound recorder Jo had last used at that unsavory dinner party the night before, and extended it toward her. There was a muted click, and Mitchell Healy's curt voice crackled into the room. "*I believe Rachel has explained all that, Joanne.*"

"Whoops." Marty tried to turn the recorder off.

Jo bit back an impatient command. "It's all right. Here, I can take it."

"*Tragedies happen in families afflicted with mental illness. It's a fact of life.*" Mitchell's voice continued from the small speakers. "*Pat and I see it every day in our work, and we both deal with the carnage that kind of sickness leaves in its wake.*"

"Either find the off button on that thing or let me whack it with a chobo." Becca tossed a small pillow at Marty. Her tone was light, but she wasn't smiling anymore. "It was bad enough sitting through all that the first time."

Jo was frozen in place, and Marty looked at her in surprise. "What's up, Doc?"

"*The best treatment in the world can't save some people,*" Mitchell Healy concluded.

"That voice wasn't there last night." Jo took the recorder from Marty and tapped keys rapidly.

"What voice?" Becca asked. "That's just Mitchell, Jo. He was really tediously there last night."

"Not him. The recorder captured another voice, along with your uncle's." Jo reversed the recording and fine-tuned the meager filters. "I'm not surprised you missed it; I only caught a moment."

"Mute the box, babe," Marty told Khadijah, who scrambled for the remote and silenced the TV.

"Jo, are you sure you didn't hear Patricia?" There was a new stiffness in Becca's shoulders.

"It wasn't your aunt, or you, or me, or Rachel Perry." Jo set the recorder to maximum volume. She thought she had zeroed in on the right thread to enhance the second voice. She hit play. "Listen again."

Beneath Mitchell's pedantic tone, between his words, after one breath and before another, a woman whispered.

"*...it's a fact of life,*" Mitchell Healy repeated.

And a woman sighed, "*He wanted me, Becca.*"

"Oh, sweet sonny Jesus Christ on a crutch," Khadijah said softly.

Jo tapped keys again, moving back into their circle. She sat on the floor carefully and played the recorded passage a third time. She heard the same message, muted and mournful but clear.

"*He wanted me, Becca.*"

Interpreting facial expressions still required study, but Jo had always been able to read the emotional nuance of voice. This one was infused with sadness. She looked up at Becca, who was staring at her in shock. "Can you confirm the identity?"

Becca just nodded. "It's her."

"That's your *mother*, Rebecca?" Khadijah slid off her knees and sat hard on the rug. "Holy smokes. I've always believed in...but I never thought I'd...holy smokes."

Jo couldn't believe her luck. This was rare in the literature, capturing a voice that had been homebound in a second location. Madelyn Healy had "left" this house and followed her daughter across the dark waters of Lake Washington last night. She didn't expect Becca to share her excitement in this milestone, but at least she seemed to be recovering more swiftly than her friends.

"Hey." Becca frowned at Marty. "Are you going to faint?"

Khadijah slid a protective arm around Marty's waist. She was decidedly pale and she couldn't take her eyes from the recorder in Jo's hands, but she shook her head.

"I'm not fainting, I'm just gobsmacked." Marty swallowed visibly. "We just heard a ghost, Kaddy."

"We did. The ghost of a mother this girl loved very much." Khadijah's tone regained its natural warmth as she regarded Becca. "Are you all right, Bec? This must be pounding on all kinds of buttons."

"Well, I haven't bolted from the room yet. That's progress." Becca's hands trembled as she swept them through her hair. "I've already moved past the whole, she's a talking dead person thing. I'm focusing on what she said."

"And you're taking her literally?" Marty looked from Becca to Jo and back. "She said 'he wanted me' when your Uncle Mitchell was droning on. Are you thinking those rumors were true? He had a thing for your mom?"

In the second it took Becca to clear her expression, Jo learned that's exactly what she believed. She wondered if Becca had taken the next step in logic, and was afraid she had.

"Messages received through EVP are rarely factually false." Becca quoted Jo. "If Mitchell wanted my mother…did he come after her? And if she resisted him, is she saying he killed her, Jo? And my father?"

They all looked at Jo with a solemnity she found disconcerting. She was neither an oracle nor a homicide detective. But she had studied these voices for years, and Becca deserved any insight her experience might offer.

"Well." She checked the recorder's settings carefully before turning it off. "It's true that ghost messengers rarely lie. But they're still human entities, Becca. Death doesn't make them suddenly omniscient or divine. Their communications can be incomplete—or factually accurate, but misleading."

"Incomplete, no woof." Marty counted the words on her fingers. "Becca, the, person, who, shot, us, is, name-name. Nine words. Your mom could make things a lot easier on us if she'd just spit out those nine words."

"We probably shouldn't count on that." Jo wished she could give Becca a better answer. "If we understand your mother correctly, Becca, this is all we know so far. She may not have committed suicide. She believes you're in some kind of danger. And a man, possibly Mitchell Healy, wanted her. Whatever that means. We can't even be certain she was referring to your uncle."

"Or even if she did mean Mitchell, that doesn't mean he killed your parents, Bec." Khadijah nodded agreement. "If our Maddie's going to be this vague, I guess we can't jump to conclusions like that."

"Gaah, why can't we?" Becca snatched a small cushion from the rug and pressed it to her face. "Let's call Mitch the shooter, award Jo a Nobel, and let me pack my chobos. I have a life to get back to."

"You say the word, baby, and we'll haul you out of here." Khadijah patted Becca's leg with the patience of a mother for a peevish child. "But I think you know you have to see this through."

Becca sighed with a harshness that told Jo to wait her out. Jo realized she had correctly interpreted an emotion-based cue, a noteworthy event.

Becca lowered the cushion from her face and stared toward the kitchen, her features set in a mature, controlled anger. "What's she expecting me to do, Jo? If we ever do find she didn't kill herself, am I supposed to drag the real murderer to the police? What kind of justice does she think I can give them after thirty-five years?"

"Maybe you're the only one she needs to know the truth." Jo watched the silent screen as Xena draped one arm across Gabrielle's shoulders. "I don't know of any homicides officially solved through EVP, Becca. *Hamlet* aside, murder victims don't often speak up to demand justice. This communication feels more personal to me. This is one woman asking another for understanding."

Khadijah was watching her with a small smile, which Jo found puzzling. After a moment, she smiled back with mechanical courtesy. She guessed she couldn't expect to understand every emotional nuance overnight.

"Yeah, getting back to that whole, Becca's mother thinks she's in danger piece?" Marty sat up and rested an elbow on her knee, no humor in her now. "We need to talk about some other possibilities. You game, Becca?"

"Sure." Becca sagged back against the couch, looking as game as a wilted flower, albeit a lovely one. "Hit me."

Marty opened her mouth, then closed it and nudged Khadijah with her shoulder.

Khadijah sighed. "We need to talk about John William Voakes."

"Okay." Becca slapped the rug and rose smoothly to her feet. She lifted a hand at their startled looks. "Don't worry. I'm still willing. But if John William Voakes is joining us tonight, we're going to need fortification."

She stepped around them and went to the low bookshelf near the arched doorway. "Jo, get some glasses from the kitchen, please. Right-hand cupboard." Becca opened the brown sack resting on the shelf and pulled out a bottle of wine. "I got this today so we could toast our ladies." She waved the bottle at the television. "This is expensive stuff. I'd rather drink to Xena, but if we're going to discuss mass murderers, in this house, after midnight—"

"Jo, sit down," Khadijah said.

Jo had gotten to her feet to go to the kitchen, but she sat again promptly at Khadijah's command. It had not been a request.

"Becca, you sit down, too. And leave that bottle over there." Khadijah's tone was still friendly, but her broad features were unusually impassive.

"Oh, come on. You're kidding." Becca seemed honestly puzzled. "Honey, it's just wine."

"You shouldn't be buying bottles of anything." Khadijah took off her small granny glasses and stared at Becca. "You can't drink, Rebecca, wine or anything else. And we won't drink around you. You know that."

Becca glanced at Jo and set the bottle carefully on the bookshelf. "I've been clean since I was twenty years old, Khadijah."

"And you've stayed that way by complete *abstinence,* remember?" Khadijah pronounced the word distinctly. "No booze, no pot, nothing. Rachel would have your head, little girl. Now is surely no time to fool with this."

Marty was staring avidly at the television, and Jo followed her gaze. Xena was engaged in battle with a villainous blond vixen. Both were spinning high above the ground on spindly ladders in a deadly ballet. The room was filled with an ominous silence, broken only by the soft purring of the static of the radios.

"If you're set on drinking that wine, I can't stop you," Khadijah said finally. "But I don't have to sit here and watch. If you open that bottle, I'll head home."

"Me too." Marty lifted her hand wistfully to the screen. "I'd have to go too. Have a heart, Bec. It's 'Callisto.'"

If anyone else in the room could read microexpressions, Jo knew her own face would reveal a strange combination of consternation, wariness, and sympathy. Becca had never struck her as someone with a history of serious substance abuse, but the strength of her friends' sudden protectiveness was telling.

"All right. No wine." The mild defiance was fading from Becca's posture. "You guys take the bottle home with you. But this only means I'm making a pot of double-chocolate cocoa after you leave."

Marty grinned in apparent relief, and Jo felt the palpable tension begin to ease. Becca looked embarrassed as she came back to them, but there was still a faint trembling in her hands. She settled on the rug again next to Khadijah, who leaned into her briefly.

"So, Mr. Voakes." Becca sighed. "Why must we have the distinct displeasure of his company this evening?"

"Do you know who he is, Jo?" Khadijah asked.

Jo nodded. John William Voakes was one of Seattle's horror stories; she doubted any native could forget his name. "Back in the early eighties, correct? Mid eighties?"

"Yeah, he was caught in eighty-three." Marty folded her long arms around her knees. "He killed his first victim in nineteen eighty-one, the older lady. Broke into her house on Capitol Hill on a Sunday afternoon and shot her when she walked in on him. Shot and killed a married couple in their apartment in the University District. In eighty-two, a single woman, a college student, also in the U-District."

"And in eighty-three, that entire family, back here on the Hill." Khadijah scratched Becca's hair lightly, as if comforting a cat. "The Walmacs—the parents and two kids. They're all buried right across the street. Were you living here back then, Jo?"

"Yes, I grew up on the Hill." Jo remembered little of the reports of the actual killings, or the spectacular news bulletins about Voakes's eventual capture and trial. By her early teens, Jo's parents couldn't pry her from her bedroom and her books long enough to follow current events. "But all I really remember about Voakes is the public outrage when he ducked the death penalty."

"This dick kills eight people in cold blood, two of them kids." Marty's tone was flat. "He sexually assaulted two of the women. I can't abide capital punishment, but the dude deserved hard labor for life. Not 'life' like a twenty-year sentence; I mean hard labor every day for the rest of his miserable life. No question."

"You would have made such a damn fine Amazon, Marty." Becca looked at her with affection. "But when did you guys get this encyclopedic knowledge about serial killers? Why John William Voakes?"

"Kaddy saw an article about him in the *Times* yesterday, so we looked him up in the archives." Marty traced a pattern on the rug beneath her bare feet. "Voakes was ex-military. He was a sharpshooter. He killed all his victims with one or two shots, not easy with a handgun. And he moved to Seattle in nineteen seventy-eight, not long before he started his crime spree. He moved here the same summer your parents died, Bec."

Becca started to speak but looked at Jo instead.

"You're suggesting that John William Voakes shot Becca's parents?" Jo slipped the recorder from her pocket.

"Don't jack the idea before we explain," Marty said.

"I'm not at all." Jo checked the device carefully and laid it on the coffee table. "Please continue."

Marty frowned at the recorder. "Well, I would, except now I'm scared Becca's mom is going to come ghosting out of that gadget at me."

Jo approved of "ghosting" as a verb. "Who knows? Perhaps we'll get lucky. You're saying Voakes may have committed a crime a year before his first known murder. A crime he never confessed to."

"He never confessed to any of them." Marty scowled. "The asswipe claims he's completely innocent, to this day. Mind you, this in spite of solid physical evidence, and getting caught fleeing the last damn scene with blood all over him."

"There's never been any doubt the man's guilty." Khadijah sounded less adamant than Marty but equally invested in discussing this theory. "The police never considered him when it came to the Healys, but…"

"The police never considered anyone but Madelyn Healy," Becca murmured.

"Right?" Khadijah nodded. "The deaths of your mom and dad were way off the cops' radar by the time the Voakes thing broke."

"The police report on your parents' shootings was not overly detailed." Jo searched her memory. "The forensics back in the late seventies were still pretty rudimentary. Based on my very limited knowledge of crime investigations, the patterns drawn of the scene and the ballistics report could have been consistent with a murder/suicide. Given Madelyn's history of mental instability and their history of arguing—"

Jo broke off, appalled that she might have misstepped again, but Becca was watching her calmly.

"So it's feasible that the cops missed the possibility of an outside shooter." Becca cleared her throat thoughtfully. "But wasn't Voakes's first known killing a robbery gone wrong? A house burglary or something?"

"Yeah, he robbed his first two victims, ransacked their places," Marty said. "After that, the cops think he just caught a taste for murder. No more robbery, just thrill killing."

"My nomination for the crappiest word coinage ever." Khadijah grimaced and turned to Becca. "But that's what we were wondering, baby. Is there any chance this maniac broke into your kitchen that night?"

"Then why am I still alive?" Becca's voice was dull. "No one robbed this place. Why would Voakes have shot my parents and left a witness? I was sitting right out here."

"This could have been his first time, if he broke in here," Marty said gently. "Maybe just to rob the place. He sees your parents, freaks out, shoots them. Out the kitchen door he goes. He wouldn't have even known you were in here. You wouldn't have seen anything."

"I wouldn't remember anything, if I had seen it." Becca rubbed her eyes. "I don't remember anything from that night, except my folks arguing, my mom handing me that damn doll."

"He raped two of the women, Becca. And your mother just said…" Marty looked away, and Jo remembered the last message with an uneasy chill.

Becca rubbed her eyes hard. "Is Voakes even still alive? Maybe we can skip over to the state pen and ask him about all this."

"Well, here's the thing." Those bitter lines formed around Marty's mouth again. "Voakes never spent a day in the pen. He was judged innocent by reason of insanity. He's been hospitalized at Western State since nineteen eighty-three."

"No, here's the thing." Khadijah drew a deep breath. "Your mother said you're in danger, Becca. There's no way she could know this, but... Voakes won't be at Western much longer. He's getting out."

❖

The muted clicking of Jo's laptop bothered her. The low purr of the static from the radios provided a partial cushion of white noise, but Jo didn't like disturbing the cathedral quiet of the living room. Becca, Marty, and Khadijah were sprawled on the couch and the floor in various postures of oblivious sleep, and she didn't want to wake them.

Jo straightened her legs beneath the low table and stretched silently. The blue glow of the screen provided the only light in the dark space, save for the ongoing flicker of the muted television. *Xena* episodes played on in a constant loop, a welcome backdrop to Jo's work.

Dawn was probably two hours off, but she couldn't sleep now if she tried. Her blood still hummed with the thrill of this study. She had examined the recording of the dinner at the Healy house second by second, and picked up no other messages—or at least no other words. She would have to tell Becca about the almost subliminal sounds that surfaced briefly at random moments throughout the recording; a woman's soft weeping.

She looked down at Becca's blond head, cushioned by the arm of the sofa a foot from her elbow. There was no need to dread telling her of those mournful sounds. Even relaxed in sleep, even given the harrowing nature of the last few days, there was a certain strength in Becca's features. Jo knew there was courage in her, or she wouldn't attempt this daunting project at all.

She gazed at Becca's sleeping profile pensively and turned back to the keyboard. She flipped past the graphs and charts mapping tonight's whispered message, the readings from the Spiricom, to the narrative portion of her notes.

RH continues cooperative.

Becca's conscious bond to her mother is ambivalent, given her anger at her perceived abandonment.

Her father remains a cypher to me. It's relevant that I have spent time in the company of Scott Healy's daughter, his brother, sister-in-law, and therapist, and I've learned virtually nothing about the man.

Jo glanced at the television and her fingers stilled on the keys. The episode was "Many Happy Returns," a silly offering of the last season, but the ending scene was moving. The warrior and the bard seated together on the cliffs at sunset, Gabrielle reading aloud from the scroll Xena had given her. Jo reached for the remote and paused the image.

Jo stared down again at Becca's still face. She moved her hands slowly over the keys, tapping out the words to Sappho's poem.

Awed by her splendor
stars near the lovely
moon cover their own
bright faces
when she
is roundest and lights
earth with her silver

Jo studied the verse, aware of the tears filling her eyes, but indifferent to them. She returned to her charts and worked methodically, the stilled image of the two women gold on the television screen.

Marty shifted on the floor, snoring with a soft, contented buzz, Khadijah's arm sprawled across her throat. The long shadows in the room began to lighten and grow blue, and Jo heard the faint piping of birds outside. At first, their gentle trilling disguised the sound at her elbow, Becca's deep sigh as she stirred in her sleep.

A dozen expressions shifted over Becca's dreaming face, rendering her a strong woman and frightened girl in swift turns. Jo reached out and almost touched her hair, her fingers inches from its lush softness. Becca murmured again, and her eyes flew open.

Jo made herself lower her hand to the arm of the sofa. "It's all right, Becca. You're safe."

Becca closed her eyes and sighed again, in apparent relief this time. She lifted her head and blinked at Jo.

"Have you been awake all night?" Becca cleared her throat and peered at her through her tumbled bangs, managing to sound maternal and disapproving at the same time.

"I'll lie down for a while later." Jo kept her voice low, as much to soothe Becca as to preserve sleep for the others. She still looked shaken. "A nightmare?"

"An old one." Becca lifted herself on one elbow and drifted her fingers through her hair. "Nothing I haven't dissected with Rachel, ad nauseam."

Becca's expression cleared, and Jo knew the topic was closed. Jo was beginning to understand every nuance of Becca's mercurial features, an honor the best psychiatrists in Seattle predicted she would never have.

Becca nodded at her sleeping friends and chuckled. "I don't know if you planned on a group sleep-in, tonight. I hope you're not too uncomfortable with all this company."

"If they don't eat my rations, I'll let them live." Jo was pleased with herself. That had sounded rather Xenic. "I don't mind them. Do you think you can sleep a little longer? Today might prove pretty busy."

Becca nodded and rested her head back on the cushioned arm. "I think Rachel has privileges at Western State."

It took Jo a moment to track her train of thought. "Really? At the hospital where Voakes is held? I wonder if there's any chance she's interviewed him."

"I doubt it." Becca yawned into the pillow. "Rachel doesn't specialize in criminal behavior; I don't see why she'd know him. But she might be able to talk to his doctors for us."

Rachel Perry might be able to get Jo into the most notorious psychiatric hospital in the state to meet with Voakes before he was released. She didn't find it necessary to clarify her intent to go solo at the moment; Becca's body was relaxing into the deep couch.

Becca blinked sleepily at the television, and a smile touched her lips. "Ah, Jo. This is probably my favorite scene ever."

Jo looked at the stilled image of the warrior and the bard, the scroll containing Sappho's poem between them. "Yes. Mine, too."

Becca's eyes were closing again. *"Awed by her splendor,"* she murmured. *"Stars near the lovely moon cover their own bright faces..."* Her voice trailed off as she drifted into sleep.

After a moment, Jo reached out and let her fingers brush gently through Becca's hair.

Chapter Eight

I don't suppose you could—"
    "Absolutely not." Becca said this as firmly as possible around a mouthful of chocolate croissant. "I'm not calling Rachel again at eight in the morning, Jo. One voice mail is enough. She hasn't been well, and this isn't a big crisis."

"Time is a factor, however." Jo was in her relentless mode this sunny morning. Becca stepped aside and let a bare-chested, studded-nippled young man zig between them on his unicycle. He tipped them a friendly wave. Ah, Capitol Hill in summer.

"Khadijah said the article indicated Voakes might be released from Western soon," Jo added.

"Are we in training to chase him? Slow down a bit, Batman." Becca touched Jo's forearm briefly. Her calves were beginning to ache with this long downhill hike. By unspoken agreement, they had avoided the street with the large window featuring mannequins. "You're really thinking we should go see this crazy serial killer? First, that Rachel can get us in, and second, that you'll be able to tell anything about what happened to my parents just by watching his face?"

"First, I'll be going to Western alone. I see no reason to expose you to a psych ward." Jo must be in butch protective mode, as well as relentless. She was also a bit deluded if she thought she could make sweeping decisions about Becca's welfare without her input. "Second, Voakes is a psychopath. I have no idea how revealing his expressions will be. I'm not sure what I can learn from him, but it's worth a try."

Jo nudged her subtly and nodded down a side street. Becca realized she remembered the necessity of avoiding the windows of the Quest Bookshop as well. She felt oddly touched by this and wished she could make up her mind whether Jo's protectiveness comforted her or chapped her butt.

They walked down the tree-shaded sidewalk toward Jo's office. Becca felt more awake and alert than the single tall latte she had consumed could account for. Nightmare aside, she had slept several hours surprisingly well on that sofa, in the company of her best friends, with Jo sitting nearby. She remembered the low music of Jo's voice, telling her she was safe. She thought of a question, wanting to hear that music again.

"Why wouldn't you let me drive us down here? All my car would have had to do was creak to a stop at intersections. It can still do that."

"Perhaps, but it's almost fifty miles to Western State." Jo fished a set of keys out of her back pocket. "We're picking up my car. I'm hoping to drive to the hospital later today, if Rachel Perry ever answers her—"

Jo broke off abruptly and touched Becca's arm. She was staring at the locked gate of her building with a fierce intensity, and Becca followed her gaze. The stinging smell hit her the next moment, a light but acrid chemical stink.

Becca claimed no great understanding of criminal trespass, but she could quote entire *Law & Order: SVU* episodes by heart, and she recognized acid poured over a lock when she gaped at it. Not some half-assed acid, either. The thick steel plate of the barred gate was gouged, not just scratched.

Jo nudged Becca back gently and grasped a high steel bar on the gate. One tug opened it a few inches, the lock rattling and useless.

"Jo, we need to call the police." Becca reached in her pocket for her cell. "Whoever broke in might still be in there."

"By all means, call them." Jo guided Becca farther back. She pulled open the barred gate and slipped through it. "Wait for them out here."

"Joanne!" Becca was exasperated. "Would you wait one macha minute? This will take all of two—"

"I doubt there's any danger, but I'll be careful." Jo's shoes cracked on the broken glass of the entry. The inner door swung open with ease, and she went through it.

Becca's cell crackled in her ear as the 911 dispatcher answered, and she snapped out information tersely, stepping back to the curb to read the house number. "Great. Thank you." She snapped her phone shut, muttering to herself. "All right. Capitol Hill cop response time, without reports of bazookas going off, at least fifteen minutes. If we had driven my car, *Dr. Call*, at least I would have the chobos in my trunk!"

She decided her nerves couldn't take this. Becca was reasonably certain no one was going to shoot Joanne Call with a bazooka in the next fifteen minutes, but she wasn't willing to risk it. She blew out a disgusted breath and stepped gingerly past the iron gate and into Jo's inner room.

"It's all right." Jo's distant voice was lifeless. "Whoever it was is long gone."

The room was utter destruction. Becca came to a dead halt and looked around in appalled silence. Every single radio that had sat on high shelves on the walls was now shattered on the hardwood floor in a jumble of broken pieces and wiring. Every tape recorder and record player had suffered the same violent fate. Half the shelves were torn down, wrenched out of their brackets by what seemed a titanic rage.

"Jo." Becca felt like she had the breath punched out of her. "Jesus Christ."

"Try not to touch anything." Jo stood across the room with her back to Becca, her hands clasped behind her, studying a smashed case on the wall. She glanced over her shoulder as Becca came toward her. "And watch the glass. It's everywhere."

Becca picked her way carefully across the floor. She glanced at Jo's large desk in the corner and wished she hadn't. The expensive computer was a shattered ruin across its oak surface. "Police are on their way."

Jo stood very still, her gaze diamond-sharp on the devices that lay in mangled pieces in the broken case. The muscles in her jaw stood out in stark relief.

"These were special to you." Becca touched her wrist tentatively. "Were they communicators—Spiricoms, like the one at the house?"

Jo nodded. "Later versions, yes. It doesn't matter. They were just...machines. Toys." She looked down at the keys in her hand. "But I have to check my quarters."

"Your what?" Jo moved toward her desk and pressed a button in the far wall. To Becca's astonishment, a recessed door slid open, so shadowed she hadn't realized it was there.

"I live on the upper level. It's doubtful they could have broken in there." Jo stepped into a small elevator. "But I need to see something."

"May I come?" Her own quivering nerves aside, Becca didn't want Jo to be alone just now. She was concerned about her eyes, which seemed eerily remote. "I'm coming," she decided, and followed Jo into a small elevator. An *elevator*, for heaven's sake, thoroughly sleek and modern; a twist of Jo's key sent it gliding soundlessly upward. Becca had sensations of both swift travel and an inordinately long distance. "Do you live on the roof of this thing?"

"The top floor. It's six stories up."

Becca hoped a mundane topic might coax that alien distance out of Jo. "You rent the entire upper floor of a building this size, right off Broadway, on Capitol Hill? In this economy? How rich are you?"

"I own the building. I'm quite rich." Jo glanced down at her impassively and stepped out as the elevator door slid open.

Becca followed, not trying to close her mouth. It was the most subtly opulent space she had ever seen, and she thought she'd seen opulent. Her uncle and aunt were pretty wealthy. Jo's "quarters" were a large, sunny expanse of blond wood floor and glass walls entirely windowing two sides. Becca was knocked dead by the view—the rolling green hills of Volunteer Park looking north, the distant crags of the Olympic range to the west—before the rest of the room registered.

The lack of technology struck Becca at once. For a woman so professionally immersed in electronic gadgetry, Jo's home seemed remarkably free of digital connections to the world. Except for one wide plasma TV, the better to watch *Xena* upon, her floor-to-ceiling oak shelves held books, print books, rather than smartphones or laptops. There was art on the walls, sparely but beautifully framed oils and watercolors, mostly unique landscapes. The impersonal aura of Jo's office was completely reversed by the understated, tasteful comfort she had created here.

Jo had walked directly to a large and lushly cushioned bed, neatly made with satin sheets, that rested in one corner. Becca shifted her eyes from it quickly. "It looks like they didn't make it this far. Jo, this place is beautiful."

Jo didn't reply. She picked up a small box from a table beside the bed. She cradled it in her hands, and only then did the rigid lines of her body begin to relax. It was a small oblong shape, the size of a book, and looked covered in velvet. Jo lifted the lid, and Becca heard a faint, tinkling music issue from the box. It played no song she recognized, a pleasing, antique melody with a Spanish lilt. This music box was what Jo had wanted to check. Its safety was important to her.

Jo drew a deep breath, closed the lid, and slid the box into her shirt. She walked past Becca toward a partitioned kitchen area. "My family made their fortune in the meat and railroad industries, dating back to the Civil War."

Becca heard the formality in her tone, a note absent in Jo's voice since their earliest meetings. She figured the shock of the break-in and destruction below merited a little shielding.

"As you've probably gathered, my work is largely self-funded." The sound of liquid splashing into a glass came from the kitchen. "At least the dead of the world appreciate how I'm investing my trust."

"Has it made it harder for you to connect with people, being wealthy?" Becca felt a pang of sympathy at Jo's defensiveness; she seemed almost ashamed to have Becca learn of her wealth. Prosperity might have erected as many barriers in this solitary scientist's life as it had opened doors. "Money can do that. Folks can be weird about it. I wonder if that made things even more lonely for you sometimes, while you were growing up."

Jo stepped around the partition, holding a shot glass filled with bourbon. Her stance was uncertain now. "With one exception, the few friends I had were more like paid staff. It was impossible to tell if their liking for me was genuine."

Jo had just revealed immensely personal information, and it mattered to Becca a great deal, but she couldn't lift her gaze from the drink in Jo's hand. She felt her stomach roil with renewed tension, remembering the scene of violent destruction below them. She was suddenly terribly thirsty.

"Becca. I'm sorry." Jo sounded dismayed, and she set the glass down on a bookshelf. "I wasn't thinking."

"Will you relax, please?" Becca was glad her tone was casual, because she was astounded by a craving that had never plagued her before. Alcohol had never been her drug, damn it. But now Jo was the one needing reassurance, for once, and she found herself wanting very much to offer that. She walked to her carefully, as if not wanting to startle a wary panther. "Just being in the presence of booze isn't going to hurt me. And all your being rich means to me is you're buying our damn lattes in the morning from now on. I'm on a social worker's salary, for heaven's sake."

Becca had reached Jo, and she did what came naturally—she slid her arms around her waist and looked up into her eyes. "I was fond of you before I knew you were rich, amiga. I like you because you're crazy smart and interesting and you hang out with the cool kids, like Xena and the Lady of the Rock." She rested her head on Jo's shoulder. "You've earned my liking, Jo. It's all you."

The side of Becca's face fit perfectly against the firm swell of Jo's shoulder. There was obvious physical power in the long lines of Jo's body, but she slid her arms around Becca carefully, as if she might break. Becca smiled into the white linen of her shirt.

"It's all you, too," Jo whispered.

Becca heard a faint, far-off whine of sirens, and she lifted her head reluctantly. "I think the cavalry is here."

"Yes." Jo's face was inches from her own.

They stood together until the bell down at the front gate sounded a chime in Jo's quarters.

❖

"It doesn't look like anything's stolen, right? Just wrecked." The cop's uniform badge identified him as N. Simmons. "You're sure you don't know anyone who might have done this, Dr. Call? No enemies, no one with a grudge against you?"

"No one, as I've said." Jo found this interview interminable. The two officers, Simmons and a black woman about Becca's age, were meticulous and thorough. They moved slowly around the shattered space of Jo's office, taking copious notes.

"It's good you didn't touch anything." N. Simmons had now said this three times, as if he needed their repeated assurance. "We'll get some techs in here to try to lift some prints. We'll need you to come down and have yours taken, Dr. Call, for elimination purposes."

"My prints are on file." Jo took her ID back from him, trying to suppress her impatience. "I've gone through security clearances to access government research."

"Very good. And we'll need contact info from you, Miss. Uh, Becca." Simmons turned Becca's driver's license over and peered at it. "Miss Healy."

"Becca Healy?" The other officer turned to her, her eyebrows lifting. "You're Rebecca Healy?"

Jo thought Becca had introduced herself quite thoroughly when the officers came into the room, but her name seemed to register with the woman—P. Emerson, by badge—for the first time. She studied Becca with keen interest, as if taking her measure all over again.

"Right, I'm Rebecca Healy," Becca affirmed politely.

"You're Madelyn Healy's daughter?"

"Right." Becca looked at Jo with muted dread.

The two cops exchanged glances.

Jo doubted the decades-old deaths of the Healys were remembered by many in Seattle. The city was large enough to offer a history of more lurid crimes, such as the depredations of John William Voakes. These two officers would have been children when it happened, and it was curious that even police would recall this case.

"You still hate dolls?" Emerson's voice was friendly, but Jo stepped quietly closer to Becca.

Emerson still carried the professional reserve of a good cop on duty, but it was easy enough to read the subtle undercurrents in her features. Jo discerned no malice in her odd question. The woman's tone was respectful, and as she took in Becca's startled expression, her face softened. "I'm sorry. You and me met once before, many years back. My name is Pamela Emerson. My dad is Detective Luther Emerson."

She waited, apparently expecting some recognition. Becca only stared at the woman blankly, but Jo made the connection.

"Luther Emerson was the SPD detective who investigated the shootings in seventy-eight." Jo's impatience fled. "You said you've met Becca before, Officer Emerson?"

"Pam. Yeah. We met the night your parents died." Pam was studying Becca with compassion as she folded her notebook into her pocket. "I'd just turned ten. I didn't need a sitter, but Dad wouldn't leave me alone that late. He hauled me over to that house with him, across from the cemetery, and ordered me to stay in the car. I sat there a while. Then I looked out the windshield and saw this forlorn-looking little white kid sitting on the front steps, all alone."

"Did you talk to me?" Becca looked unsettled but fascinated. "Jo, I don't remember any of this."

"I'm not surprised, after what you'd been through." Pam hooked her fingers in her belt and swept some broken glass slowly away from Becca's feet with her boot. "I don't know how they lost track of you long enough to let you escape to the porch, but you seemed pretty wretched. So I rummaged around in the backseat for one of the toys my dad kept back there, for little kids. I came up on the porch and handed you a baby doll. You wanted nothing to do with it, to say the least. You chucked it into the bushes." Pam chuckled softly. "I understood. I never had much use for dolls myself. But we sat together for a bit."

"Is your father still alive?" Jo bit her lip, realizing her bluntness, but Pam just nodded.

"Retired ten years now, healthy as a horse."

"Would it be possible to meet with him?"

"You mean this afternoon?" Pam threw a sardonic glance at her partner.

"Well, sometime soon. I have questions for him."

Becca's cell chimed in her pocket and she pulled it out. "Rachel," she mouthed. She flipped open the phone and stared at it. "Rachel? I'm fine. But you know…I can't possibly sum up any of this at this time." She handed the cell to Jo. "Here."

Jo took the phone and Becca walked over to Pam Emerson. She held out her hand and the officer took it.

"Thank you, Pam, for being kind to me that night." She smiled at Jo. "I'll be waiting outside, okay? Please don't be long." She stepped carefully out of Jo's ruined office.

"You think she's all right?" Pam asked.

"Becca will be fine." Jo hoped she told the truth. She lifted the cell and spoke tersely. "Dr. Perry? Joanne Call. You need to get me in to Western State Hospital to see John William Voakes. Today, preferably."

CHAPTER NINE

Jo decided to let Becca answer the doorbell. She wanted to use her best digital recorder to interview Voakes, and it required careful calibration. She squinted into the dim light of the only standing lamp in the living room and adjusted settings until she realized the bell had rung for a third time.

"Becca, would you please get the door?" Jo rolled her eyes. Her tone was inordinately sweet, even to her own ears. She'd bitten back her annoyance at the interruption and compensated by sounding like a cloying nanny cooing to a toddler. She supposed she still had an urge to shield Becca, given their morning, and she was capable of answering doorbells herself.

She took the two stairs to the entry in one long stride and pulled open the door. Rachel Perry stood on the front porch, carrying a small bouquet of tulips, shading her eyes and looking toward the large cemetery across the street. The sun cast dappled shadows across her face. For a moment she resembled one of the still statues in that burial ground, dignified and ageless. She turned to Jo with a tentative smile.

"Hello, Joanne." She extended the flowers to Jo. "Fresh from my garden. Becca's fond of these."

"Good afternoon, Rachel. Thank you."

"Becca said she wanted to say hello to an old friend in Lake View." Rachel nodded toward the cemetery. She seemed curious, but refrained from questions. "She asked me to tell you to meet her there."

"Ah." Jo frowned down at the flowers. It was past noon, and a good hour's drive to Western State. "I hadn't realized Becca had left the house. I was rather caught up in my...in any case. I'll join her there."

Rachel nodded. She reached into the tasteful purse draped over her shoulder and drew out a crisp folded sheet of paper. "I knew you wanted this quickly."

Jo accepted the page with a rush of relief. She had asked Rachel to fax this reference to Western, but it would be good to have it in hand as well. "I appreciate this. I was going to have you fax a copy to my office, but..."

"I'm so sorry to hear of the break-in, Joanne. It must have been a nasty shock for you both, walking in on that scene."

"Yes." Jo scanned the letter quickly. "Police are looking into it."

"Do you think there's any connection between what was done to your office and the work you're doing with Becca?"

Jo looked up sharply. The fine lines around Rachel's eyes had deepened since she last saw her. Her worn features revealed concern, but not accusation. "That thought had occurred to me, yes. It could have been a random act, but the timing is suspicious."

She realized she was keeping an infirm woman, Becca's close friend, standing on the front porch, and she flushed. "Rachel, excuse me. Please, come in."

"It's all right, Joanne." Rachel patted Jo's arm. "I only stopped by to give you the release. Becca's waiting for you, and I know you're wanting to get started. Please let me know if there's anything else I can do to help."

Rachel turned and made her way carefully down the steps to the sidewalk. She looked small and frail, but she offered Jo a friendly wave.

"Rachel?" Jo remembered her promise to Becca. She set the tulips and the letter on the stoop and came down the steps slowly. "I brought up some painful memories for you the other night. I apologize if I was insensitive." She blew out a breath. That had sounded okay to her. "I know you worry about Becca. I want you to know I'll take every precaution to make sure she's all right."

Rachel watched her face, reading her as if she were as adept with microexpressions as Jo, as she might well be. "I do worry about our friend, I admit it. But if my feet were held to the flames, I'd have to admit Becca is an intelligent and perfectly capable woman, and I trust her. And she trusts you, Joanne."

Rachel stepped closer, and her voice was soft but clear. "I hope I'm not saying this for the wrong reasons; because I'm tired, or not at my best, these days. But I'm going to allow myself to be completely selfish for a moment. If there is any—*any* explanation for the death of Becca's parents other than Maddie Healy's psychosis, I want you two to find it." She paused. "I care for Becca very much, and I want to believe she can find some kind of peace with this. And I admit I would love to live, just one day, without feeling I failed her family. I'll do anything I can to help you learn what happened that night."

Jo nodded. She watched Rachel walk to her car, her mind clicking through every nuance of her expressions. She was sure of it. Rachel was telling the truth.

❖

The rolling hills of Lake View Cemetery were sparsely populated again today, at least by the living. Jo could hear distant rhythms of reggae from adjacent Volunteer Park, a vast, friendly montage of playing fields, museums, and stages. Seattle was gearing up for the weekend's Gay Pride celebration, and the endless pre-parties were well underway.

As expected, Becca waited for her in the friendly shadow of the Lady of the Rock. In spite of the distractions of her trashed office and the interview with Voakes, Jo experienced a moment of simple pleasure at the sight of her. Becca was sitting back on her hands in the lush grass, gazing up at the Lady's strong face. Her own expression was thoughtful and calm.

"Rachel provided a letter of reference." Jo wished she had opened this conversation less abruptly, but Becca only smiled up at her.

"Yeah, she thinks seeing Voakes won't be a problem." Becca extended one hand to Jo. After a brief silence, she said, "Um, catch a clue, please? I eat four pounds of chocolate every day."

"Oh." Jo took Becca's hand and pulled her gently to her feet. She rose gracefully, in spite of her claim of gluttony.

Becca brushed grass from her hips and nodded at the Lady. "Do you ever wonder where she's pointing?"

Jo looked up at the statue's extended right hand, the delicate fingers gesturing into the distance. She turned and peered over her shoulder in that direction. "It seems she's pointing toward the cemetery's restrooms."

Becca laughed. "Yes, I realize the restrooms lie over there. But this statue must have been cast a century ago, and far away from here. I've always wondered what her sculptor wanted us to see."

Jo remembered the line from Derrida that Mitchell Healy had quoted the other night. "Another question of ghosts to be solved."

Becca smiled her understanding. "Can I show you something?"

"You may."

They began walking north, away from the fading music from the park, until Becca nudged Jo slightly east.

"I'd like to avoid that patch, if you don't mind."

The distant field was dotted with life-sized memorial statues, and Jo understood. Becca led her down a winding path of smaller gravestones to a wide plain of recessed metal plates. She wondered if Scott and Madelyn Healy lay beneath this sad ground; Becca had never said where her parents were buried.

But they stopped beside a larger plot, a gathering of four plaques, all the same size, of the same cold brass and bearing identical dates of death. The Walmac family. Voakes had been fleeing their home when he was caught.

"These graves were as popular an attraction as Bruce Lee's, for a long time." Becca spoke with the hushed tone reserved for the dead. "Being the victims of a notorious serial killer brings a little unwelcome fame."

They winded Jo, these stark, unexpected remnants of four lives lost to the insanity of John William Voakes. Two parents and two young children, obliterated in one night. Jo stared at the graves, gripped by horror and sympathy that felt visceral. She cursed herself for leaving her sunglasses on the table in the house. She must still be as shaken by the day's events as Becca had been, though Becca seemed relatively centered, right now.

"I took the clinical track in my graduate work. You focused on research." Becca clasped her hands behind her, studying the plaques. "By personal history and professional training, I know more about the nuts and bolts of mental illness than you. The families my foster kids come from are rife with it. I've seen craziness up close before. It doesn't scare me."

"Neither of us has anything to fear from Voakes."

Becca nodded. "That's why I'm coming with you to see him."

Jo blew out a slow breath. "This isn't just mental illness, Becca. This is being in the presence of a man who murdered eight people."

"And there's a small possibility, no matter how faint or unlikely, that he murdered ten." Becca paused. "I think my knowledge and experience could be helpful to you today. I also think I have the right to see the face of a man who might have killed my parents."

Jo tried hard to summon a logical response to either or both of these arguments, and a dimple appeared in Becca's cheek.

"I see we're going to have to hold another session of Becca School. Class?" She took Jo's hands, making it no easier for her to be logical. "Look, I love you wanting to look out for me. I really do. Marty and Khadijah can be protective, too. I don't know what it is about me that brings out this…shepherd thing in you guys."

I can't stand the thought of anything hurting you, Jo explained silently.

"But my friends don't get to infantilize me. I'm not five years old anymore." Becca pressed her hands. "Watch my back, by all means. I appreciate it. But if you try to baby me, you're only going to piss me off. Okay?"

Jo summoned another sigh from the soles of her shoes. "Okay."

Becca lifted herself on her toes to kiss Jo's cheek. "And stop looking so miserable. I can defend both of us with my mighty chobos better than you can with your spooky Spiricoms, anyway."

"That's probably true." Jo resisted the urge to touch her cheek. "Well. Rachel told me today that she trusts you, and she's known you longer than I have. I guess I can do no less."

"She said that, huh?" Becca glanced over her shoulder, and her smile faded. "There's something else you should see." She took Jo's hand, and they walked slowly down a small rise, beyond all that remained of a slaughtered family.

The graves here were older, but without the antique quaintness of earlier decades. Jo placed these headstones in the mid-eighties, reasonably well kept, their epitaphs still readable as they passed. Becca didn't have to point out the grave they were looking for. Jo saw the cut tulips resting on the sparse grass beneath the stone.

Loren Mitchell Perry
1968–1983

Jo did the math swiftly. "Rachel's son?"

Becca nodded. "Rachel gave him my uncle's name, to honor their friendship. Loren was a little older than me, I only met him a few times. I guess he turned into a pretty wild kid. He had problems with drugs. He was killed in a motorcycle accident when he was fifteen."

Jo looked at the wilting flowers Rachel had left on her son's grave. "And his father?"

"He left the picture early on. Rachel hardly mentions him. She raised Loren alone." Becca folded her arms, as if cold. "She was devastated. My aunt and uncle were really worried about her. It took her years to come back from this."

"I can only imagine. I'm sorry she had to go through it." The words came naturally to Jo, an encouraging development.

"Rachel was strong when I needed her, when I was five years old. And she'd found herself by the time I needed her again, when I was sixteen." Becca's voice had been warm, but now it grew more halting. Jo kept her eyes on the grave, sensing Becca needed privacy for this. She was *sensing* now, with this woman.

"Heroin was pretty cool in this town in the nineties." Becca's posture was elaborately casual. "Though most of my friends had the sense to avoid it. Not so with brains, here." She shook her head. "I don't know what I was thinking, what possessed me. I'd always been such a *good* little dweeb. But smack is unforgiving stuff. I shot up once, with an impossibly cute girl whose name I can't even remember now. Then I shot up a second time, alone. I was in trouble very quickly."

Jo grasped the seriousness of the trouble Becca had flirted with at the tender age of sixteen. Seattle was shamed by a sad history of loss stemming from the periodic, intense romances its youth held with chemicals. Heroin had been the go-to hit for the wealthier set in the nineties, just as meth was the fix sought by street kids in the past decade. The casualties could be gruesome. "Rachel helped you with this addiction?"

Becca knelt and pulled a small weed from the base of Loren Perry's headstone. "You know Mitchell and Patricia put me in counseling with Rachel after my parents died. They insisted I see her again when I was sixteen, when they realized my…problem. Khadijah and Marty flat-out finked on me to my aunt and uncle. You can imagine how tickled I was about that at the time, but they did the right thing. They may have saved my life."

She looked up at Jo. "Rachel did excellent work with me. Not just with kicking, with the loss of my parents, the phobia, everything. I meant it the other night, when I said I consider her one of the best psychiatrists in the city." She gestured at the headstone. "And she did this work four years after the death of her son, who also struggled with drugs. I was about the same age Loren was when he died. It couldn't have been easy for her."

"No, I'm sure it wasn't." Becca's fine fingers smoothed the grass at the head of the grave, and Jo missed the friendly warmth of her hand in her own. "Rachel told me she supports us fully in this study, Becca. She still has your back."

Becca looked up at her over her shoulder, and the sun sparkled off her smile in a way that made Jo wish for her sunglasses again. "I know she does. As I have before bragged, I have excellent taste in friends." She held out her hand and Jo took it easily, as if she had been helping Becca rise for a lifetime. "So, amiga. Let's go visit a serial killer."

CHAPTER TEN

B ecca kept giving the queen's wave out the window of Jo's Bentley, the small, curved-palm salutation that Elizabeth bestowed upon the British masses. Jo eyed her wryly from behind the wheel after Becca blessed their third pedestrian.

"I can't help it. I climbed ten rungs up the socio-economic ladder the moment I stepped into this thing." Becca stroked the butter-soft leather of her seat. "This isn't a car; it's a royal chariot. Can we drive by Marty and Khadijah's place? I just want to wave at them before we peel off and leave them in our dust."

She'd hoped to coax a smile from Jo and it worked, if only briefly, a slight lifting of one corner of her sensual lips. Becca still worried about what the morning had cost Jo, the shock of seeing her prized possessions destroyed.

"They'd only want to come with us." Jo's mirrored shades shifted toward the rearview mirror as they merged onto I-5. "Which probably wouldn't be a bad thing."

"You think so?" Becca was surprised. "Are you getting fond of my buddies?"

"I like them both, yes. But even more, I've always liked the idea of a clan. A family of strong women having our backs, in your words, as we confront a killer. It's a pity Rachel's letter only introduced us, and we couldn't get an entire Amazon tribe through Western's doors."

So the woman who abhorred crowds secretly longed for a clan of her own. Becca almost remarked on Jo's growing ability to talk openly about her heart, but she stopped herself in time. She hoped such personal revelations would become normal conversation between them, not worth special note. "I think that's why the Amazon tribe in *Xena* appealed to so many lesbians, right? Partnered or not, we're still searching for a clan, that extended family. That notion has always drawn me, too."

That slight smile crossed Jo's face again, and she reached for the dash and clicked a recessed button. A moment later a rich trickle of music filled the posh interior of the Bentley, and Becca grinned. "Oh, you're kidding. Perfect."

The iconic theme music from *Xena: Warrior Princess* was a more than fitting soundtrack for the day's quest, and its familiarity filled Becca with a chiming comfort.

She lay her head against the cushioned headrest, enjoying the music and the cool purr of the elegant car's all but silent air-conditioner. Seattle was too unjustifiably proud of its sometimes heat-choked summers to feature air-conditioning in most apartments, and the one in Becca's poor jalopy had gone to its rusty reward years ago. She allowed herself a small, selfish hope that Jo would never grow so uncomfortable with her wealth that she'd dispose of it all, or if she did, that she'd sell Becca this car really, really cheap.

"What about your father, Becca?"

Becca turned her head on the rest and looked at Jo quizzically. She might be talking about feelings more readily, but she still needed help with question clarification. "My father?"

"I've heard so little about him. I know the focus of our study is your mother, but it seems odd to me that such a major player in this family drama is so rarely mentioned."

"Well, from our dinner the other night, you know my dad didn't always get along with his older brother." Becca traced a pattern on the cool glass of the window with her fingertip. "A point in his favor, I've always thought. But he and my mom fought all the time, too. He had a temper. He tried to take care of me when she was sick. And as far as I remember, he did that pretty well. My dad was always nice to me."

Becca realized she had summed up the whole of her father's life as she knew it. She erased the pattern she had drawn on the window with a slow sweep of her knuckle. Scott Healy was a montage of blurred pictures in her head, his face always far above her; he had been tall, and not prone to stooping to get eye-level to a toddler. But the face Becca remembered had almost always been smiling. His kindness to Becca had been tinged with a harried, anxious quality, but it had felt genuine. When he raced home at noon to fix Becca lunch, he always created the unique bowl of cheesed SpaghettiOs that had been her small self's passion for years.

"We'll have to consider your father a suspect, Becca."

Becca's reverie came to an unpleasant, jangling halt. "Come again?"

"We already know the police investigation of this case, and the forensics, were spotty. They eliminated Scott Healy because of the placement of the gun on the kitchen floor, its position between the two bodies…" Jo glanced at Becca contritely. "I'm sorry. I'm just pointing out that otherwise, your father is a rational suspect. He had motive and opportunity. Your parents were involved in an emotional argument that night. It's possible that he's the one who fired the first shot and then killed himself."

Becca was abruptly younger again; not a helpless five-year-old, but a stubborn and resentful teen. She clenched her fists on the seat in denial. "So, first we considered Rachel a suspect. Now it's my father. Jesus, John William Voakes is looking better for this all the time."

"I consider Voakes the least likely of possibilities." Jo either didn't hear or ignored the warning in Becca's tone. "The theory Marty and Khadijah proposed about him is intriguing and technically feasible, but—"

"Jo, would you please remember we're talking about my family here?" Becca snapped off the air-conditioner against a chill. "If we're going to try to prove my mother innocent, only to condemn someone else I love to taking the rap for this—"

"We're going to try to find out the truth." Jo's voice was kind, but firm. She opened her hand on the seat between them. After a long moment, Becca accepted this unprecedented gesture, and rested her hand in Jo's. "I'm afraid there's no promise of a happy end to this story."

Jo's palm was smooth and cool against her own.

The looming presence of Mount Rainier, its base shrouded in an almost perpetual mist, hovered off the far horizon as they drove south toward the town of Steilacoom. Its volcanic history aside, the stately mountain stood as Seattle's constant guardian, and Becca had always drawn solace from its craggy peaks on the rare sunny days it was visible. Her parents had loved Rainier, she remembered. They had taken her for picnics in a lush field of wildflowers in its foothills. A small painting her mother had made of that field was framed on Becca's wall, above a picture of her parents.

The mountain's silent regard worked its magic again, filling Becca with a tentative courage as they sped toward the most notorious mental hospital in the state. The mountain strengthened her, and so did Jo's hold on her hand.

Western State Psychiatric Hospital, called the Insane Asylum of Washington Territory when it opened in 1871, was notorious only by lurid local legend, for the most part. Its incarceration and lobotomy of actress Frances Farmer in the forties ensured a kind of lingering, whispered infamy. Some sources claimed Farmer was never lobotomized at Western at all, but the shameful procedure had definitely been practiced here.

From the visitor's lot, they were only seeing a small portion of the grounds—Western sprawled across two hundred and fifty acres—but the main complex didn't seem particularly sinister. They might have pulled up in front of a dated, rather grim high school.

"This is your first time here, correct?" Jo touched her keychain to lock the Bentley in the sun-drenched parking lot.

"I toured the place a long time ago, when I was in grad school. Doesn't look like much has changed since then." Becca walked beside Jo toward the entrance, taking faint comfort in their twinned, elongated shadows streaming over the concrete.

"Given your career, you'd know more about this place than me. Any impressions you'd like to share?"

"Let's see." Becca smiled at this courtly acknowledgement of her credentials. "Western really has a decent reputation in psych circles, in spite of its detractors. The staff here is good. Patient rights are respected."

"And anyone in western Washington who's declared mentally disabled as part of a criminal case receives treatment here?"

"Right. Western has wards for both civil and criminal commitments." Becca paused as Jo pulled open the heavy glass-paned front door. "I seem to remember that long-term patients die kind of young here."

Jo held the door and stared at her, and Becca shook her head.

"I don't mean that anyone kills them off. Or that there's abuse, or neglectful treatment. It's just a sad little factoid that stuck in my head—people die young here. I guess even with the best intentions, most places like this just aren't able to nourish life, in all the ways that count."

Jo touched her back to steer her gently inside. "It seems this one nourished Voakes well enough, for more than twenty-odd years."

"I have a feeling someone like John William Voakes doesn't have much interest in spiritual nourishment." Becca wished they hadn't invoked his name, just inside the doors of his prison. He seemed much more a living, breathing reality here. She wished briefly for formidable bars on the opaque glass windows of the reception area, rather than wired screens.

"Dr. Joanne Call, Rebecca Healy." Joanne produced their IDs and Rachel's letter, and handed them to the staff seated behind the large desk, a uniformed guard and a smiling younger woman in civilian garb. Visitors were first welcomed to Western by the muscle of the guard and this girl's warmer greeting, two forms of reassurance for family members who wanted both safety and humanity for their loved ones.

"Oh sure, Dr. Call, I think you're expected." The woman spoke into her headset, nodded, and pushed back her chair. "Would you like to follow me?"

Becca couldn't imagine anything filling her with more giddy delight.

They moved past the screening station into a larger, open area peopled by the hospital's more functional patients, men and women awaiting late-afternoon visiting hours. They were dressed in clean, if mismatched street clothes, and could have been any small group of slightly bored people waiting for the clock to inch forward, until you looked more closely. The glossy sheen of heavy medication masked the features of almost every patient, blunted their expressions and slowed their movements. Few met Becca's gaze as they passed.

Their escort swept a key card to open a large side door as Becca read one of the many framed posters of guidelines that hung on the walls. What was all right for a visitor to bring *(non-perishable/ factory sealed food items that are to be stored in the patient's snack locker)*, how visitors were to interact with patients they didn't know *(courtesy communications only)*. Becca thought she remembered the forensics unit was in a separate complex of buildings on the east section of the grounds, but she and Jo were led down a carpeted hallway that seemed to contain administrative offices.

"Ah. Dr. Call?"

The young woman left them in the care of a lushly mustachioed official who circled his desk to greet them. He stood several inches shorter than Jo, and smiled at them both with a kind of benign distraction. "I'm Ben Chavez, the hospital's public information officer."

Jo had slipped into her off-putting staring mode, so Becca finished the introductions politely. "I hope it's all right if I sit in on this interview, Ben. Will we be meeting with Voakes here, or over in the forensic center?"

"I'll be happy to walk you over there right now." He patted his pockets and finally produced the key card that admitted them through a series of doors. They emerged from the main building onto a tree-shaded complex of sidewalks extending in several directions.

Chavez took off briskly, Jo pacing him with her long legs, Becca trotting gamely to keep up.

"So I'm just going to go into my Western State Hospital speech, and please feel free to tell me if you know all this." Chavez shaded his eyes against the lowering sun and nodded at the surrounding buildings. "We house over eight hundred patients here, at any one time. Employ almost two thousand staff. We work with the Psycho-Social Rehabilitation model, which involves—"

"We're trying to understand why release is being considered for someone with a criminal history as extensive as John William Voakes's," Jo broke in.

If Chavez was thrown by Jo's abruptness he didn't show it. Becca supposed a public information officer in a state hospital had to be able to switch gears smoothly. With the blurb in the paper about Voakes's planned release, Chavez had probably been fielding such terse questions for weeks.

"Well, keep in mind that Mr. Voakes was found not guilty by reason of insanity, a verdict that's not too likely today. His crimes were committed just before the legal reforms around the insanity defense kicked in, in the mid-eighties. All the public outcry over Hinkley's assassination attempt on Reagan led to—"

"And Voakes has been deemed no longer insane?" Jo sounded merely curious now, not abrasive, but Becca still winced at the sidewalk. "Is that why he's being released?"

"I believe the determination has been made that Mr. Voakes is no longer a threat to the community. That's the legal wording for the release criteria in place at the time he was committed." Chavez's tone was sympathetic, as if expecting to weather their outrage. He swiped his card at the door of a smaller circular building. "A technical distinction, mostly. But it's important to note that residents committed here due to homicide often stay a lot longer than they would have spent in prison. Mr. Voakes has been with us for twenty-six years."

Pointing out that Mr. Voakes had taken eight lives—ten?—seemed moot at the moment. But Becca heard an underlying tension in Chavez's voice. He was polished and professional and he worked by a script, but other than that he seemed to be a decent guy. She wasn't nearly as adept in reading subtle facial expressions as Jo, but she wondered if his eyes held the slightest shadow of fear.

"I really wanted you to see this." Chavez stopped at the entrance to a large circular room and perched his hands on his hips. A dozen people sat at computer stations around one side of the space, peering intently at their screens. Three staff moved from one to the other, offering guidance with what looked like grocery budget spreadsheets. These patients presented in more traditionally healthy ways than those in the general visiting area, Becca noted. Their casual clothing held some sense of personal style, and haircuts were recent and well done.

"This is our Program for Adaptive Living Skills, or PALS." Chavez sounded genuinely proud. "These residents no longer need in-patient treatment, but they still face some challenges living in the community. It's an amazing program, really. Intensive life skills training, field trips into town. Residents are monitored, assessed, and tested every step of the way before they're released."

The focus and industry of everyone in the room was impressive, but Jo obviously shared Becca's confusion as to why they were there. They were nowhere near the complex that contained the forensic center.

"And you're showing us this, because?" Trust Jo to be direct.

"John William Voakes lived in this program for the past twelve months. And as I said, residents are monitored, assessed, and tested every step of the way before they're released."

"Voakes lives here. Not in forensics?" A dark suspicion bloomed in Becca's mind. "He's already out, isn't he?"

Chavez kept his eyes on the far wall. "We engaged in some deliberate misinformation in our statement to the press, Becca. I'm afraid some sleight of hand was necessary to avoid any public drama around the release. Mr. Voakes was transferred to an excellent transitional living program in south Seattle two weeks ago. Where he will continue to be—"

"Monitored, assessed, and tested, every step of the way," Jo cut in. "May we speak to his psychiatrist?"

"Well, that would be Dr. Hasef. I'm afraid he's on vacation until—"

"Thank you, Mr. Chavez. I think we're finished here." Jo turned on her heel.

❖

Jo stalked ahead of Becca to the Bentley, frustration stiffening every line of her body. Becca followed silently, the oppressive shadow of the hospital falling away as they emerged into the twilight of the parking lot.

Becca heard the faint chime as the passenger door unlocked beneath her hand, but she didn't open it. She looked back at the looming hospital thoughtfully, imagining a different life.

Jo tapped her keys on the roof of the car impatiently, waiting for Becca to get in. "Yes, Becca? Something?"

"Just thinking. Wondering how things would be, if they had happened just a little differently. If my mother had fired that gun, but only one shot. If she'd killed my father, but not herself. I'd be coming here to visit her, wouldn't I?"

Becca stared at the implacable edifice of Western State until she felt Jo's hand brush the small of her back. Jo opened the door of the Bentley, waited until Becca was safely settled in its plush seat, and closed it with a quiet click.

Light lingered long in the sky this time of year, and Becca watched the last gold rays bathe Rainier's face as they drove back to the city.

CHAPTER ELEVEN

Jo waited until the twilight faded and it was fully dark outside. "You're sure you're up for this, Becca? It's been a very long day."

"If we really have to do it at night, yeah, I guess I'm up for it." Becca stood across the living room, looking at Jo as if she were a dentist about to inflict an unanesthetized root canal. "You're sure it can't wait for some nice, sunny morning?"

"I'm afraid it has to be dark. The shootings occurred at night. We want to reproduce the conditions of the catalyzing event as closely as possible."

"I guess I'm still not sure why this walk-through thing is necessary, period."

"Walking through what happened will re-create a scene that holds great emotional resonance, for both you and your mother." Jo made herself be the factual guide Becca would need to get through this. She went to the last of the radios and tuned it in. The Spiricom was set at full range. "Voices have been known to speak in moments of mutual memory—in the presence of a loved one who's talking about a shared experience."

"Can't we do this at the Lady of the Rock, then?" Becca's smile told Jo she was being facetious, perhaps a way of whistling in the dark. "I can talk about the shared experience of our picnics there; those are emotionally resonant. And Mom can float by and give us her recipe for peanut butter sandwiches."

"I wish we could. That would be much more pleasant." Jo wished Becca weren't standing clear across the room. If she were beside her, Jo might be able to touch her shoulder as casually as any of her friends. "But I'm afraid your mother didn't come back to talk to you about your picnics. Her messages all relate to the night she died."

"I understand. I was kidding." Becca drew her hands through her hair. "Okay. How do we start?"

Jo went to one corner to make herself as unobtrusive as possible and clasped her hands behind her. "Please start with the day, before it happened. Everything you remember about that day."

"All right. It was my birthday. Dad had to work, but Mom took me to a movie that afternoon. *Grease,* I think. I remember my little baby dyke self crushing out on Olivia Newton-John." Becca spoke methodically. "And my folks threw me a birthday party later. Cake, presents, the works."

"The party was held in here?" Jo asked.

"No. In our backyard." Becca drifted to a window and looked out at the dark yard. "It was a big deal, lots of neighborhood kids. Rachel brought her son, Loren. My aunt and uncle were there. Mitchell flirted with my mother most of the party."

Jo looked up. "You remember this, Becca?"

"Jo, I've been through this day at least a hundred times in therapy. The details are pretty clear. And that one's no big surprise; Mitchell still flirts with every attractive woman he sees. I grew up watching him do it."

Jo nodded. "Go on."

"That's all I remember of the day." Becca was quiet for a moment, her face reflected in the dark pane of the glass. She turned from the window. "The next thing that's clear is all three of us, in here. It was late enough for me to be in bed. Past time, in fact. I was sitting in a corner with my new coloring book. I was miffed that my birthday was over, and they'd forgotten about me again."

"They," Jo said. "Your parents?"

"Right."

"Would you go there, please? Where you were sitting."

Becca hesitated. She crossed to a distant corner and settled on the floor. She was far away from Jo across the large room and looked as small and forlorn as she must have felt that night.

"Do you remember what your parents were arguing about?"

"Money. Mitchell." Becca shrugged with a casual note that rang false. "Dad working too much. I really don't remember, Jo. All the arguments kind of blended together in those years. I learned not to listen."

Jo resisted an urge to press her on this point. "And you were drawing in a book?"

"Coloring. I had my new coloring book." Becca swept her palm across the wood floor in front of her. "My mother must have realized I was upset, and she brought me my favorite present, the... doll. Then she went into the kitchen. Then my dad followed her. Then there were two shots."

Jo knew they had to dissect this pedantic narration, but she dreaded this. "Do you remember where your parents were standing? Before your mother handed you the doll."

Becca gestured briefly at the open area in front of the sofa. "I'd gotten the doll for my birthday, and I loved it. Mom must have wanted to comfort me. She brought me the doll and then she went into the kitchen."

Jo walked to the sofa and picked up the small pillow resting against its arm. She made her movements slow and gentle as she crossed the room to Becca. Becca's gaze was locked on the pillow, and she looked bleak and afraid. Jo reached her and held out the pillow. Becca started to lift her hands to take it.

Two pops sounded from the small globe radio, and Becca's hands froze in place.

Two quick, muted snaps. Their sound didn't boom through the room. They were more distorted, elongated echoes, but Jo still felt ice water sluice through her veins.

"J-Jo?"

"*Listen*," Jo snapped. Silence was crucial right now. She clenched the pillow and stared at the radio, but there was only a brief crackling of static and it lost the signal. Jo let out a stale gush of air and looked down at Becca. "You're all right?"

"Yes."

"Sonic remnants are quite rare in the literature." Jo walked quickly to the Spiricom and studied its backlog, her scalp prickling. "I've never personally heard one recorded. It was a kind of echo, Becca. A reproduction of crux indices that match your mother's—"

"*English*, Joanne?"

"I'm sorry." She brought the Spiricom back to Becca, quelling the excitement in her chest. "Sometimes it's possible for a messenger to project other sounds, other than their voice. That's what happened here. I think we just heard the shots that killed your parents."

"Yes. I gathered that much." Becca's stomach was still roiling. She was desperately glad that she hadn't had to touch that pillow, and the relief was even stronger than her shock. "Those sounds are contained in this house, then?"

"No." Jo sat next to her, and that suited Becca fine. "This message wasn't generated by the house; it came directly from your mother. Would you like to see how I know?"

I'd like to keep hearing your voice. "Show me."

Jo displayed the small glowing screen of the Spiricom, which was laced with two identical patterns, two waves made of thin spirals of color. Jo touched the one on the left. "This is a sonograph of your mother's voice, three days ago, telling you to run." She touched the other wave. "And here is a graph of those two strange shots."

Becca stared at the screen. "They're exactly alike."

Jo nodded. "Completely disparate sounds, but they both originated from the same source. Broadcast from the same radio station, as it were. Becca, the timing of this capture is interesting to me. I was just about to hand you the doll when we heard the—"

"You know, it's nights like this that I'm bummed I forgot to get married." Becca had absolutely no notion where that had come from, and judging by Jo's puzzled expression she wasn't alone.

"I'm sorry?"

"No, I'm sorry. Stupid, random thought."

She'd just felt so lonely, suddenly, even with Jo seated beside her. Staring at a graph of her dead mother's voice, Becca had been swept, not for the first time or the hundredth, by an old longing for the familiarity and comfort of a life mate. A wife she had lived with for years, someone who knew all about her, knew what this meant to her. Someone she'd never found, and she'd stopped looking.

Becca made herself focus, and she rubbed Jo's forearm as if brushing away lint. "What were you saying?"

"The timing of the…" Jo was quiet for a moment, watching her. "I've wondered about that. Wondered why."

"About?"

"Why you've chosen to be single."

Becca grasped this gift of distraction from painful memory and was grateful Jo allowed it. "You're assuming being single is my choice?"

"Of course."

Jo's confidence in her desirability made her smile. "Eh, I'm not sure about that. I've always wanted what Marty and Khadijah have. Even what my aunt and uncle have. They really care for each other."

"Then why don't you have it?" Jo sounded logical, as if asking why Becca didn't have a Bentley. A partner seemed just as remote a possibility at this point in her life.

"Not really sure. Maybe because no one can claim my parents modeled a happy marriage." Becca had relied on this psychological chestnut all her life to explain her loneliness, but it had felt like an excuse, never entirely honest. "I haven't dated many people. Never been with anyone for more than six months. I'm still good friends with most of them."

"That doesn't surprise me." Jo set the Spiricom at her side.

"I haven't been Sister Becca, mind you." Becca wanted to lighten the mood a little. "I've had enough sex, especially in my wanton youth, to satisfy a…"

Becca trailed off, feeling her face warm with color. Jo hadn't asked about her sex life, for heaven's sake, and given their previous conversation about attraction, she'd rather not go back there tonight. She rested the back of her head against the wall.

"Anyway. It's probably not going to happen for me, the partner thing, and I've accepted that. I thank whatever gods may be that I have so much love in my life, married or not. I'm so lucky, Jo, in my friends."

"Your clan."

"Yes. Exactly."

They sat quietly together, and Becca felt her eyes drifting shut. It was late, and she knew it was time they got up and stretched out on their nice comfy living room furniture. They should sleep and dream among the radios and the Spiricom, and wait for shots to be fired or women to scream or weep. Becca shuddered with misery.

She was vaguely aware of her head sliding slowly, then resting on something both soft and firm, something like Jo's shoulder. She started to apologize, but realized she was asleep, and dreaming of the gentle brush of Jo's lips in her hair.

CHAPTER TWELVE

The night passed badly. Jo doubted Becca slept at all, despite the comfort of the living room's deep couch. The crease in her brow never quite disappeared, her body never fully relaxed into the cushions. Jo knew this because she kept watch over her from her armchair, their wakefulness accompanied by the soft hum of empty static from the radios. She was beginning to realize how much she was asking of Becca, these long nights in the house of her nightmares.

Thursday dawned hot and clear and remained so, a trend Seattle's burgeoning LGBT clan prayed would last through Pride weekend. Jo weaved around another couple seated in the grass in Volunteer Park, still stymied by their destination. She had her preconceptions about meeting with a retired police detective, and they involved huddling around a small table in a dark bar, not traipsing through the gayest park in the city, the busiest week of the year. She glanced behind her to make sure Becca was keeping up.

"Was Pam Emerson specific about this little rendezvous? It's a rather large park." Jo knew she sounded testy, but stepping over the legs of yet another pair of men engaged in full liplock did that to her. Did none of these people hold jobs? This was more of a crowd than she would ever willingly tolerate for long.

"Pam said they'd be down by the reservoir." Becca took Jo's hand, a gesture increasingly common between them that pleased her inordinately. They passed the Asian Art Museum and headed downhill, toward the large cement pool of crystal blue water dancing in the sunlight. Jo vaguely registered the beauty of the Olympic range in the distance before she heard a sharp whistle.

"Hey, Healy!" Pam Emerson waved at them, a friendly enough welcome. She was seated on a blanket in the thick grass beside a portly man who proceeded to dash Jo's remaining preconceptions about retired police detectives.

Luther Emerson didn't bother to greet them as they joined him. Clad in a voluminous yellow and red Hawaiian shirt, he reclined on the blanket, braced by a portable backrest, head back to receive the sun. His full jowls were dusted with white bristles. Large sunglasses masked his eyes, and a truly disreputable cloth fedora perched on his head. The only note stereotypical of police officers was the open box of Mighty O doughnuts balanced on his formidable stomach.

"This courtly gentleman here is my dad, Luther." Officer Emerson was more readily Pam today, casual in frayed shorts and a halter, apparently on a day off. Jo would have preferred her to be finding the men who broke into her office, but she had to appreciate her setting up this meeting.

"I retired in two-aught-aught-two." The man's voice was a rumbling bass, and that appeared to be all that he had to contribute to the conversation. Somewhat prissy lines had formed on either side of his mouth, and he kept his sunglassed gaze on the water.

"It's nice to meet you, sir." Emerson was clearly in his seventies, and Jo had been raised to speak respectfully to her elders. If this elder had unclasped his hands from atop his large stomach, Jo would have shaken one of them exactly twice, but he didn't. Becca sat in the grass beside Pam, and Jo glanced at her to be sure it was all right if she took the lead, because she was learning to do such things. "We want to talk to you about the deaths of Scott and Madelyn Healy, in nineteen seventy-eight."

"So my daughter tells me. And I believe I have just stated that I am retired." Luther freed his hands long enough to scratch his throat with two blunt fingers. "I have been retired for ten wonderful years."

"Yes, your daughter also mentioned your retirement." Jo slipped her recorder from her pocket and switched it on. "I'd like to record our conversation."

Luther lifted his sunglasses a bare inch and stared at the recorder balefully. Jo caught a glimpse of yellowed eyes before he lowered the glasses again, but he didn't protest.

"You've just got to give him time to warm up," Pam said. She leaned back on her hands, apparently enjoying the sun herself. "He's like a real rusty old car. Go ahead, Pop, have another doughnut. I think there's one tiny little vein in your left foot that isn't clogged all to hell."

"Good-bye, tiny vein." Luther reached into the box and drew out a chocolate iced monstrosity that Becca regarded with rapt fascination. To Jo's surprise, he offered the doughnut to Becca, and his voice changed entirely, warming with courtesy. "Hello, Miss Healy. It's good to see you've grown up into such a strong and lovely lady."

"I'm Becca. And you've just answered my heartfelt prayer, sir." Becca accepted the doughnut with equal friendliness, not to mention overt greed. She broke the pastry apart and handed half to Pam. "I'd say you're very good at your retirement, Mr. Emerson."

"Luther. I am indeed." He pulled a jelly doughnut out of the stained box and bit into it. Jo supposed that if she wanted one, she'd have to help herself. "I've had ten blessed years away from midnight calls to homicide scenes, Becca. Threw my pager in the terlit my last day at the station. I leave all the flatfoot work to this one now." He waved his doughnut at Pam.

"He thinks he's insulting me with the flatfoot thing." Pam edged one dab of icing from the corner of her mouth delicately. "I've been almost twenty years on street patrol."

"Gonna be walking a beat the next twenty, too, you can't stop playing lesbian avenger at the station." Luther regarded Becca over his sunglasses. "Miss Thang here thinks she has to be the voice of social justice at every roll call. Gets damn tiresome, and it holds her back."

"As he still bitches to all and sundry who will hear." Pam snickered. "He's jealous I look so good on my bike."

This had the tone of an old and loved bickering between father and daughter, with no real malice. The man was obviously comfortable enough with gay people to sunbathe in their midst, and there was pride in his voice when he referred to Pam. Which was all nice for them, but Jo had the urge to move them on to actual information. Besides, Pam Emerson was smiling at Becca with a familiarity she didn't especially appreciate.

"Luther, you performed the preliminary investigation at the house on Fifteenth Avenue that night, correct?" Jo positioned the recorder on the blanket.

"Lord, she's that Mariska Hargitay woman," Luther muttered. "Yes, your honor. I'd just made grade. Not easy back in the seventies, a black man making detective."

"I hear that," Pam murmured.

"And do you feel you conducted a thorough and conclusive investigation into these deaths?"

"You were one lost little girl, the first time we met." Luther's tone mellowed again as he spoke to Becca. "I sure felt bad for you and never forgot your face. Wondered about you, over the years." He jutted his chin at Pam. "We both have."

"Thank you." Becca patted his gnarled hand. "I understand Pam was sweet to me that night, too."

"In any case," Jo snapped, flapping a butterfly out of her face. "Luther, did you ever consider the possibility that Madelyn Healy didn't fire the gun—that there was an outside shooter?"

"Oh, I always liked the sister-in-law for it."

Jo stared at him. Then she and Becca stared at each other. Becca summoned words before Jo could.

"The sister-in-law. You mean my *aunt*? My Aunt Patricia? Patricia Healy, *that* aunt?"

"Patricia Healy, wife of Attorney Mitchell Healy of Kirkland." Luther's mouth was brooding now, his eyes hidden by the black glasses. He sucked jelly from his thumb with a wet slurp. "So look. There was no forced entry. There was an outside door giving access to the kitchen, and it was unlocked. The Healys weren't known to own a handgun. The thirty-eight was unregistered. We never traced it. Yeah, a third party could have come in, fired the shots. I wrote all this in my reports."

No, he hadn't. He definitely hadn't. Jo cleared her throat. "Not in the reports I've seen, sir."

A humorless smile crossed his whiskered face. "Oh, I'm not doubting my words got changed around a bit. I was new on the unit, which made me both green and black. Besides, Mitchell Healy, Esquire, had some powerful contacts, even back then. He was making a run for a state senate seat at the time. We weren't encouraged to look into things real close."

He tipped his glasses and looked at Becca. "I'm sorry if that means I did a disservice to you, those many years ago. I guess it bugged me enough for the details to stay clear in my mind. But it's also possible the call on that case was right on, ma'am. I'm afraid your mama was just not real well."

"I understand that." Becca still looked disoriented. "But my *aunt*?"

"Oh, that." Luther pulled another doughnut out of the box, frowned at it, and dropped it back in. "That's just one of them snapshots. Don't mind me. I'm old."

"No, tell her, Pop." Pam was watching Becca sympathetically. "I don't care if it is far out. You had good instincts, even back as a rookie."

"Okay." Luther sighed deeply and hunched lower against the backrest. "So cops get these snapshots in their heads. Just glimpses, fast impressions. And when your aunt and uncle came over to pick you up that night, Becca, Patricia Healy insisted on seeing the bodies. Wasn't necessary. Her husband already ID'd them. But I took them both back in that kitchen, and that's when I got that snapshot. Their faces stay with me, almost as much as yours did."

Jo glanced at Becca uneasily.

"Far as I remember, neither of 'em looked at your daddy, Scott Healy, not even a glance. That stuck with me at the time. Both Mitchell and Patricia zeroed in on Madelyn Healy right away, and that camera went off in my head, pop. I saw this flash of...anguish pass over your uncle's face, Becca. He couldn't hide it. And in that same quick second, your aunt? She looked satisfied. Just as pure and strong as her husband's grief, was that woman's look of satisfaction."

"Luther." Becca folded her legs beneath her, elaborately calm. "Why in the world would Patricia Healy shoot my parents?"

"Are you aware of the fact that Mitchell had romantic feelings for your mother?"

Becca looked at Jo and closed her eyes. "I've heard a rumor to that effect."

"Well, whoever passed on that rumor spoke the truth, I'm afraid." Luther yawned hugely. "S'cuse me. I did get to dig that far. Gossip with the hired help was that Mitchell Healy's eye had strayed more than once in his marriage. He'd had several ladies on the side. His wife seemed capable of overlooking this, but then she's an odd duck. Word was Mitchell had been putting the moves on Madelyn Healy, but she wanted nothing to do with him."

"So you're describing a motive for Becca's uncle for these deaths." Jo, who distinctly disliked Becca's uncle, was more than willing to go there again. "He was a spurned lover. A passion killing."

"Could be." Luther scowled at the beautiful view. "But I got to go by that snapshot in my gut. Mitchell Healy wasn't the one looking pleased with himself that night, looking down at that dead woman. That was Patricia."

They sat quietly for a while, and Jo fought back the urge to break the silence. The birdsong and the sparkling water were soothing, there was friendly laughter around them, and Becca needed this break.

Becca's gaze was pensive on the distant mountains, and she sat with a stillness that made her seem just as remote. Her fine fingers drifted through the grass, much as they had at the headstone of Loren Perry's grave. As Jo watched, Pam Emerson's hand moved exactly as she wanted her own to, and rested lightly on Becca's hair. Becca looked over her shoulder and smiled at Pam, who winked at her.

Jo understood, clinically, that there was nothing sensual or flirtatious in Pam's gesture. A snapshot of her own appeared to Jo, of the motherly comfort the Lady of the Rock offered to the weary girl whose head rested in her lap. Pam's face held only friendliness and a similar maternal warmth. The mild tousling she gave Becca's hair could have come from Marty or Khadijah. Regardless, Jo found herself mired in a wistful regret, a mild jealousy completely foreign to her, that Becca was smiling into a different pair of eyes.

"Why don't you three toddle off sometime soon and let me get some sleep?" Luther yawned again, his capacity for company apparently worn thin. "How am I supposed to pick up any cute boys with all you women hanging around?"

"Pop, you're the straightest mean old black man on the Hill." Pam stretched and rose smoothly to her feet. "I think the cute boys are safe."

"Not if they're rich enough." Luther's chin settled into his chest, and he twined his fingers again over his belly. "Good-bye, Becca. Good-bye, other one. Take good care. I am retired."

Pam walked with them up the gentle slope away from the reservoir, though Jo didn't see a particular need for an escort. She glanced past Becca and saw the way the muscles in Pam's arms gleamed in the sun, her easy athletic stride. Police officers who walked a beat had to be fit, and Pam obviously worked out a dozen times a day. Jo sighed.

"He means it, you know, the good-bye bit." Pam stuck her hands in the pockets of her denim shorts. "He won't want to talk with you again. He's really told you all he remembers about the case, anyway."

"Oh, I think he cleared things up for us nicely." Becca gave her a wan smile. "My aunt shot my parents. Unless it was my uncle. Or my father. But that was an incredibly good doughnut, and I like your dad."

"I like him, too," Pam said, and Jo began to feel that the two of them were walking alone together. "But you do get some take away from this, Becca. My dad was open to the prospect of an outside shooter. And you're trying to prove your mom didn't do it, right?"

"We're trying to find out the truth." Becca sighed. She looked up at Jo and slid her arm through hers, and the beauty of the sunny day hit Jo at last.

"Yo, *Emerson*!" One of a group of three women lounging on the steps of the Asian Art Museum hailed Pam. "Seven o'clock!"

Pam and the three women broke into a rapid, rhythmic sequence of claps that mystified Jo. They unleashed a raucous cheer.

Becca grinned up at her. "That was the Storm clap. There must be a game tonight."

"Must be a game? Y'all don't follow the Storm?" Pam eyed them, askance. "My missus and I get season tickets every damn year."

Hearing Pam had a missus warmed Jo toward her considerably, as did Becca's light hold on her arm.

"So I'll check in with the station before tip-off, see if there's any developments." Pam lifted her chin at Jo. "We dusted your place for prints, Jo. No catches yet. The dude or dudes wore gloves. Most of your block's retail, so there weren't neighbors nearby late at night to hear anything. We're still digging, though."

"Pam, I'm not crazy about the timing of this." Becca looked pensive again. "What if whoever did this is trying to threaten Jo? Warn her off? That break-in was really violent."

"I think that's a possibility we have to keep in mind." Pam regarded Jo soberly. "Any guesses as to who might not like the questions you've been asking lately?"

"Someone with a stake in hiding the truth about what happened." Jo realized her answer was so generic as to be useless. She wanted to erase the new shadow that had filled Becca's eyes.

"Well, you keep your eyes and your ears sharp. It's just as well you two are together most of the time, right now." Pam was watching them with an odd smile. "Safety in numbers. Okay, I'll check in with you peeps later on. You've got my numbers; you can call me any time."

"Thank you, Pam." Jo tried to summon a sufficiently butch tone for Becca. "The bastard who did it is lucky, you know. If he'd touched my *Xena* DVDs, he'd be dead meat."

"*Xena*?" Pam turned back to them, her face dawning with light. "I knew there was something I liked about you guys!" She raised one fist and gave a cracking good rendition of Xena's trilling war cry.

CHAPTER THIRTEEN

An hour later, it was Becca's turn to wait beside the Bentley, drumming her fingers on its glossy hood while Jo closed the clasps on her shoulder bag with meticulous care. Jo glanced up and seemed startled by her glare.

"Something?"

"Cut tulips require something like water, Jo. They don't thrive if they're left on a bookshelf."

"Becca, I've explained I did not deliberately leave Rachel Perry's cut tulips languishing on a bookshelf. And I've apologized. Not sure what more I can offer at this point."

Jo sounded as impatient as Becca felt, and she curbed a snappish response as she slid into the Bentley. Neither of them was sleeping well. She knew that. Becca was comforted by Jo's presence in that sad house, but Jo had to be even more exhausted than she was, after three straight nights in that damn armchair. Becca would insist she log some hours in a real bed soon. She looked out the window and sighed inwardly, feeling the blood rushing to her face. Hot flash, it had to be. She was much too tired to feel this sudden arousal, simply picturing Jo's lithe length stretched out on a bed.

She studied Jo's profile as she turned the powerful car smoothly onto Fifteenth, her weary features more chiseled today. "Can we stop on the way and slap my Aunt Patricia around? Make her talk?"

"Of course." Jo seemed relieved by the lightness in Becca's tone. "May I pound on your uncle? Of all our suspects so far, he's the easiest to dislike. Well, short of Mr. Voakes."

Becca nodded, her gaze drifting to the window again. Marty and Khadijah had disliked her Uncle Mitchell from their first meeting. Her best friends had been polite to Patricia, who treated them with the same puzzled, distant benevolence she showed Becca, most of the time. Patricia could be brittle, and she was fiercely loyal to Mitchell. But Becca could not, for the life of her, picture her pulling a gun on her parents.

"Luther Emerson said Mitchell was running for a state senate seat back when the shootings occurred." Jo sounded thoughtful as they took the interstate south. "Do you know what happened to his political aspirations?"

"I'm clueless there. I never knew he'd had any." Becca remembered that revelation in the park. "No one's ever talked about any kind of political campaign. But there was a lot going on with my family at the time. That newsflash might have gotten lost in the drama."

She fell silent to drink in Mount Rainier as they crossed the West Seattle Bridge. The mountain was still resplendent in the afternoon sunlight, and she appreciated Jo's companionable quiet. The Bentley's tires glided soundlessly across the expansive bridge, the blue waters of Puget Sound and the rising orange cranes of the docks to their right. They were bound for Tukwila, a small suburb south of downtown Seattle, a neighborhood Becca had never had cause to explore much.

"What can you tell me about Horizons?" Jo asked. "Surely it's a secure facility, right, if it's housing John William Voakes?"

"You know, I don't think it's a lockup program." Becca had heard of Horizons at one or more distant staff meetings, but she remembered little about it. "I know they're contracted through DSHS with Western State to house people who don't need hospitalization any more, but aren't ready for independent living. I had no idea they accepted ex-patients with a history like Voakes."

They fell silent again as the Bentley purred down Ambaum, a broad street choked with traffic even in mid-afternoon. Most considered West Seattle a tony neighborhood, and parts of it certainly were; there were mansions overlooking Puget Sound that stole your breath. But the families Becca worked with were usually impoverished, and some of them lived in the poorer neighborhoods braiding off this street.

She felt her stomach knot, knowing they were minutes from meeting an honest to hell lost soul. Accepting Luther's doughnut had been a bad call, but he had all but forced it on her.

The neat grounds of Horizons lay nearer the wealthier district. It resembled a manicured horseshoe of an apartment complex more than a therapeutic halfway house. Becca counted eighteen well-kept units lining the tree-shaded walk as they approached the main office.

"You would be Joanne Call and Becca Healy. Correct?" The woman striding to meet them looked about Rachel's age, and she moved with the vigor and energy Rachel used to have in abundance. "I'm Dr. Emily Kelley. I'm clinical director here."

She didn't offer her hand, and she stopped a good two yards from them. Her tone was polite and her manner poised, but Emily Kelley was obviously ticked off. Becca had seen the same brittle body language in some of her countless supervisors when they felt unfairly disempowered. "Would you come this way?"

Dr. Kelley was already going that way, and whether they followed seemed a matter of indifference to her. Becca stumbled in her wake, and Jo's hand was fast and sure beneath her elbow. Emily slowed to a stroll as she led them around the side of the building.

"It seems the two of you have powerful friends." Emily glanced back at them, her tone milder now. "The call from Western didn't leave us a lot of room for negotiation. John's team here didn't get a vote as to whether you met with him."

"And what are your objections, exactly?" Jo was reliably willing to forego small talk.

"Well, you're not journalists. That's a plus." Emily sighed and slid her hands into her pockets. "I suppose Ben Chavez was afraid you'd run straight to the media if you weren't granted an audience. We're going to have to brace ourselves for that onslaught anyway, as soon as John's presence here becomes common knowledge. Hello, Paula."

Emily nodded pleasantly to a blunt-featured woman who passed them on the shaded walk. She'd spoken the woman's name with palpable warmth, unlike her formal pronunciation when she referred to Voakes.

"But to answer your question, Dr. Call, I object to this interview because we don't want to make a sideshow of this man, or this program. Horizons has had a remarkable success rate transitioning the chronically mentally ill into the community. We do valuable work here."

"And we won't be detracting from that success." Jo's pace was stolid. "We just want a few minutes with Voakes, and we'll be on our way."

"You wouldn't be getting a few minutes if John weren't willing. I'm honestly not sure why he's agreed to see you today. He told us when he transitioned here that he wouldn't meet with reporters or with guests he doesn't know. And he knows no one."

"Was he told our names?" Becca asked blandly.

"Of course."

It wasn't hugely relevant. Voakes hadn't necessarily agreed to see them because he recognized Becca's name. But she saw Jo's sharp eyes register the fact, a brief flickering of their cobalt light.

"I couldn't even tell John the purpose of this interview." Emily ducked under a low lattice awning and motioned them through. "Ben was vague about your interest, in the extreme."

Jo opened her mouth, but Becca touched her arm. "Emily, I have personal reasons for being here. My parents were shot to death in nineteen seventy-eight, and we think there's a possibility John Voakes knows something about what happened."

Emily Kelley stopped and turned to them, and Becca got the distinct impression she was in this work for the right reasons. Emily's weathered features held compassion, the kind of old and weary compassion of a veteran of the wars, someone who has worked with the marginalized for a very long time. In social service, Becca had known women who genuinely cared for the length of their careers, like Emily—and women who went through the motions, well-intended but empty bureaucrats. Like her aunt.

"I'm sorry for your loss, Becca. But I have to ask if I should call in a public defender to sit in on this meeting."

"We'll do whatever you think is best, but that's probably a little premature. If you can see your way clear to letting us go ahead, join us for this talk. Jo and I will back off if you get uncomfortable with any road we take."

Emily nodded, her gaze on the vast vegetable garden spread out before them. "What chances do you think our people have getting jobs out there, thanks to rare cases like John William Voakes? The mentally ill are being demonized again in this city. Have you felt it, Becca?"

Becca nodded. Lurid headlines had surfaced over the past few years of isolated atrocities committed by Seattle's truly malignantly crazy. Most of them had histories with Western State.

Emily nodded at two men walking back toward the complex, who both waved friendly greetings. "All our people take the rap for the sensational cases, and the vast majority are completely harmless. Better than harmless. They just want to live independently, give back to their communities…"

Emily trailed off, and she smiled at Becca for the first time. "I have a feeling I'm preaching to the choir. All right. I'd rather you take the lead on this, Becca, rather than Dr. Call." She glanced at Jo. "No slight intended. And if I pull the reins at any time, I expect you to stop immediately."

Emily walked on. Becca turned to Jo, disconcerted. She had assumed Jo would handle this. She wasn't certain she was prepared to be in charge of a sensitive chat with a serial killer.

"You can do this," Jo said and followed Emily.

And just like that, Becca found she agreed. Jo must have been listening in Becca School. She knew what she needed in this moment, not a shared anxiety, but the calm and immediate confidence of a friend. She squared her shoulders and kept them that way as she saw John William Voakes dig a sharp trowel into overturned earth.

An elderly white man knelt by a furrowed row of cabbages at the far end of the large garden, digging slowly into the soil with the glinting trowel. A wheelchair waited nearby. A young man, an immensely big attendant, stood next to Voakes, his muscled arms crossed. Becca knew the old man was Voakes and the big man was staff—the latter was glaring, not at Voakes, but at them, protective of his client.

"John's visitors are here." Emily greeted her staff quietly, and the man lumbered to meet them. "This is Peter, John's personal attendant."

"I didn't realize he was so old." Becca's throat was drying as she watched the frail man struggle from his knees into the wheelchair. "Isn't Voakes in his sixties?"

"Yes, mid sixties," Emily replied. "But he's dying. That's why he's here."

Peter had reached them, and he planted his solid bulk in the middle of the paved path, blocking their way. He regarded them stonily, confident that his stance would intimidate them enough for a few moments of awkward silence, at least.

But he hadn't counted on Jo, who either had no notion of body language or simply lost that awareness when she chose to. Jo closed the distance to Peter and stood very, very close to him, her breasts brushing his folded arms, her height making it possible to stare directly into his wide brown eyes. A breeze whipped a lock of Jo's dark hair in his face, but he didn't dare blink.

Becca walked rapidly to them, in case a sensitive chat was needed.

"You're guarding a serial killer, not a monk." Jo's low voice was calm, but those spooky eyes were inches from Peter's. "We're not going to harm him. I'm sure you'll be standing close by to ensure that. As will your boss, who has approved this interview, so *step aside*."

Peter stepped aside. Jo stalked past him, then turned and waited for Becca. Emily shook her head at Peter and followed Jo. Becca took Peter's arm and walked with him, ignoring his surprise and discomfort. She knew this kid. She had worked with him a hundred times in entry-level positions.

"Peter, the work you've chosen to do. It's not a sprint; it's a marathon." She gave the kid's arm a friendly squeeze. "You've got to learn to pace yourself. I can see how passionate you are about your job, but your kind of passion burns us out. If you don't learn to take care of yourself, you'll flame out and be gone from this work in two years. That's a promise."

"Okay," the kid whispered. He looked a little dazed.

"Good luck." Becca squeezed Peter's arm again, fond of him because of his genuine zeal and devotion. Equally sure he'd be gone in two years. She released him and summoned all her energies to meet a murderer.

John William Voakes was her nightmare of what Rachel might become—skeletally thin, weak to the point of infirmity. Shriveled and trembling, he sat crab-like in the cushioned wheelchair, his bony hips not filling the width of the seat. His balding, freckled head was lolling to one side, and Becca couldn't see his face. From a remote corner of her mind, she could empathize briefly with Peter's protectiveness toward his fragile client. She and Jo, Peter, and Emily, stood in a small circle around the chair.

"John, you've been expecting this visit." Emily's tone was oddly flat, devoid of sympathy, and she darted Becca and Jo a look of warning. "I know you're ill, but you're much more alert than you're pretending to be."

And John William Voakes rose smoothly from the chair, his head bobbing up, strength suffusing his thin limbs, and Becca took a ragged step back. His short, stumpy form stood erect easily, and his rheumy eyes lit up when he saw Becca. A snapshot of his merry, smiling face went off in her mind, and she knew she would carry the image the rest of her life.

Jo moved swiftly between them, just a small step, but one that placed her squarely between Becca and Voakes, and Becca lowered her head and released a small gasp of relief.

"If you feel you've delivered enough shock value, John, I'll ask you to sit down."

Emily didn't raise her voice, and Becca trusted Voakes wasn't doing anything too alarming. She imagined him and Jo Call locking eyes, and was glad she couldn't see it. Then she decided she had to see it. She moved from behind Jo and regarded the man fully.

John William Voakes was indeed studying Jo avidly, his head cocked to one side. And inevitably, Becca was reminded of the banality of evil. She had looked into the faces of fathers who tried to smother their infants because they cried at night, and most of them held this same bizarre, discordant look of normality.

Apparently, his little surprise had cost him. Voakes was weaving on his feet now, and the color was draining from his face. Jo's silent immobility, her flat gaze, might have prompted this weakening, but he was obviously a sick man. He looked at Becca again.

The lower lids of Voakes's colorless eyes were rimmed in moist red. He held out his hand to Becca, and his voice was gentle and wetly sibilant. "Hello, Clarice."

Becca stared at him, ignoring his hand, and he lowered it to his side.

"I'm sorry, Miss Healy." Voakes smiled again. Typical of Western State long-timers, his dental care had been lacking. "I've wanted to greet you with that for years."

"John, I told you to sit down. Now," Emily said. "It wasn't a suggestion."

Peter started as if nudged awake and brought the wheelchair around behind Voakes. He had to touch the back of its pedals against Voakes's legs gently before he broke his gaze from Becca's and settled stiffly into the chair. She could smell him from where she stood, a mixture of fresh earth and rank sweat and illness.

"Let's do this back in your room." Emily's voice hadn't warmed. "It's past time for your afternoon meds. Peter?"

The big kid pushed the wheelchair slowly away from the garden, allowing some distance to grow between them. He leaned down and murmured something to Voakes, who nodded limply, his fatigue authentic now.

"We had one of our units outfitted for hospice services." Emily walked with them, her sandals clocking slowly on the cement walk. "There's room for a hospital bed, IV stands, and the chair. Nurses from the hospice at Swedish Hospital visit morning and night to keep him comfortable."

"What's wrong with him?" Jo might be asking for an estimate on a plumbing repair.

"Colon cancer, widely spread. He's on palliative care. No further treatment is possible, so they're just keeping him free of pain."

"That's kind of them." Jo waited while Peter inserted a keycard to unlock a private cottage at the edge of the walk. "He's being kept separate from your other residents?"

"They avoid him. He's hardly an escape risk, but we never leave him unattended. Let's let Peter get him settled." Emily stopped them outside the door of a spacious bedroom. They watched as Peter parked the wheelchair beside the white bed and helped Voakes into it. He moved with the wincing hesitance of an elderly man with a terrible disease.

"So basically, he was brought here to die," Jo said.

"He was allowed to come here because he's dying. As a young man, John used to make his living as a gardener. He filed a plea to spend his remaining time here, tilling vegetables that will go to area food banks."

"Giving back to the community," Jo said dryly.

Emily shrugged. "It's a matter of months. Maybe weeks."

Becca was fixed on Voakes, and she started a little at Emily's touch on her arm.

"Are you all right with this? It's got to be hard for you."

"I'm fine. Thanks, Emily." Becca meant it, on both counts. They entered the bedroom, which smelled sharply of disinfectant.

"So this is supposed to be fifteen minutes." Peter sounded brash, perhaps to atone for his earlier face-off with Jo. He handed Voakes a small paper cup and a plastic beaker with a straw, and waited until he downed the pills with two painful swallows. "That's all he's got in him, once these meds knock him out. You still okay with this, John?"

Peter seemed to hope for some denial, but Voakes nodded weakly, sinking back against the stiff pillow. Peter raised the railing on the bed and elevated its front so Voakes sat erect. No effort was made to supply chairs for them, but Becca would rather stand. In addition to the disinfectant, the room was filling with the odor of a sweaty, dying old murderer. She felt Emily's gaze on her and realized the floor was hers.

"I want to ask you about the summer of nineteen seventy-eight." Becca was relieved. Her voice was steady, and she could feel Jo's solid presence behind her. "You were living in Seattle at that time, right?"

"Yes." Voakes eyes were closed, his stubbled face gray and slack.

Becca knew of no delicate way to phrase this, and delicacy wasn't called for. "I want to know if you shot two people in a home on Capitol Hill, in June of nineteen seventy-eight. Three years before the deaths of the Walmac family."

"You might have me mixed up with James Anthony Williams." Voakes's voice was thready, but it had lost the wet, lisping tone. "Don't worry about it. It happens all the time."

"What?"

"James Anthony Williams. Gary Leon Ridgway. Westley Allan Dodd." Voakes thumbed spittle from the corners of his mouth. "The multi-murderous in this part of the country seem to go by more than our fair share of names, don't we?"

"Shannon Harps." The name of the woman murdered by James Anthony Williams on Capitol Hill in 2008 swam up out of the murk of Becca's memory, suddenly sharp and clear, because she was angry. She didn't like the crafty pleasure surfacing on Voakes's face. If he wanted to riff on the names of notorious madmen, the innocents slaughtered by them would be remembered, too. "I'm talking about shootings that happened thirty years earlier. I'm asking if you know anything about that night."

"John, you don't have to say anything, now." Emily was eyeing the recorder Jo held openly in one hand. "If you want an attorney present, we can arrange that."

"I'm not really mentally competent enough to know if I need an attorney." Voakes grimaced against a sudden pain. "So nothing I say without one can be held against me. But thank you, Dr. Kelley." He lifted one veined hand slightly, then let it drop back on the thin spread. "Can you come a little closer, Miss Healy? I'm not seeing very well, these days."

Becca kept her distance. "You don't have to see me. Are you going to answer my question?"

"I've pictured you, lots of times." Voakes closed his wrinkled eyelids briefly. "You were such a blond, pretty little thing."

"John." Emily's tone was suddenly sharp. "Perhaps you should mention, at this time, that you're very familiar with the history of the Seattle crime scene. Your doctors are aware that you kept newspaper articles on area crimes long before your arrest."

"That's true." A kind of sulking contrition tugged Voakes's mouth downward. "I read all about your parents' deaths, Miss Healy. I saw the photograph in the *Post-Intelligencer* of their orphaned little blond daughter. I don't mean to imply that I laid eyes on you *personally*."

Voakes's red-rimmed gaze drifted over Becca, from head to foot. He could see her perfectly well, and a shudder went through her.

She was rapidly recalculating everything she thought she knew about psychopaths. Most of them had blunt affects, little facial expression or vocal inflection. There was no psychotropic medication for this kind of atavistic madness. But even in his last illness, Voakes was animated, revealing a kind of mild, sneaking enjoyment of this attention. Becca remembered that aspects of the sociopathic brain had more in common with reptiles than humans, and that seemed to fit him perfectly.

"I haven't heard you deny it," Becca said.

"I haven't really heard enough to know if I should deny it." Voakes sulked for a moment, plucking at the sheet, apparently striving for some combination of pathos and ambiguity. "Why the sudden interest, if I can ask? I mean, you could have asked me about this years ago. You've always known where to find me."

"I've never been interested in finding you, Mr. Voakes, and in five more minutes, I'll never think of you again," Becca lied. "We don't have any way of making you tell us the truth; you'll either answer me or you won't. The state of your conscience when you die is entirely up to you. But you need to make this decision, now."

Voakes considered this, or pretended to. Becca felt Jo's strong, breathing presence behind her, and she matched her breath for breath.

"All right. I'll tell you the absolute truth, but then you have to do me a favor. Quid pro quo, Clarice. You'd be granting my dying wish."

Becca bit back an automatic refusal, acknowledging Emily's look with a slight nod. "No promises. But I'm listening."

"I'll even go first." Voakes brightened, showing a flash of that malign merriment. "Then you can decide if you want to grant my last wish or not. The state of your conscience when I die is entirely up to you. Are you ready?"

Becca waited.

"I didn't kill your parents." Voakes sagged into the bed, color returning to his face. His meds probably contained painkillers that were beginning to kick in. "The police got it right that time. Your mother killed your parents."

Becca looked at Jo, whose gaze was fixed on Voakes's haggard features. She met Becca's gaze and nodded once. Voakes was telling the truth.

"Can I have the doll?" Voakes's eyes were closed, his face turned toward the window, slatted light falling over the bed.

Vertigo slammed into Becca, and she swayed on her feet. She fought to clear her head with a fierce act of will.

"That little rag doll you were holding that night. I assume you kept it, such an important family heirloom. I'd like to be cradling it as I fall asleep for the last time. I think it would comfort me."

Becca found her voice. "How do you know about the doll, Mr. Voakes?"

"Oh. You were clutching it in that photo I mentioned, the one in the paper."

She looked at Jo again, mostly because she needed to see her in that moment, but also because Jo had made a thorough study of every police report and newspaper article related to the shooting.

Jo shook her head.

"Okay, it's time to wrap this up." Peter scowled at Emily. "We said fifteen minutes. He's starting to fade."

"What about my dying wish?" Voakes sounded plaintive.

Becca had had enough. She turned with admirable balance and coordination and walked out of the room. Emily followed her closely, looking ready to perform CPR, if necessary.

They would debrief with Emily. They would drive back to Capitol Hill. On the way, they would try to explain to each other how Voakes could have seen a doll in a photo that didn't exist.

But first Jo stopped in the doorway of the bedroom long enough to speak to John William Voakes for the first time, and pass on her own parting wish.

"Die soon, and badly."

CHAPTER FOURTEEN

The Bentley purred silently back over the West Seattle Bridge before either of them spoke.

"Did you watch Oprah Winfrey?" Jo asked.

Becca pulled her gaze from the downtown skyline looming ahead, the black celery stick of the Columbia Tower, and frowned. "Jo, are we really in the mood for celebrity chat right now?"

"This is important." Jo knew one reliable way to comfort Becca was to feed her, but Jo had never learned to cook. She wanted to take her to the best restaurant in the city, but there were two problems with this plan. First, she had only seen Becca consume unhealthy food, and second, Jo didn't think she could stand one more minute in the company of strangers.

"All right, sure. I liked Oprah's show."

"Good." Jo clicked her signal to exit off I-5. "The doll wasn't a state secret, Becca. Even Pam Emerson mentioned your reaction to a doll that night."

"But you said the only photo of me that was ever in a paper was that kindergarten portrait. That was outrage enough. There were never any shots of me holding a doll."

"Yes, but Emily Kelley pointed out that we weren't privy to the conversations that could have happened over the years in a state mental hospital. She told us about the forensic unit at Western, the gossip there. Voakes could easily have heard details about your parents' deaths any time in the past two decades."

"Maybe. What did his face tell you? Did you learn anything?"

Jo cruised silently through the Central District, trying to find words to describe the extraordinary aberration that was John William Voakes. "I've never seen anything like him. According to his expressions, he never lied once."

"*What?*"

Jo shrugged. "I'm saying that his microexpressions are useless as a means of detecting false statements. Most people show some flicker of guilt when they lie, or at least a fear of getting caught. Your friends are right about you, Becca. You're too inherently honest. You broadcast lies like a beacon. Voakes has no perception at all that lying is wrong, so there was no guilt or fear. He seemed to be telling the truth when he denied killing your parents. But he gave the same signals when he claimed he saw the picture of the doll in the paper, an outright deception."

"Which doesn't exactly vindicate him." Becca rested her head against the seat, looking disturbingly spent. "So John William Voakes stays on our list, along with Rachel, my uncle, my aunt, my mother, my father. Hell, Jo, maybe I shot the gun myself and blocked it all out. Maybe I thought it was a toy. Two unlucky shots…"

Jo had actually considered this most horrific of scenarios early on, and dismissed it out of hand. "Becca, you were five years old. They would have to be two incredibly unlucky shots, one after the other. And a five-year-old wouldn't have the knowledge or presence of mind to stage a murder/suicide."

"I was a pretty precocious five-year-old. And where *are* we going? Oh."

Jo waited until Becca's face lit up, then she sighed in relief. She nodded at the glass doors of Ezell's Famous Chicken. "I understand Oprah Winfrey announced on her show that Seattle's Ezell's had the best fried chicken she ever tasted. I know you like chicken. You wanted some the other night, when Marty and Khadijah came over for the Xenathon, but you suggested going to *KFC*…" Jo uttered the letters with distaste.

"You know, Jo?" Becca looked entirely serious, as if she were telling an unvarnished truth. "You can be a very sweet woman.

A good friend. I don't think you give yourself enough credit for that."

She unsnapped her seatbelt and leaned over to kiss Jo lightly on the cheek. "Come on. Aren't you hungry? You're buying."

Jo ducked out of the car, smiling, resting her hand on her cheek.

❖

Becca had the best intentions of waiting until they had settled in the house and fired up a *Xena* episode before attacking the chicken, but she made short work of her share on the drive back to the Hill. Some of Jo's share, too. She didn't understand how anyone could steer a luxury car while consuming greasy poultry without so much as a smeared lip, but Jo managed it. Becca went through twenty napkins with relish.

She was growing drowsy by the time they pulled up to the house. The triple punch of a long day, a heart-to-heart with a serial killer, and a full meal had about done her in.

She saw the wrought iron gates of Lake View Cemetery across the street reflected in the polished glass of the Bentley's window as Jo keyed off the engine. "You realize I'm using a solid week of vacation leave for this, Jo? We could be at Cannon Beach. We could be at Lake Crescent." She glanced at Jo and blushed. "I mean, I could be. Just saying, I've taken more relaxing vacations."

"You'll deserve a real break after this." Jo extended her long arm across the back of the seat and regarded Becca. "You would deserve a luxury vacation, in any case. Seeing Western and meeting Emily Kelley have opened my eyes a bit about your work. You deal with people in crisis every day, and you have for your entire career. I can tell how good you are at what you do, Becca. You were diamond sharp with Voakes, but genuine and warm with Pam's father. Your compassion comes through so clearly."

Becca set off the tiny little vacuum cleaners behind her eyes, not wanting to tear up, hoping to keep Jo in the gentle space she had amazingly created. "Sometimes I think I spend my days applying Band-Aids. The poverty and mental illness and addiction I see in my work seem unbeatable. Feels like all I've done is deal with a constant series of mini crises my entire career."

"A thousand Band-Aids, a thousand small works of healing that actually helped someone." Jo shrugged. "Seems like an honorable career to look back on to me."

The interior of the Bentley was growing warm in the late afternoon sun. Becca glanced at Jo's hand on the back of the seat. Her thumb would only have to move a mere inch to brush the back of Becca's neck. Jo sat motionless, her eyes on the steering wheel, and Becca felt a weary sadness seep into her. This was a woman dealing with a profound disability, and she didn't have the right, or enough hope right now, to push things further.

"Listen, I'm bushed." She gave Jo's knee a sisterly pat. "I could conk out easily for a nap in that armchair. You have to be tired, too, so I'll swap you for the couch."

Jo slid her arm slowly from the back of the seat and unclasped her belt. "We can fight about it inside."

They walked together up the shaded steps to the porch, and Becca found enough energy to be proud of her lack of stomach knot. Dread used to shoot through her at the very sight of this place, and simply walking into it took an act of will. She was besting this house slowly, with Jo's help, with late-night *Xena* parties here with her friends. A murderer of a family, a house haunted by tragedy, eating fried chicken in luxury cars. Becca was learning to face down her demons.

Or she was, until she saw the body of the bloody, mutilated child slumped beside the front door.

❖

The first indication Jo had of anything amiss was Becca's sharp gasp, then her body slamming into her own with an impact powerful enough to send them both hurtling backward down the stone steps.

Jo twisted instinctively and managed to save her spine the first smashing blow of the step, but the swell of her shoulder took a painful crack. Her body helped cushion Becca's landing, but they both tumbled helplessly because she was thrashing like a banshee. The bone of Jo's ankle smacked against another stair before she could bring them to a halt.

"Becca, hold still!" It was all Jo could yell, mindlessly and several times, while she tried to pin Becca's wrists to the cement walk. She was afraid she would hurt herself, and she kept trying to cushion the back of Becca's head with a hand she needed to restrain her.

Becca was trying to talk. Jo could hear words mixed in with her terrible gasping, but she made no coherent sense. Her eyes were filled with horror and then they fluttered shut, and her body sagged abruptly beneath Jo's hands.

"Becca? Christ." Jo looked around wildly. Where was a medically knowledgeable pedestrian when she needed one? Her hands hovered over Becca's still figure. She didn't seem to be hurt. Air was still whistling in and out of her chest, so at least she was breathing.

Jo crouched beside her, tapping her clammy hand ineffectually. Then she cursed and lifted Becca into her arms. Her dead weight made Jo stagger as she lunged to her feet, and her ankle and shoulder protested painfully, but she managed to wrestle them both up the wide stairs. If getting Becca out of this sun and a wet compress didn't bring her around quickly, she was calling medics.

Jo was dimly grateful she'd gotten the door unlocked before Becca smacked her. One good kick would widen the opening enough to carry her in. She clenched her teeth, wincing as she maneuvered her head around the doorjamb, and then she saw the bloody doll on the cement step. Jo stared at it until Becca stirred sluggishly in her arms.

"Hey. Let's get you inside." Jo felt Becca's small nod against her shoulder. Her body remained slack, but she lifted one hand to grip the back of Jo's neck.

Jo back-heeled the door curtly, then waited until she heard it latch behind them before carrying Becca down the two stairs to the sofa. She lowered her into it carefully, then sat at its edge. "Becca?"

"T-trigger."

"Yes, I saw it." Jo rested her hand on Becca's forehead. "I'll call Pam Emerson. You'll never see it again."

Becca nodded again.

"You look awful," Jo said. "Can you talk to me?"

Becca wrapped her arms around her waist, holding herself tightly, trembling so hard Jo imagined the couch vibrated.

"Becca, you're safe, I promise you." Jo fought a wave of helplessness. "Tell me what you need from me."

Becca fumbled with the front pocket of her jeans, pulled out her cell, and handed it to Jo. "Rachel." Her voice was slurred, as if she were drunk, and Jo was getting scared.

"Right away." Jo flipped open the cell and found the number quickly. After an interminable few moments, during which Becca lay motionless except for the tremor, Rachel Perry answered.

"Becca, thank goodness." Her tone was warm, and Jo could hear light classical music and the tinkling of cutlery in the background. "I'm at the benefit dinner for your aunt's shelter. Please have some emergency that—"

"Rachel, it's Joanne Call," Jo broke in. "Becca needs you."

"Joanne?" Rachel sounded startled, but then spoke calmly. "Is Becca all right?"

"No. She's had a bad shock." Jo tried to mirror Rachel's control. "We're at the house on Fifteenth."

"Do you need to get her to a hospital?"

"She's all right physically, but she's…there was a nasty trigger."

"Joanne, I'm on my way." The music was fading even as Rachel spoke. "Tell her I'll be there soon. Just keep her quiet and sit tight."

"She's coming, Becca." Jo folded the cell. "Can I get you some water?"

Becca shook her head.

Jo watched her silently for a few miserable moments.

"I'll b-be okay, Jo." Becca covered her eyes with her hand, and her mouth twisted before she turned her face into the sofa's cushion. "Just give me a few minutes alone, okay?"

"Of course," Jo whispered. On the rare occasions she cried, she preferred privacy, too. But Becca's request was the only thing that could have wedged her from the couch, in that moment. She rose and made her way to the front door. She checked to make sure Becca hadn't moved, then slipped out onto the porch.

The mutilated doll drew Jo like a macabre and malodorous flytrap. She crouched in front of it, as dispassionate as it was possible to be, given her still-racing heart.

Jo didn't know what kind of doll five-year-old Becca had been clutching the night her parents died. Voakes had referred to a rag doll, and that didn't describe the ugly little present someone had set on this porch in the few hours they had been gone. It was roughly as big as a human toddler, an unusual size for a doll but without the realistic features of a mannequin. It was pink plastic and naked, stripped of whatever clothing it had come packaged in. The chubby cheeks were generic, its single eye was the classic desirable Caucasian blue. Fine blond hair, chopped brutally by unskilled hands, stood out from the scalp in chunks.

The doll's pink chest was splashed with red, possibly fingernail polish, but an entire bottle of it. The "blood" began at the shattered socket of the left eye, which had obviously been shot out with a gun. Jo tweezed the white hair in two fingers and pulled the doll forward. Most of the back of its head was gone.

She heard a single sob from inside the house, soft and quickly suppressed. Rage shot through Jo, fury that anyone would dare frighten Becca like this. Before she could stop herself, she clenched her fingers powerfully over the doll's ruined head. She wrenched it off the plastic neck and hurled it from the porch, then heard it bounce into the bushes below.

"Jo?" Becca's voice was faint, but it drew Jo to her feet and back into the house like a clarion summons.

They would wait together for Rachel Perry. If Becca wanted Jo couchside while she spoke to Rachel, the wrath of hell itself would not move her.

❖

And Jo was banished to the porch again.

The wrath of hell hadn't dismissed her; that had been Becca. Apparently, she wanted private time with Rachel. That was fine with Jo. Her shoulder throbbed from its smack against the step. There was aspirin in the medicine chest in the upstairs bathroom, but she had nothing better to do than sit sentinel out here on the stairs and guard Becca from Patricia Healy.

"I'm afraid she's right behind me," Rachel had said as Jo helped her up these same steps. "Patricia's still saying her good-byes at her fundraiser, but she insisted on joining us here soon. It's possible my racing to the exit, squawking in alarm, tipped her off somehow."

Jo had seen Rachel safely settled beside Becca, then let herself out quietly to prevent any pending aunt-ambush. She used the time to wrap that monstrosity of a doll in a tarp and lock it securely in the trunk of her Bentley. She would turn it over to Pam Emerson in the morning. She considered parking the Bentley around the corner, to better distance Becca from its malicious cargo, but didn't want to leave the porch unguarded.

The sun was taking its seasonally sweet time setting, its last gold rays bathing the cemetery across the street. Jo rubbed her shoulder pensively, wishing she could see the Lady of the Rock from here. Imagining this benevolent light kissing the Lady's face, illuminating the young girl resting her head in her lap. Jo had seen a reflection of this image of the cemetery's Pietá in Becca and Rachel, just now. The maternity of the older woman's hand, resting on Becca's hair. They touched each other so easily, Becca and her people.

It was full dark before a classic Rolls with Patricia Healy behind the wheel glided to a halt in front of the house. Wasp-waisted in a jade gown befitting a formal dinner, Becca's aunt hurried up the stone steps, her head lowered. She almost stepped on Jo, and stumbled in surprise.

"Joanne, I didn't see you." Patricia righted herself, looking flustered. "Is Becca inside?"

"Yes. Rachel is with her. They've asked for some time alone." Jo could read the indecision in Patricia's face, so she simply stood up. With psychiatric aides like Peter and nosy aunts like Patricia, her height could prove an advantage. "I'm sure they won't be much longer."

Patricia blinked up at her. "Oh. That's fine. We'll wait out here, then." She turned carefully on the wide step and managed to arrange herself gracefully to sit on it, gown and all.

Reluctantly, Jo resumed her seat one step above her.

"Can you explain what happened? Rachel didn't share many details."

"I'll let Becca tell you about it." Jo heard the genuine worry in her voice, but she didn't feel up to cozy conversation right now.

"That girl has certainly been through the wringer." Patricia sighed and slipped off her shoes and placed them neatly side by side on the step. "Funny. I still think of Becca as a girl, but I was her age when she came to us. And I felt as old and decrepit as a redwood then, suddenly dealing with this traumatized little child."

"Hm."

"Becca's becoming a lesbian was never an issue for us, by the way." Patricia smiled up at Jo. "Both Mitch and I think you all should have every civil right on the books. We support your community entirely."

"Hm." Jo remembered Mitchell's fondness for search engines, but she doubted anything in her online presence revealed her sexual orientation. She wondered at Patricia's presumption.

"When Becca first came out to us, we thought she might just be lining up with her friends, Marty and Khadijah. They're a lesbian couple, and they're both terrific women. I hope you get to meet them someday."

"Hm." Jo found she was actually missing Uncle Mitch's interruptions. At least they provided some respite from Patricia's incessant chatter. Was Rachel transplanting Becca's liver in there? What could be taking so long?

"Thank God Marty and Khadijah knew to come to us, back when Becca was in so much trouble years ago." Patricia sighed again and plucked at the folds in her gown. "Becca went through a period of serious drug use, Joanne, when she was sixteen. Mitch and I were quite alarmed. She managed to beat it, but we've thought of her as rather fragile ever since. The violent loss of her parents, heroin addiction. And now this, tonight—whatever this is. You can understand why we're worried."

Jo wondered if Becca had had any nasty STDs in her adolescence that her aunt might want to disclose out of her hearing, but she managed not to ask. This felt like some clumsy effort to discredit Becca, to make Jo doubt her judgment, and she resented it. The front door opened and Rachel emerged, alone, on the porch. Jo left Patricia to flounder to her feet unassisted to join them.

"She's more comfortable, now." Rachel spoke quietly, as if still in tending mode. "I ended up giving her a Seconal." She made a clicking sound of regret. "Becca stays away from meds when she can, but we both agreed it was a good idea tonight. That doll must have been a horror, Joanne."

"A doll?" Patricia looked from Rachel to Jo and back. "Oh dear, that doesn't sound good. May I see her?"

"Becca's finally sleepy. It isn't a good time for more visitors." Rachel slid her arm through Patricia's. "Why don't you give her a call tomorrow, Patricia? She promised to join me for breakfast in the morning, just to check in. I'll want to see how she's doing then."

Jo released a small breath of relief. "Is there anything I should know for tonight?"

"Just stay in close proximity, in case she dreams. I made her go upstairs to lie down in a real bed, by the way. The woman needs sleep." Rachel peered up at Jo and patted her wrist gruffly. "You could do with some rest, too, Joanne. You have to take better care of yourself."

"Oh, look who's talking." Patricia pursed her lips. "Rachel, you're out on your feet."

Nothing about Rachel had registered for Jo, except her welcome presence, while Becca needed her help. Now she realized how right Patricia was. Rachel seemed shrunken in on herself, hunched and old in the finery of her silk dress. Jo remembered the bird-like thinness of her arm as she helped her up the steps.

"Let me drive you home," Patricia said. "Or you can sleep at our place, Rachel. That might be best."

"Don't be silly, Patricia, I live six blocks away. Just help me down these infernal steps, and I'll be fine. Good night, Joanne."

"Good night, Joanne," Patricia repeated, guiding Rachel solicitously down the stairs. "Please call if Becca needs anything."

"Where are your shoes?" Rachel asked.

Jo hitched her thumbs in her pockets and watched the two women thoughtfully as they made their way to the street. Their expressions had revealed two things in the last thirty seconds, more clearly than any message whispered from beyond the grave.

Rachel's concern for Jo's personal well-being had rung entirely false. Jo supposed she found this understandable. But so had Patricia Healy's concern for Rachel.

CHAPTER FIFTEEN

I t's all right. I'm awake." Becca heard the bedroom's hardwood floor creak beneath Jo's foot. She assumed it was Jo, and not some creeping, doll-planting interloper. It had better be, since she'd left her chobos downstairs. She was too drowsy to turn over on the wide bed and actually look.

"I'm sorry," Jo said, apparently apologizing for her mere presence in the darkened room. "I felt it was necessary to bring this up."

Ah. Jo moved around the bed, and Becca could see her shadowed form set the Spiricom on the low table beside it. She seemed surprised to find the small globe radio already there.

"That yellow ball seems to tune in on my mom the best." Becca yawned. "If she speaks up tonight, she'd better mind her manners and whisper."

She felt Jo settle gradually onto the side of the bed, and her silence finally prompted Becca to turn over. Her limbs moved with a drugged languor, and she blinked sleepily.

"It's not the same bed," Becca said.

"What?"

"The furniture in this house has been turned over several times over the years. I made Rachel reassure me about that, more than once. My parents slept in this room, but it wasn't in this bed."

"I never assumed it was." Jo sounded puzzled and troubled. "Becca, you scared the hell out of me tonight."

"I know." Becca felt genuine sorrow about this. She knew how she would have felt if Jo were suddenly, frighteningly unconscious. "Thank you for looking after me so well."

"It didn't seem there was much I could do. How are you now?"

Becca thought about it and decided to tell the truth. "I'm better. Rachel pumped me full of drugs, and I'm calm now, and sleepy. But I'm afraid I'm going crazy, Jo."

It came out so casually, it sounded so reasonable, and Becca's eyes filled again with helpless tears. As if she could see them, Jo wrapped her hand in hers.

"Tell me," Jo said. That's all she said, and Becca found she could.

"Bipolar disorder tends to run in families. You know that. I'm beginning to think I've caught my mother's bug. These fugue states I go into. They feel psychotic. I may be losing my grip here."

Jo waited, but that's all Becca could get out right now. The tears ran down either side of her face, trickling through her hair to the pillow.

"You're not having manic episodes, Becca, not as I understand mania. And if you're having intense reactions to this phobia, that just seems good common sense to me. In the past, the danger has always been in your mind. These days your subconscious is reacting to what has become a very real threat."

Jo's logic wasn't reaching Becca, but her voice was. That low, rich alto, the thoughtfulness of her speech. Unfortunately, it wasn't calming Becca; it was just making it possible to open the floodgates further. She managed to keep her own voice level. "That's basically what Rachel told me."

"Rachel knows you very well. You have a therapist you trust, and loving friends to see you through this. You'll be fine."

"My mother had those things, and she wasn't fine."

That did it. Becca was undone. Even as sobs convulsed her, she knew Jo and Rachel were right. She knew she wasn't going to end up on a back ward of Western State, but it was so dark outside and Rachel had only given her one Seconal, and it wasn't enough.

Whatever unlikely wisdom had told Jo when to be silent must have told her now that more than words were needed. Becca felt her long body ease down onto the bed, stretching out beside hers. Jo's arm draped lightly across her waist, and Becca curled into her shoulder.

They held each other while Becca wept, and for a long time after her tears finally stopped. Then Jo's hand brushed beneath her chin, and Becca lifted her face to meet her kiss. Their lips blended with a sweet softness, melding with a natural ease, a perfect fit. Becca's body filled slowly with a different kind of languor, a liquid, trickling warmth.

"Becca." Jo lifted her head, and Becca wondered at the honest regret in her voice. "I've never made love to anyone. I don't know how. And I don't want to learn tonight. I just want to hold you."

And Becca was saddened all over again that Jo was afraid this would be considered heresy; both that she was inexperienced, and that a moment of such loving physical intimacy had to lead inevitably to sex.

"Don't you know this is enough?" she whispered. "Becca School is back in session, dear Dr. Call. You're giving me exactly what I need."

Jo's body relaxed against hers, and Becca could feel sleep claim her in seconds. Her exhaustion had finally kicked in, and Becca was relieved there was some hope Jo might actually sleep through the night. There was some hope she might too now, well and dreamlessly, with Jo draped around her like a comforting cloak.

Becca turned her head toward the side table. She couldn't see the little radio or the Spiricom, but the soft crackle of static drew her.

"Mom?" she said softly. The word felt strange in her mouth. It wasn't one she had spoken aloud often, certainly not as a name. At five, her mother had been "Mommy," and Becca had been "little girl."

Jo had said the Spiricom might make two-way communication possible. Becca wondered fuzzily if her mother was awake out there, in whatever shadowed land she inhabited now.

Her lips still vibrated from that kiss, that unexpected gift. She hoped fervently that Jo wouldn't regret it in the morning, either the kiss or the welcome embrace of her arms tonight. Becca felt a sleepy but powerful hankering to talk to Khadijah or Marty or Rachel, to have a long and thoughtful chat about the fact that she was falling in love for the first time in her life.

She sighed, and her eyes drifted closed. No one could really advise her on the risk of this romantic folly, about whether loving Jo would ultimately heal or hurt them both. Becca's wandering mind summoned an image of the Lady of the Rock, and she took comfort from the statue's maternal gaze.

"*Becca.*"

Becca's eyes flew open, and she started so hard only the depth of Jo's weariness preserved her sleep.

Her mother's voice was different.

She had spoken only her name, but Becca heard the change clearly. For the first time, there was no grief in her mother's tone, no fear, no pleading. Madelyn Healy was speaking to her daughter as she had never been able to in life, as one woman to another, and her voice was rich with love and a kind of shy, pleased approval.

"*Becca…it's right.*"

Becca stared into the darkness, her heart pounding. She felt Jo's soft breath stir her hair, and she understood.

Becca smiled, spiraling down into sleep, filled with a new, growing faith in two things. Her mother had been a wise woman, and they were both right about Joanne Call.

CHAPTER SIXTEEN

Yes, Pam, I believe I've admitted you told us to call you at any time." Jo grimaced and stepped deeper into the bushes, lifting small branches with one hand and clasping her cell with the other.

"Yeah, and last night would have been a *very good time.*" Pam Emerson's voice crackled in her ear. "I could have been there in ten minutes, Jo, damn."

"Well, I'm bringing it to you now." Or half of it. If Jo couldn't find the doll's stupid head, Pam would have to make do with decapitated evidence. "It will only take me ten minutes, too."

"You shouldn't even have touched it," Pam pointed out.

"Too late for that. Ah." Jo bent awkwardly and snagged the doll's head with her thumb through the hole in its eye. At least the hideous thing would be intact.

She straightened and saw Becca across the street. She was standing by her battered Toyota, the sun shining on her hair, regarding Jo quizzically. "You're right," she told Pam, "I should have called you last night. I apologize. I was…distracted."

"How's Becca?" Pam's irritation softened. Jo remembered she knew of Becca's fear of dolls. She had tried to comfort her with one, the night of the shootings. She felt an unexpected flicker of relief as Pam Emerson clicked solidly in place as a member of their clan.

"She had a rocky night, but she's better today." Jo concealed the head of the doll at the back of her belt, wincing as her sore shoulder tweaked. "She's seeing her therapist for breakfast."

"That's a good idea. And I'm seeing you at the station in nine minutes?"

"Nine minutes." Jo folded her cell and walked down the driveway. She gave Becca a brisk wave of farewell, went to the back of her Bentley, and opened the trunk. She slipped the doll's head into the tarped bundle containing its body, closed the trunk, and walked straight into Becca. "Omph."

"Whoops!" Becca steadied her, smiling up into her eyes. "Sorry, Batman."

"No harm done." Jo liked the feel of Becca's hands on her arms, and the fact that she kept them there even after she was steady. "You're off to see Rachel?"

Becca nodded. "I told her I'd meet her at her place. The way she looked last night, I don't want her out running around. What about you? You haven't spilled your plans this morning."

"Well, I'm going by my office to start cleaning up." Jo considered lying by omission, but remembered her ongoing lessons in Becca School. "But first I'm bringing the doll to Pam Emerson. It's in the trunk."

Becca's hands tightened on her arms, but only briefly. She looked toward the back of Jo's car, then back at her. "Okay. Sounds like a good plan."

"Did hearing that trigger you?"

"No." Becca really did look fine. "It's a little hard to explain, but if I'm not actually looking at a doll, I can think of it as an abstract. It's as if you were terrified of spiders—you wouldn't be crazy about a dead tarantula in the trunk, but at least you'd know it wasn't going to crawl up through the seats and eat you."

"That makes sense." Jo drank in the warmth of Becca's jade eyes. The light in them deepened.

"It's Capitol Hill, so I can do this." Becca's voice was lower now, silken, as she stepped closer. "But in case you have issues with public displays of affection, I'm giving you fair notice that I'm about to kiss you."

Jo actually did appreciate that notice, because touch generally was still hard for—

And then she forgot touch had ever been hard for her as Becca's arms slid around her neck. She lowered her head and their lips met.

It was really, really nice.

Jo didn't have words for some things.

Becca must have agreed because she wrapped her arms around her, the kind of hug she was so justly famous for among her friends. Jo had never been so warmly and thoroughly hugged in her life, but Becca was pressing her shoulder and she squeaked.

Becca released her. "What was that?"

"Nothing."

"You're six feet tall and you just went off like a poodle. What's wrong?"

"Nothing."

"Joanne, if I wanted the stoic butch routine, I'd read fan fiction. What is it?"

Jo grinned in spite of herself and shrugged. "We took a tumble down the front stairs last night. I'm fine. It's just a bruise."

The light faded from Becca's features. "Are you sure? Should you see a doctor?"

"I'm sure."

Becca looked up at her pensively. "I don't know whether to trust you with this. You're not very good at taking care of yourself, I've noticed. I'm still not sure what you need, at any given time."

"Please consider Joanne School in session now." Jo lowered her head until her forehead touched Becca's, and the words flowed as naturally as rain. "Don't you know this is enough? You're giving me exactly what I need."

The breath went out of Becca and she seemed a bit weak in the knees, an effect Jo had never had on a woman, to her knowledge, nor had ever wanted to. She kind of liked it.

Becca stepped back and pulled her cell out of her pocket. She flipped it open and tapped keys, then mouthed "voice mail" at Jo. "Rachel? Let's make it dinner tonight, okay? I'm so much better. And something has come up here that's kind of pressing. I'll call you later."

Jo frowned. "Becca, this is a terrible idea."

"No, it isn't. I will check in with Rachel, but it can wait for tonight." Becca slid her cell back in her pocket. "I want to hear what Pam has to say about the doll. Just don't let me see it. And you're not cleaning up all that broken glass in your office alone with a bruised shoulder."

"Becca—"

"And you're letting me drive." Becca plucked the keys from Jo's fingers, chimed open the door, and slid inside the Bentley.

"Becca—"

"Trust. Trust builds relationships." Becca patted the wheel cheerfully. "Get in, please."

"Building trust, hell, you want my Bentley," Jo grumbled. She made her way to the passenger's side, unsettled by this change in plans, but resigned to it.

Becca pulled away from the house, smiling broadly.

"Spare us the queen's wave, please." Jo clicked her seatbelt shut. "Keep both hands on the wheel."

"I'm an excellent driver. Lots of parking tickets, but that's Seattle. Not one moving violation in twenty years."

"I'm glad to hear it." Jo tried to maintain her sulk, but Becca's obvious pleasure as she steered the elegant car down Aloha was infectious. She turned on the radio, clicking past NPR to a classic rock station, and regretfully turned to business. "We need to tell Pam about our talk with John William Voakes."

Becca nodded. "Yeah, she might be able to connect us to the cops who investigated him. I'm hoping she'll have a lead on whoever trashed your office."

"Well, none of our usual suspects fit. Even if Voakes could have snuck out of that guarded room the other night, he's too physically weak to do such damage." The same could be said for Rachel Perry, and Jo couldn't imagine the pristine Patricia or Mitchell Healy wreaking that havoc. "Becca, the station's at Twelfth and Pine."

"Oh. Right." Becca hit the turn signal. "Sorry. I was just grooving on the ride."

Jo looked at her. Pam Emerson had given her nine minutes to reach the station, and she had spent one of them kissing Becca. She couldn't regret that. But the rest of her time had fled long ago, and Pam was waiting. She opened her mouth to say so. "Go ahead. We can cruise for a while."

"Yeah?" Becca darted her a delighted look. "Hot doggy. I'll just go around the block."

She clicked the signal the other way and turned onto Denny. Apparently, the block would include all of Seattle's downtown district, but Jo sat back to enjoy the ride. They both deserved a little respite under the morning's mild sun and blue sky, and she was able to relax against the plush seat.

"*Becca!*"

The static of the Bentley's radio crackled hard, and Madelyn Healy spoke.

"*Becca, the gift held blood.*"

"Jo?" Becca sounded suspiciously calm. "I think our brakes are out."

❖

Becca kept mashing the pedal to the floor, but the effort was increasingly futile. The elegant car shuddered and picked up speed as they rolled down Denny.

"The Bentley has the finest emergency brake ever made." Jo calmly grasped the hand brake that rested on the console between them and pulled it up. There was one jagged pause in their forward motion before the car rolled on.

"Well, shit," Jo suggested.

Becca was afraid she might. Denny was a long, straight avenue that sloped sharply down toward the Space Needle, and it intersected with busy streets. They were hitting the end of the morning rush. Becca gulped in air, gripping the steering wheel fiercely.

"Can you turn toward the sidewalk?" Jo clenched the dashboard.

"Wish I could." Becca darted her eyes left and right, relieved there was a pocket of space around them. Grinding the wheels against open curb would slow them, but no curb was open on Denny. Becca had a choice of crashing into parked vehicles or roaring up on a sidewalk and killing one of many pedestrians. There was time to jump out, but someone could still be killed by this car if they did. "Oh Jesus, Jo, Fairview."

"Just keep us steady."

They were rolling down toward one of the busiest intersections connecting to downtown. Becca caught a dizzy flash of a bilious green building coming up on the left—a walk-in haven for homeless youth—seconds before she saw two ragged kids crossing the street in front of them. Becca slammed on the horn.

"Right!" Jo yelled, but Becca was already spinning the wheel hard. She saw the kids' two white faces jerking toward them. A Prius loomed next to them in the same instant. Becca made the wheels kiss the curb, some alien logic in her mind telling her not to over-correct.

Horn blaring, the Bentley skittered between the two gawping young people and the Prius, but even with Becca's caution, their momentum sent the car tipping wildly, lifting up on two wheels. It slammed level on the pavement again and coasted through the intersection.

Becca's mother, the Lady of the Rock, or some god Becca still wasn't sure existed had to be looking out for them. Fairview's miraculous red light allowed the Bentley to swerve around the one passing car. The street was leveling and they were slowing, and Becca was able to turn them into the wide dirt lot of a factory on their right.

They rumbled to a stop inches from the chain-link fence bordering the lot.

Becca still gripped the wheel, her eyes wide and staring, not wanting to believe she had pulled it off. She turned calmly to Jo.

"Are you all right?" she barked. "Are you all right?"

"Why wouldn't I be all right?" Jo snapped irritably, still gripping the dashboard as tightly as Becca held the wheel. "I'm sitting right here. You did it, Becca. You saved us."

"Now we're getting the hell out of this car." Becca turned the key and the oddly hissing engine quieted. Jo seemed to read her mind, and they elbowed open their doors. If the brakes of this thing had so obviously been messed with, she wouldn't be surprised if a bomb went off under the hood. She wanted them out of there.

They walked stiffly together across the lot, stood side by side, and stared at the treacherous Bentley.

Jo flipped open her cell. "Where are we?"

"Denny and Terry Avenue."

Jo clicked keys and spoke tersely into her phone. Her tone was stoic as she talked to Pam Emerson, but Becca could feel her trembling beside her.

Jo snapped her cell shut. "What's the matter with you?"

Becca looked up at her, puzzled. "Besides almost flattening two homeless kids, I'm fine. What do you mean?"

"You're so calm."

"Oh. I'm in crisis mode." Becca clasped her hands behind her, enjoying the familiar, but temporary, cerebral tranquility that saw her through emergencies. "Trigger my phobia and I'll freak right out, but throw me a threat that makes sense and I can usually handle it. Social work. I promise I'll be a basket case by tonight, though."

"Well, I'll have my nervous breakdown now, then." Jo was pale as chalk.

"That's okay. Go ahead. I think there are two rules in good relationships: I get to drive, and only one of us gets to go crazy at a time." Becca tugged Jo's sleeve gently. "Come on. Sit down. We found a patch of shade."

They settled together into the dirt in the shadow of the building. Becca wrapped Jo's cold hand in hers and held it on her knee, and they were quiet for a while.

"The gift held blood," Jo said.

Becca closed her eyes, her tranquility fading fast. "I don't know what that means. I don't understand what gift she's talking about."

"We heard her voice just before we realized the brakes were gone."

"Was she warning us? Trying to get us out of the car?"

"Your mother spoke in the past tense. The gift *held* blood. It didn't sound as if she was warning us of a current danger."

"You had just mentioned John William Voakes before she spoke."

"True." Jo was watching her closely. "Becca, I can fly us both to the finest hotel in London. We can be there in ten hours."

"That's tempting." Becca had a terrific craving for a chocolate truffle and a stiff drink. She let the prospect of escape play out behind her closed eyes, a luxury suite in an exotic city, far away from bloody dolls and severed brake lines. She knew she couldn't do it. "Jo, please, get out of here if you can. I'll understand. I can't go with you. She's my mother. But you didn't bargain for any of this. I don't want you hurt because of me."

"I won't grace that suggestion with a reply." Jo was steadier now, color returning to the high planes of her face.

And through the post-crisis calm and questions of ghosts and murder mysteries, Becca found room to marvel all over again at their shadows on the thin grass. Jo's tall figure outlined darkly beside her smaller one, leaning against her. She still couldn't believe her shadow might be finding a twin; but there Jo was—breathing and real and, thank Christ, safe for now.

Becca heard the far-off whine of a siren approaching. Pam Emerson was setting a land speed record. The Bentley sat sadly in the distant corner of the sunny lot, both its front doors open.

"What gift?" Becca whispered to the air.

CHAPTER SEVENTEEN

"Tell me again, who could have gotten to your car last night?" Pam had ushered them into a coffee shop, a break from the growing heat of the day and a chocolate opportunity for Becca. Still feeling a little unsettled, Jo watched Becca delicately consume a fudge cupcake.

"Jo?" Pam nudged her.

"Sorry. Anyone could have gotten to my car last night." Jo sipped her latte. "It was parked on the street."

"But you had visitors at the house, right? Not me, only the good Lord knows why, but other visitors?"

"Yes. Rachel Perry and Becca's aunt came over. But I was outside on the front steps while they were there. I saw them come and go. Neither of them went near my car."

"Damn. Okay. What are you two going to do for wheels?" Pam flipped through the pages of her notebook.

"I've leased something." Jo expected the BMW to arrive shortly. She'd given the service the address of the coffee shop. "What about my office, Pam?"

"Damn place is clean of prints. We drew a couple of boot outlines from the floor, but they're real generic boots. We'll have the doll tested. Guess we'll have to overlook any prints left all over it by some slimy scientist."

Jo sighed, penitent once again. "I've apologized for touching the doll three times now."

"Well, keep at it."

Becca snickered into her coffee, and Jo wondered again at her resilience. Becca looked centered again, fully herself. They watched the Bentley roll by, hitched to the back of a tow truck, its image wavering across the shop's paneled windows. It was nothing. A machine, a toy.

"And we have one hit from a hooker."

"Excuse me?" Jo frowned.

"A working girl was standing at the corner of Broadway and Roy, late Tuesday night." Pam consulted her notebook, her tone sardonic. "She saw 'a man' walking away from your office shortly after midnight."

"A man," Jo repeated.

"Real helpful." Pam nodded. "A white man, she thinks. Average height, average weight, nothing distinctive at all. Just that he was wearing a long coat, which no one needs in Seattle in late June in the middle of the night."

"So he could have been hiding something in it?" Becca asked.

"A crowbar, a baseball bat. Might be." Pam folded her arms. "Okay. I'm strongly suggesting the two of you stay the hell away from that house. He knows you're there. This perp burned through an iron lock with acid. He wouldn't have any problems getting to you."

"Well, that would be true wherever we went." Becca drew her hands through her hair. "I don't want to live my life looking over my shoulder every day. I hate this. And that house is still the best place to hear my mother." She looked to Jo for confirmation.

"That's not necessarily true. We've heard your mother speak from the Healys' place and from my car radio. She seems to travel with us. We haven't heard her in that house since—"

"She talked to me in that house last night."

"Excuse me?" Pam asked. "The what? The mother what, now?"

"My dead mother." Becca was smiling at Jo's abruptly arched eyebrows.

"You heard her again last night?" Jo was confounded. "She spoke to you? Becca, you might have mentioned this!"

"She wasn't talking to *you*," Becca told Jo politely. "It was a private conversation."

"All right." Jo drummed her nails against the glass tabletop. "If it's not too private, what did your dead mother *say?*"

"Well." Becca hesitated, and that connection beamed again between them, light and effortless. "She told me I was right to be falling in love with you."

Jo stopped drumming on the table. She found herself smiling back, not a broad grin, just a small lift of one corner of her mouth.

"The mother *what*, now?" Pam seemed to relent and slapped Jo on the back. "I mean, congratulations. I'm real happy for y'all. But you're talking about hearing Madelyn Healy's voice?"

"We have a lot to tell you, Pam." Becca patted Pam's hand with real sympathy. "And we will fill you in, I promise. But right now, we have to make plans for the day. My hip is vibrating for the fourth time, and I think it's Rachel, yelling at me for missing our breakfast."

Jo shook her hair out of her eyes, the motion needed to break that tingling bond with Becca. "Right. We stay in the house, then."

Pam sighed. "Guess we can step up patrols in the neighborhood, but that won't cover it. You guys own a gun?"

Becca shook her head in the same moment Jo nodded, and she looked at her in surprise.

"I'm licensed to carry a Magnum six thirty-two. It's a revolver, Becca. A hand gun."

Pam whistled softly. "What's the caliber on that?"

"Three twenty-seven. I'm quite accurate with it." Jo was berating herself for not retrieving the weapon the last time she had been home, the day they found her ruined office. She had taken only the music box with her, Consuelo's gift. She spoke to Becca softly. "I thought you'd be uneasy around a gun. Given your history."

Becca nodded, then shook her head. Then she nodded again, and shrugged helplessly. "I am. Uneasy with guns. Thank you for thinking of this. But I also think we need some protection."

"I never, never advise civilians to arm themselves." Pam regarded them pensively. "But arm yourself, Jo. I'm not sure why a scientist dense enough to handle evidence is sharp enough to carry a classy weapon like that, but go get that gun. You a good shot?"

"I have many skills." Jo winked at Becca.

"All right." Pam thudded Jo's back again with the flat of her hand, and if she kept punching the bruise below her shoulder, Jo was going to deck her, but she liked her catching the *Xena* reference. "I'm coming by your place tonight. Don't know how long I can stay, but it won't hurt to have a visible police presence there for a while."

Jo lifted her chin at Becca. "Would you like a calling of the clan?"

A natural shorthand had developed between them. She knew Becca understood her.

Becca grinned at Pam. "Bring popcorn, please. And prepare for at least three *Xena* episodes."

❖

Becca made her way upstairs, pulling on the bannister as covertly as possible. She felt Jo's concern following her as palpably as touch.

"Those recordings of ghost voices flat knock me out." Pam's dazed voice drifted up the stairs. "Wish we could call Becca's mother to the stand, let her fry the son of a bitch who's messing with her girl."

Becca pictured the little yellow globe radio perched on the railing of a witness stand and had to smile through her stupor. *Xena's* closing theme was fading in the living room, and the voices of Marty and Khadijah murmured below. Becca glanced over her shoulder and caught Jo's gaze, and nodded reassurance.

She just needed a few minutes alone. The warm company of her friends was wonderful, but Becca was worn out. She trudged into the bedroom her parents had shared for six years and sat carefully on the side of the wide bed.

She and Jo would sleep in the living room again tonight, after their clan left. The presence of her friends was infusing that space with a protective vibe, Becca could feel it. And she and Jo both knew that room was the true center of the house, the holder of whatever strange energy opened to the other side. She would bring down the Spiricom and the globe radio and let Jo set them up again.

She picked up the little yellow ball and held it in her hands. A mild hissing issued from it, empty air.

"Maddie," Becca whispered to the globe. "Mom?"

Nothing but static.

"I feel a little like Hamlet, talking to poor Yorick's skull," Becca murmured to her mother. "Are you there?"

Static.

"It took us hours to sweep up the glass in that office today. Jo could have hired a crew to do it, but I know cleaning her space herself was important to her." Becca examined a shallow cut at the base of her thumb. "I'm glad you like Jo. That you like Jo and me."

Becca didn't like the small smudge of blood near her palm. She wiped her hand on her knee uneasily and stared at the radio. "What gift held blood, Mom?"

She waited, but Madelyn Healy was especially far away tonight. Becca repeated the question, slowly and clearly, and waited again. Not even a faint crackle in the soft burr of sound.

"We're doing everything we can imagine to do to find an answer. I'm sure you realize this. I just hope I don't let you down. It's the only thing you've ever asked me to do, solving this puzzle. Short of learning to tie my shoes and whatnot. I'd like to come through for you if I can. Wish us luck."

Khadijah's laugh pealed below her, and Becca smiled. "I wish you could have known my friends, Mom. I think you would have handpicked these guys for me. You know what, you might have been sick, but you must have done so much that was right. I have good friends, good work. Maybe even a chance at love now. I spent my first five years with you, the most crucial years in anyone's life, and you gave me a strong start."

Jo, who said she didn't do people, was right. Becca held feelings for her mother beyond the anger, the grief; more gentle feelings. She was talking to her now as if deep cups of cocoa and all the time in the world lay before them.

"I had dinner with Rachel tonight. She's in bad shape, Mom. Scary weak. I know the two of you were friends. You cared about her. Look after her if you can, wherever you are." Becca lowered the ball radio to her lap. "I guess that's it. Good night."

It was time she got back downstairs. She knew Jo was worried. She lifted herself to her feet and picked up the Spiricom, cradling it and the radio in her arms. Becca looked around, trying to remember what else she had brought up here.

She slid open the drawer to the bedside table to retrieve her bottle of lotion, and instead found a bottle of Scotch.

❖

The scant sliver of a moon was shielded by tattered streams of clouds, the late-night air mild and cool on Jo's face.

She sat out on the front steps feeling guilty about this brief escape from the house, but enjoying it nonetheless. It wasn't a heinous desertion. Their company had left hours ago, and Becca had been curled on the sofa, sleeping peacefully when she slipped out. She drew smoke deeply into her lungs, feeling mildly guilty about this indulgence too, but—

"You *smoke*?" Becca's low voice behind her was incredulous.

Jo clenched her eyes shut and sighed out a white plume. "I guess there would be no point in denying it at this time. In my own defense, this is my first cigarette in two years. I found an old pack in my bag." With real regret, she rubbed the glowing tip against the stone step.

"Well, *cripes,* don't kill it!" Becca padded quickly closer on her bare feet and sat on the step next to Jo. The soft white of her T-shirt glowed against her skin, even in the meager moonlight. She held out two fingers expectantly.

Jo passed her the still-smoldering tube, surprised.

"You know we're both going to hell for this." Becca drew shortly and closed her eyes in pleasure. She stuttered out her next words to keep the smoke in. "We're the only two people left in Seattle who smoke."

Jo nodded gravely. "In some circles, it's a greater social stigma now than drug abuse."

"In lesbian circles, smoking is second only to being single, as proof of a character disorder. This is written down somewhere." Becca exhaled a cheerful gust of smoke. "I think eating too much chocolate and fainting at the sight of dolls made the list, too."

"I'm fairly certain you'll find wealth and long-term virginity on the same list." Jo was proud of herself for this light-hearted reference, and gratified when Becca laughed, but something nudged at her. "I'm kind of surprised you're tempting fate, Becca. Khadijah mentioned complete abstinence is how you've stayed clean and sober, and nicotine is certainly a dr—"

"Yeah, well, I may not be as much of a die-hard junkie as some people think." Becca pulled in smoke again, her eyes suddenly hard. "I've beaten that."

Jo wished for better light. Becca's features underwent a fascinating change, angry and almost feral for an instant. Then she was Becca again.

"In my own defense, this smoke is my first in six years. I don't think either of us want to puff like chimneys again, Jo. But tonight, it's nice."

Jo accepted the cigarette back, willing to agree. They finished it in companionable silence.

"I tried to reach my mother earlier." Becca snugged her T-shirt down around her knees. "While I was upstairs. The lady ain't talking."

"We know so little about windows." Jo scrubbed the glowing butt thoughtfully against the step, then slipped it into the crumpled cigarette pack. "Those brief periods of time when voices are able to come through. There seems to be no rhyme or reason to your mother's timing."

"Becca. Not true." Becca tapped two fingers. "Her first message, and I heard it twice."

Jo understood where she was going, and remembered Madelyn Healy's second message. "Becca, run."

"He wanted me."

"The gift held blood."

They sat in brooding silence. At least Jo wasn't alone in her frustration; Becca shared her impatience to make sense of all this. She saw Becca's hands lying loose in her lap and lifted one. She touched the small, neat Band-Aid at the base of her palm. "Did you wash this out? It's a wonder we're not both slashed to ribbons after sweeping up that lake of glass today."

Becca nodded, but she was staring at her hand, and Jo could feel her trembling.

"Becca?"

"It's fine. It's just a scratch."

Jo closed her fingers gently over Becca's wrist and felt the rapid patter of her pulse. Becca looked up at her, and gradually, her trembling quieted, and the thrumming beneath Jo's fingers slowed to a steady beat. Becca's features changed, the anxiety draining away, replaced by an already familiar expression of friendly invitation.

"I'm listening," Becca said.

"I've never courted anyone," Jo whispered. "I'm not sure how to do it. Especially given our tendency to encounter life-threatening emergencies every time we…"

Becca was just smiling at her. She was going to be absolutely no help. Jo turned her head and cleared her throat, worried about smoke on her breath. She wished she could go inside and brush her teeth, but even she knew certain moments could be lost forever and must be taken when offered.

Jo had very little historical data to rely on as to whether she was a good kisser. Apparently, there was some art to it. But this was only their second kiss, and she wanted to do her best. She tried to do what came naturally. And she enjoyed it, very much. She worried whether Becca was enjoying it too, and to Jo's consternation, their lips popped apart as she yawned. Not a subtle, suppressible yawn, an irresistible jaw-cracker, and then Becca was doing it, too.

They leaned against each other and indulged in a mutual, whooping yawn that ended in a tired giggle, and Jo was not a woman who giggled. Her performance anxiety fled and she was filled with both relief and a creeping, numbing exhaustion.

Becca scratched Jo's back lightly. "I'm useless in a kitchen, other than making cocoa. I make dynamite cocoa. Are you game?"

"I'm game. Then we sleep."

"Then we sleep. Perchance to dream." Becca accepted Jo's hand to help her to her feet. "Sorry, I went into Shakespeare mode for a moment earlier tonight. I must still be there."

Jo followed her to the silent house, hoping dreams would leave Becca alone for the night. Pam Emerson was due early in the morning for a brief check-in, and Jo wanted to stop by the archives at the UW Library for some research. She hoped to learn more about John William Voakes, and about Mitchell Healy's aborted political career.

Jo was willing to trust fate would grant them at least one peaceful night before the craziness began again.

Chapter Eighteen

Jo dreamed of smoke, and even from the depths of sleep she clenched the arms of her chair like a vise.

Thick clouds of white swirled around the Lady of the Rock, hiding the cloaked woman and the girl kneeling beside her. Jo coughed into the bend of her arm, her eyes watering, and tried to see the Lady's face through the gray billows and choking stink.

The statue swam abruptly clear and sharp into view. The Lady's head turned slowly, the stern face shifting down to look directly at Jo. Her pointing fingers lowered protectively to spread over the girl's vulnerable back.

The stone lips moved. *"Save my daughter."*

It was Madelyn Healy's voice, and the deep cathedral voice of the Lady, the voice of Artemis herself, for all Jo knew. Fear sliced through her and she jerked awake.

The living room was roiling with smoke.

The small lamp they had left lit near the entry was dark, casting the room in heavy shadows. The tiny lights from the radios were blurred by a shifting fog that stung Jo's sinuses, galvanizing her with an atavistic, cellular awareness of danger.

Becca was thrashing on the couch even before Jo gripped her shoulders. She came awake with a wrenching gasp.

"Fire," Jo barked. "We have to get out of here."

"I'm running!" Becca flapped Jo's hands off her arms, scooting off the couch. She coughed explosively. "Jesus, Jo!"

"I don't see flames." Jo bent and snatched up the Spiricom, then wrapped Becca's hand in hers. "Stay low and breathe shallow."

They inched around the furniture and made for the two stairs leading to the entry, adrenaline singing through Jo in a painful rush. The darkness in the room hung like a heavy curtain barring their way, but there wasn't far to go. Jo listened so hard her scalp twinged tightly, and she heard it seconds before they reached the front door— the faint, low buzzing of a drill.

Damning caution, Jo grabbed the latch of the door and pushed. It budged half an inch and caught.

Someone was barricading the door, their way out. Someone who apparently was still kneeling on the other side, finishing his work.

"Jo?"

"Stay behind me." Jo was dimly grateful she hadn't removed her boots before falling asleep. She unleashed a powerful kick. The heel crashed into the door, but it held fast. The whirring sound on the other side cut off. Jo was caught up in a paroxysm of coughing. Becca clenched her forearm, and she straightened quickly. "All right, head for the kitchen. The side door."

Jo pushed Becca in that direction, and hoped very much she could trust her memory of the large room, the layout of the furniture. The smoke was thick enough now to make visual navigation impossible, but she remembered where she left the bag holding her gun and Consuelo's music box. She kept one watering eye on Becca's progress as she moved as quickly as she could into the living room.

"Uh, no, negatory on the kitchen." Becca was apparently back in crisis mode. Her voice was loud but unafraid.

Jo whirled and saw the red light fluttering through the crack beneath the swinging kitchen door. She heard the crackling of flames for the first time.

"Jo, the south window," Becca called. "It's big enough!"

Jo found the bag and snatched it before joining Becca. They groped toward the far wall.

Her fumbling fingers found the catch at the top of the long window and turned it. Jo pulled up the wooden frame with one titanic heave, and punched the wire screen hard. It clattered outside onto the lawn, and Jo heaved the Spiricom and the bag after it, freeing her arms to help Becca.

Becca lifted one leg over the window ledge. "This won't be pretty," she grunted, "but I'll make it."

Jo helped Becca clamber through the window and drop to the sloping grass outside, a fall of some six feet, and jumped after her. The fresh air hit Jo's face in a welcome rush as she landed on all fours beside Becca. The impact was enough to punch the breath from her aching lungs, and she hovered for a moment, head down, until she could take in air again.

She reached out and grasped Becca's wrist.

"Okay," Becca gasped.

Jo hauled them both bodily to their feet, and they ducked away from the eaves of the smoking house. Jo was fully erect when she saw him.

"Becca, get the gun," she snapped, and she was running full-bore one second later.

"*What?*"

Jo could hardly stop to explain. The man had made it to the top of the porch stairs, and he hadn't heard her yet, he wasn't even hurrying. Jo caught a quick impression of a slender figure in dark clothes carrying a toolbox. She targeted it and went airborne, sailing off the top of the steps and tackling the man halfway down.

Jo was gratified not to take the brunt of the landing this time, her second trip down these wretched stairs. She crashed solidly on top of the man and he flailed beneath her, even before their bodies tumbled to a halt on the front walk.

They were nearly matched in size and weight. While Jo was fairly muscular, their stalker was thin and sinewy, almost wasted. But unlike her opponent, Jo wasn't practiced at personal combat. He bucked under her, smacking Jo in a place that might have incapacitated her, had she been male.

"Wrong gender, asshole," she hissed in his ear. She snarled her fingers in his ragged hair and jerked his head back, then absorbed a painful punch in her side from his elbow.

They grappled on the concrete, and he twisted out from under her. Jo's chest burned with old smoke and she devoted herself to simply hanging on to the prick, not letting him get away. He got off one smacking punch to Jo's brow that almost dazed her, but her arms wrapped around him in a death grip.

He twisted and rolled and he was on top of her, gasping harshly. His small gimlet eyes were slitted. Jo felt his cold hands wrap around her throat, and she heard a crack.

The man's head snapped back and he stiffened. His hands around Jo's neck went slack. He started to tumble to the side and Jo encouraged this, growling and throwing his sagging body off hers to sprawl on his back on the sidewalk.

Dread filtered through Jo's shock, not that the man might be dead, but that Becca would have to live with having shot him. She clawed her hair out of her eyes and saw her, Becca, who ate four pounds of chocolate a day, holding an Amazon stance in the scant moonlight with one chobo balanced over her shoulder like a baseball bat. Jo noted vaguely that Becca also carried the Spiricom and Jo's bag, crisis mode having rendered her amusingly thorough.

"I could only find one in the dark," Becca gasped, waving the chobo. "Are you all right? Are you all right?"

Jo didn't have the breath yet for speech so she just lifted a hand in reassurance. The man was still heaving for air, too. At least he wasn't dead. Becca had clubbed him neatly and well. He was out cold. Jo took his hair again, none too gently, and turned his head. She realized she could see his features, outlined in red light. Behind them, the house had begun to burn in earnest.

"Do you know him?" she rasped at Becca.

Becca knelt gingerly at his side, gazing at his face with wide eyes. "I don't think so. I'm not sure. He's alive, right?"

"He's alive." Jo heard him moan, a rumble deep in his chest, and she was taking no chances. She searched him swiftly, swiveled, and sat solidly on his back, pinning him to the ground.

"Good idea." Becca plunked herself down on his legs, eliciting another groan, but the man lay still beneath them.

"You went back into a burning house," Jo panted, "for your *sticks*?"

"I smacked him good, too," Becca pointed out proudly. "You sure you're all right?"

"I'm peachy." Jo touched her brow and winced. She lifted her head and heard the far-off whine of a siren. "I think we woke the neighbors." The clattering of the toolbox down the stone steps would have roused the dead. She nodded across the street toward the cemetery. "Perhaps all of them."

"Good." Becca sighed. She took Jo's hand and cradled it on her knee.

They sat side by side on their unconscious stalker and watched the house of Becca's nightmares erupt in flames. The night air crackled now with the ugly snap of burning wood, and scarlet light flooded over them. Becca rested her head on Jo's shoulder, an odd take on a couple seated before a romantic fire, and they waited together quietly, content, for the moment, with safety and silence.

❖

Becca's first bout of shakes had taken her and passed by the time Pam Emerson pulled up in her efficient Kia. The neighborhood was still awash in revolving red lights and the flickering gold of the smoldering house. Their arsonist had been treated by EMTs and was strapped to a gurney, and Pam had grilled her and Jo thoroughly. Becca was distantly aware that they were standing in a puddle of water, one of several left dotting the ground by powerful hoses.

Dawn was at least an hour away. Smoke still wafted through the street, but the fire was under control. At least the adjoining houses were no longer in danger from showers of sparks. Clumps of people stood on the dark sidewalk on either side of the property, kept at bay by firefighters and assorted police. The distant warbling of radios cut through the air at intervals.

Becca looked around for a place to sit, but benches were in short supply. She had allowed Jo to leave her long enough to put her bag in the rented BMW, but she still cradled the Spiricom in her arms. Becca realized she was stroking it like an electronic cat, and she leaned against Jo ruefully.

"I'm glad you saved this. You already lost one very pricey vehicle and every precious toy in your office in this deal. At least we salvaged your favorite Spiricom."

"We salvaged everything that's precious to me, Becca." Jo slid her arm around her shoulders with an ease that touched Becca as much as her words.

She closed her eyes against Jo's breast. With the house in flames, Jo had rescued her Spiricom, and her bag, and Becca. Becca had rescued only her chobos and the flat bottle of Scotch she still carried in her shirt.

"Okay, ladies." Pam joined them, looking rumpled in the shorts and loose tank top she probably slept in, but her dark eyes were snapping and alert. "Medics checked you both out, right?"

"Yes, we've been checked." Jo shrugged off the light cotton blanket the EMT had insisted on draping over them. "What do you know so far?"

"Well, the gentleman over there is awake. Might have a concussion, but he'll live. We're running him to Harborview's ER. No ID, and he won't tell us his name, no big surprise. But we'll print him, and I intend to sit with him for the next twenty hours or so, and ask him lots and lots of questions." Pam smiled like a shark. "We'll find out who he is."

Jo nodded. "I'm taking Becca to my place. We'll call you once we've had some sleep."

"Can I talk to him first?" Becca couldn't believe she was suggesting this, but it felt important. "Now, before he's fogged up by meds?"

Pam squinted at her. "Yeah, if you're up to it. He might spill something to you he wouldn't to us. He's strapped down," she added unnecessarily, but Becca appreciated the sentiment.

She looked up at Jo, who stayed right beside her as they made their way to the cluster of police and medics around the gurney. Pam spoke to two of them, who parted to let them come closer.

The man wasn't as young as Becca had assumed. That was her first impression. This was no kid. He looked older than her or Jo. And sick, or at least chronically malnourished. His weathered face turned toward them, and he stared at Becca.

"All right, Smoky," Pam addressed the man dryly. "Those rights I read you are still in effect. You remember, anything you say, can and will." She lifted her chin at Becca.

Becca cleared her throat, and the circle around them fell silent. "Do I know you?"

The man didn't answer, and for a long moment Becca thought he would refuse. Then he smiled, displaying the distinctive, ruined teeth of a chronic meth user. His voice emerged in a harsh drawl.

"You tell my daddy hello for me, Becca."

Becca stood still. He said no more, and she didn't ask anything else. She didn't have to. She recognized his voice.

"Becca?" Jo's warm breath stirred her hair, but she couldn't move.

Music played in Becca's head. The experience didn't feel psychotic or particularly alarming, just a soft and happy sprinkling of notes.

Olivia Newton-John, a song from Grease. *Becca had just seen the movie, and loved it. A brief but clear vision of a party outside on the grass. A cake with candles. Hands holding out a wrapped present, the one that delighted Becca the most that day. The box that contained the doll she would clutch so desperately late that night, after her parents died.*

"The gift held blood."

The hands that gave her the wrapped box at the party were the same ones that pressed the doll into Becca's arms that night. And they were not her mother's hands.

Finally, the medics wheeled the gurney away and loaded it into a waiting ambulance.

"Hey." Pam touched Becca's arm. "What gives, Bec?"

Becca shook her head. She looked up at Jo, moved out from under her arm, and walked toward the cemetery.

She was starting to remember who shot her parents, and she wanted a drink.

CHAPTER NINETEEN

L eave us alone." Jo's words were abrupt, but Pam was clan
and she understood; she just nodded.

Becca wasn't hurrying and so Jo didn't either, but she was
unstoppable as a truck, or a brakeless Bentley. Barefoot and still
clutching the Spiricom, Becca found no hindrance in the barred iron
gate of Lake View Cemetery. She simply climbed over it. Jo could
have caught her there, but she let her walk ahead, into the silent
darkness of the grounds beyond.

Jo tried to count down from a hundred, but only made it to
seventy before she had to follow. She climbed the gate mechanically
and dropped to the other side. Becca's white T-shirt glowed in the
distance. The moon was thin but intensely bright and shed patches
of silvered light on the grass. Jo knew this path by now, and could
have found her way in complete darkness.

She came over the small rise and stopped short, and her
heart gave an uneasy snap in her chest. The Lady of the Rock was
shrouded in smoke.

Perhaps a breeze had carried the smoke from the burning house
this far, but no smoke Jo had ever seen held the ethereal, witchy
quality of this shimmering fog. The Lady's face was masked by its
light tendrils, and it swirled at the base of the statue, around Becca,
who sat leaning against it. Jo corrected herself. She had seen this
eldritch mist before, cloaking the Lady in her dream, and gooseflesh
rose on her forearms.

Becca sat still, her back stiff against the base of the statue. Jo couldn't see her features clearly from here, but she was holding something in her hands. She stared at it with a fierce concentration Jo could read in every line of her body.

Jo walked closer, and her heart gave another uneasy pang when she realized Becca held a small bottle. But when she looked up at Jo, there was no uncertainty in her. This wasn't the laughing Becca or the frightened one, this was the Amazon.

"I've beaten this," Becca said. She held out the bottle to Jo.

The mist swirled around Jo's knees as she went to Becca and took the bottle from her. In deference to the sleeping dead around them, she made her way to the path between graves before twisting off its cap. Jo poured out the liquor on the ground, mumbling some vague version of a prayer of thanks. She rested the empty bottle at the side of the path and returned to the Lady.

The statue awaited her silently, holding watch over both her daughters.

Jo sat in the soft fog beside Becca, who cradled the Spiricom in her lap now. She said nothing, and Jo wished fervently, not for the first time, that this woman came with some kind of online manual. She didn't know what to say.

"You know who he is, don't you?" Jo asked finally.

"Yes, I think I do." Becca was gazing at the Spiricom.

"Once we weren't sitting on him, he looked familiar to me." Jo grimaced. "My head's just too busy right now. I can't place him."

Becca handed her the Spiricom. "Tune this in, please?"

Jo looked around. They couldn't hope for much beneath the open canopy of the sky in the expanse of a cemetery, but she complied, turning dials. To her relief, the small screen flickered with light under her touch.

"I'm going to ask you to do something hard, Jo. I don't want you to ask me any questions right now."

"You're asking me to stop breathing."

"I know." Becca leaned her shoulder against her briefly, and a ghost of a smile crossed her lips. "But there's a lot to work out in my head before I can be sure. And we need to talk to other people first. Be patient with me, okay?"

"Becca…"

"Try."

"Okay."

Becca took the Spiricom back and held it in her lap. The screen cast a mild gold light across her face.

"Hey, you." Becca spoke as easily, as normally, as if she were sitting across from her mother, sharing a cup of cocoa. "I hope you're listening. I want you to know I understand what happened now. Not all the details. I still don't understand why. But I know who, Mom."

Jo felt a shudder go through Becca, a quick and hard grimace of the soul, but it passed.

"You didn't do it. You didn't kill Dad. You didn't leave me." Becca's eyes filled with tears, but she smiled with a sweetness that made Jo fall in love with her all over again. "I get that. You never would have left me."

The Spiricom hissed softly. Madelyn Healy answered from a great distance, and her voice was calm and free.

"Thank you, little girl."

"Rest well."

The hissing fell silent. Becca touched a switch on the Spiricom, and the small screen went dark.

"I doubt we'll hear from her again. I think she's gone." Becca looked at Jo wistfully, as if she were newly orphaned. "You were right. That's all she wanted. She didn't do it, and all that ever mattered to her was my knowing that."

Jo slid her arm around Becca's waist and let her rest against her. Questions were all but exploding out of her throat, but she curbed them firmly. "Tell me what you need from me."

"This is what I need from you. I want you to sit here and hold me until the sun comes up. Then you're going to drive me to my place so I can get some clothes."

"And then?"

"My mother may not need justice, but I do." Becca's voice grew quietly savage. "We're going to visit my Uncle Mitchell."

CHAPTER TWENTY

Patricia Healy waited for them in the open doorway of her stately house.

In Jo's experience with Becca's aunt, Patricia had been anxious and rather remote, but never haggard, as she appeared this morning. She wore a tailored ensemble appropriate for the office, but her skirt and jacket were rumpled, as if they'd been donned the day before.

When Patricia saw Becca, she slumped against the door in visible relief and lowered her head. She said nothing; only stepped back and opened the door wider to admit them both. Jo learned something else as she walked into the elegant entry. Judging by the fumes issuing from Patricia Healy, she was drunk as a lord.

The neighborhood was wealthy enough to foster trees that attracted songbirds, and their lilting music drifted through the Healy house. It wasn't a fitting score for Jo's mood, which was leaning decidedly dark. Her nerves were wound like clock springs turned tight, her body shaky and weak. She tried to mirror Becca's composure as they walked into the large dining room.

Mitchell Healy had apparently passed a more peaceful night than any of them. He sat at the cherry wood table, neatly robed, silver hair brushed, legs crossed at the knee. He was lifting a cup of coffee to his lips but paused when he saw them.

Jo realized his sleep wasn't as untroubled as she'd thought. His eyes were ringed with shadows. When he saw Becca, he betrayed the same quick flicker of relief that Patricia had shown. As far as Jo knew, no one had yet notified the Healys of the arson. She didn't understand why they seemed so attuned to Becca's recent danger.

"There, I told you, Pat." Mitchell set down his cup, got up, and went to Becca. He took her arms gently, and she allowed it. "Becca, you look just fine. Your aunt has worried herself into a frenzy for nothing. Doctor." Mitchell nodded tersely at Jo.

She returned it, just in case Becca's dictum that Jo be nice to her family was still in effect. She kept an eye on Patricia, who had followed them into the dining room. She wore her alcohol as if it were new to her, moving with the studied care of the inexperienced inebriate.

"Please sit down." Mitchell led Becca toward the table. "We can't offer you much in the way of breakfast, I'm afraid. We weren't expecting company this early on a Saturday morning. But there's cof—"

"Mitchell." Becca removed his hand from her arm carefully. "You need to tell me why we were almost killed last night by a man who's been dead for thirty years."

Mitchell went still. Jo saw a spark fire behind his eyes—clear disbelief, denial. But Patricia's features, even blurred by drink, revealed only acceptance.

"Loren Mitchell Perry." Becca spoke the name with no venom. "I've never forgotten his voice. Even as a kid, Loren spoke with that affectation, that tough drawl. Rachel's dead son set the house on fire last night, with Jo and me inside."

"Oh, sweet…" Patricia sagged into a side chair, but Becca kept her eyes on her uncle.

Mitchell sighed harshly. "They've caught him?"

"He's in police custody," Jo said.

"Becca, you can't be sure about this." A shadow of the attorney surfaced. "You're saying this man *sounded* like a boy you last heard decades ago—"

"It was Loren, Mitchell." Becca sent Jo a humorless smile. "I've learned to listen to voices very carefully. He told me to tell his father hello. Loren was named after you."

Mitchell's face was undergoing an extraordinary series of reveals. The disbelief became fear, then denial again, and something quite close to hatred.

"I always thought that was an honorific," Becca said. "Rachel naming her son after you, to salute your friendship. But now I'm thinking that's not true. Loren looks like you now, Mitchell."

"I may have sired him," Mitchell said at last. "He's not my son."

Mitchell went to Patricia and took her arm with an awkward tenderness. He steered her into a chair at the table and sat beside her. He clasped Patricia's hand on the glossy surface, looking fully his age now, and waited while Becca and Jo pulled back other chairs and joined them. "This woman forgave us both, Becca. Your aunt is a more generous and loving person than you've ever realized."

He released Patricia's hand long enough to lift a delicate cup to his lips. His throat moved as he swallowed, giving him time. "Very early in my marriage to Patricia, Rachel and I were…together, for a few nights. It was a terrible mistake for us both. For all three of us." Mitchell's newfound candor seemed to desert him and he drifted off, staring at the table. "I can't believe this. I can't believe he's come back. Forgive me, Pat. You tried to tell me."

"Of course you didn't believe it, dear." Patricia lifted her head and spoke clearly, with the careful diction of the drunk. "You always believe the best of the people you love. It makes you blind sometimes." She looked at them dully. "Rachel insisted on keeping the baby. On raising him alone. Loren became addicted to hard drugs when he was still quite young."

"The boy was a monster before the drugs, Pat." Mitchell's face hardened, any tenderness gone. "Rachel moved heaven and earth to help that child. Nothing reached him. He was a thief and a bully and a miscreant before he was ten years old."

Patricia merely nodded, and they fell silent. Becca seemed content to wait them out, but Jo was less so. She had promised not to grill Becca, but that vow didn't hold for her kin.

"So Rachel Perry, a psychiatrist experienced in treating chemical dependency, brought up a drug-addicted son." They flinched at Jo's brusqueness, but Becca only watched her. "And in spite of all of Rachel's maternal efforts, Loren persisted in being a bad seed?"

"Well." A new, subtle wave of contempt passed over Patricia's face. "Rachel had problems of her own, back then."

"Pat." Mitchell's tone was wooden, and Patricia nodded again.

Jo decided to let it pass. "Mitchell, why is there a headstone in Lake View Cemetery marking the grave of Loren Perry?"

"All right." Mitchell sat back in his chair. "If you must hear the whole, sordid story. When Loren was fifteen, he was suspected of molesting two young girls in the neighborhood. Police were going to arrest him any day. His solution to this was to get drunk and smash his motorcycle all over Mercer Street."

Mitchell spoke calmly as if giving a formal disposition. "Loren was comatose in Harborview for several days. I admit readily that I called in favors, pulled some strings. We had new identity papers drawn for him. He was transferred to an excellent hospital on the east coast. He lived there until he was eighteen. Then, I'm happy to say, we lost track of him entirely."

"Not entirely, apparently," Jo pointed out. "The grave?"

"It's empty," Mitchell said. "As I said. I called in favors."

"You and Rachel arranged all this." Becca stirred at last, sounding dazed. "She agreed to have Loren locked up in some hospital for three years? To lose track of him, as you put it, for thirty years?"

"Do you know what having a son convicted of child molestation would have done to Rachel professionally?" Mitchell scrubbed his napkin across his lips. "She had no husband to support her. Not that she considered the impact on her career, mind you. I did. I was the one who cared that this creature was ruining Rachel's life. All she cared about was saving Loren from arrest, giving him a fresh start."

"What kind of hospital houses a mental patient for three years." Becca wasn't asking a question, and Jo knew she was picturing a distant facility much like Western State. "What kind of pit did you find to launch Loren on this fresh start?"

"It was better than he deserved, Rebecca." Mitchell tossed his napkin to the table. "I don't know why he's come back into our lives now, unless he imagined that harassing my niece would result in some kind of payoff. That he could bleed me dry financially, to call him off."

"Oh, you know better, Mitch." Patricia pushed back her chair and went to a side table, her step halting. She poured an amber liquid into a small glass. "Rachel's son never made any effort to contact us. Not the entire time he's been terrorizing Becca."

"Pat, don't start again." Mitchell's voice lowered. "You're not used to it, and you've had more than enough."

"That's certainly the truth. I've had enough of your blindness. I knew it was Loren the second Joanne told me about that fucking doll. Forgive me, Becca." Apparently, Patricia was apologizing for either the profanity or the alcohol. She turned her back to Becca and downed the glass in one shot. "It's time you stopped protecting her, Mitchell."

"Patricia, I've told you I'm not going to entertain this paranoid delusion of yours again."

"Becca almost *died*. Hasn't that even registered with you?" Patricia spun, and her bloodshot eyes brimmed with tears. "Doesn't it matter to you that this girl we raised almost lost her—"

"*Of course it matters.*" Mitchell rose sharply enough to knock back his chair. He stared at Patricia, the tendons in his jaw standing out. "But Becca is safe now. That is *all* that matters. And now you'll have to excuse me, as I'm due in court."

He walked toward the stairs, his back bent, his shoulders curved toward his chest. Jo knew of no court that held sessions on a weekend. Mitchell looked back at Patricia. "Leave her alone, Pat. You're wrong about her. She would never have hurt me like that. The woman's dying. Let her be."

Jo was trying hard to listen through her exhaustion. Becca sat very still as her uncle left the room.

"It's his career that's over now, you know." Patricia filled her glass again and made her way back to the table. "I don't think that's quite hit him yet. Once they identify Loren, this whole sad shit sack of history is going to come out."

"Mitchell said, 'She would never have hurt me like that.'" Jo struggled to find an inroad through this maze. "He was referring to Rachel Perry? Was he saying that Rachel wouldn't have hurt him by bringing their son back to Seattle?"

"No, Joanne, I'm afraid not." Patricia sipped from her glass now, rather than bolting it. "Mitch wasn't talking about Rachel dragging Loren back into our lives. He was referring to a much older injury his darling Rachel inflicted on this family. I think Becca knows that."

Becca watched her silently.

"Mitch's career was essentially over the night your parents died, dear. His hopes for political office, gone. There was scandal involved. Vicious rumors about Mitch and your mother. I thought for a time that he might even be named a suspect."

Patricia turned the glass of amber liquid in her fingers slowly. "Your uncle is a man of many passions, Becca. I've always known that. Rachel. Other women. Your mother. I've never doubted my husband's love for me, never. But he loved your mother more. More than any of them. More than me. I've always known that, too."

Decades of drunken emotion passed over Patricia's aged face in the sun-filled dining room. "There was something special about Madelyn. Even I saw it, and I'm heterosexual as a brick. There was some spark in her. Some kind of innocent purity. You have it too, Rebecca. It drew Mitch like a flame. And Scottie knew it."

She put down the glass and rubbed her face in her hands. "They *hated* each other, Mitch and his brother. I'm sorry, Becca, but hatred is the only word for it. I honestly suspected Mitch of the killings myself, for a moment, as I looked down at the bodies. But I was wrong."

Patricia focused on Becca with effort. "I didn't know for sure. Not until I realized Loren Perry had come back. Are you ready for another hard truth, Becca?"

"Yes," Becca said.

"I hated your mother because my husband wanted her desperately. I'm still glad she's dead. But I credit her with this much—Maddie was faithful to your father. She never let Mitchell touch her. He's been truthful with me over the years, about every one of his little peccadillos, and I believe him about this. Do you?"

"Yes," Becca said.

"Good." Patricia downed the rest of her glass, and Jo couldn't stand it anymore.

"Pardon me," Jo said. "What injury did Rachel inflict on this family?"

Becca got up. "Come on, Jo."

"Are you going to see her?" Patricia asked, her voice soft now.

"Yes."

Patricia rose too and came around the table, weaving only slightly. Jo was torn between an impulse to take her arm and support her or tear her arm off completely, but Becca allowed her to clasp her hands.

"Do you know how I've managed to hold on to a solid marriage for forty-seven years, Becca? By accepting the fact that the people we love can be flawed. Even deeply flawed. And choosing to love them anyway."

Becca looked down at Patricia's trembling hands.

"Forgive us," Patricia said gently. "We do love you, the best way we know how."

"I know that. I always have."

Family, Jo thought. Clan. There could be such a chasm between the two.

Becca leaned forward and kissed Patricia's cheek. "Get some sleep."

She held out her hand and Jo took it, and they walked together toward the entry.

"Becca?" Patricia's voice drifted behind them. "She was taken to the hospice at Swedish Hospital last night. She doesn't have long."

Becca nodded, and they left the house.

CHAPTER TWENTY-ONE

Finding parking was unusually difficult, and Jo focused on that minor annoyance. She circled the BMW around Swedish Hospital twice, a process that took twenty minutes. Pedestrian traffic was thick on Seattle's First Hill, people of every gender swarming the streets. It was the morning of Gay Pride.

Becca was a still presence beside her, her hands in her lap. An Olivia Newton-John song surfaced on the car's generic radio setting. Jo could smell the sweet freshness of Becca's hair as she listened, her gaze distant out the window.

Before driving to the Healys' house, they had gone to Becca's second-story apartment in a working class neighborhood off Lake City Way. To Jo's disappointment, Becca had asked her to wait in the car. She had been gone long enough to shower, and she returned carrying a small satchel. Jo thought glumly that her own clothes still smelled of smoke, and she rolled her side window down.

"You're all right?" Jo asked again.

"I am. I'm fine," Becca replied again.

That settled, Jo finally turned into the hospital's subterranean garage. She circled its depths for several years before finally pulling into a narrow wedge of a parking space. She keyed off the engine and suppressed her automatic urge to open the car door, to get on with things. Jo rested her hands on her knees and waited until Becca spoke.

"Mitchell was saying that Rachel would never have robbed him of the love of his life. He still won't believe Rachel would have hurt him that much, all those years ago, by killing my mother."

Jo had worked this much out in her head. She waited.

"I'm not fine," Becca said finally.

"Of course you're not."

"I think I've done pretty well." Becca's voice was starting to shake. "Last night, at the fire, talking to Loren. Earlier today, with my uncle and aunt. But now I have to see Rachel, and before I do, I might have to fall apart a little. I'm s-sorry—"

"You never have to apologize to me for your tears, Becca."

Becca rested her head against the swell of Jo's shoulder, which had been created solely for this purpose. She cried for a while, and Jo sat with her. Like Becca, Jo knew who had shot Scott and Madelyn Healy. Also like Becca, she didn't yet understand why, but they could take time now for this.

"Should we find a vending machine inside? It would have chocolate bars." Jo was serious.

Becca actually smiled and knuckled tears out of one eye like a child. "Yeah, that would be good. But maybe later. We need to get out from under all this concrete so I can make a call."

"You're sure, Becca?"

Becca nodded. She got out of the car, and Jo followed her through the labyrinthine passages of the parking garage into the light. Becca flipped open her cell, pressed keys, listened, spoke at length. When she was finished, she pulled open one of the double doors to the hospice unit, and Jo followed her through.

"Good morning." Becca spoke to the young nurse behind the reception desk. "We're here to see Rachel Perry."

The nurse looked startled. "This early? Is Dr. Perry expecting you?"

Jo glanced at the nurse's nametag. "Monica, this is quite important. To Dr. Perry, as well as to us." She allowed the girl to absorb Becca's expression, and her own.

"Well, we've finished with morning meds. But I do need to check. Dr. Perry just joined us last night." Monica lifted a headset and touched buttons. She turned away from the desk and spoke quietly. She turned back and nodded. "Room sixteen. It's down that hallway, last door on the left."

"Thank you." Becca laid her hand on the counter, then turned and looked up at Jo. She was faltering again; Jo could read it in the sudden sheen over her eyes.

"I've got your back," Jo said.

Becca steadied and took Jo's arm. Jo nodded at Monica, and they entered the long hall.

Jo's work had made her familiar with the workings of end-of-life care, and she knew a good hospice could be a good place to die. This was a good hospice. There was no chemical smell of disinfectant, just the pleasant freshness of the morning air through several open windows. The carpet beneath Jo's feet was thick enough to muffle their steps, but tailored to accommodate a wheeled gurney when necessary. The walls were painted a soothing blue with a cream accent, and framed paintings were positioned low, in the view of people in wheelchairs, on stretchers.

They passed three staff in the corridor, young attendants who smiled pleasant greetings. The unit was mostly silent. Jo heard no moans of pain, no demented cries. A hospice provided palliative care. It existed solely to make the dying process as painless as possible, and if that meant heavy medication, so be it. But they tried to help patients find meaning in the journey as well—closure with family, legal arrangements, spiritual consolation. Jo wondered which of these services Rachel Perry would choose to access.

They stopped before Room 16. Without pause or ceremony, Becca lifted her hand and knocked on the door.

"Come in, Becca."

Rachel wore a soft velour robe the color of dawn, closed high around her neck. She stood with her back to them, looking out a large oblong window, a patchwork of colorful stained glass. The room was large and well furnished. There were few personal belongings among the tasteful décor. Rachel traveled light.

She turned and smiled at Becca. In the brief time since the nurse placed the call, Rachel had brushed her hair and applied lipstick, but her posture was bowed and she looked ancient. All Jo could read on her worn face was fierce relief and genuine love.

"I knew you'd be all right. I *knew* it."

"No, Rachel, you didn't." Becca closed the door behind them and stood close beside Jo.

Jo waited, and so did Rachel, but Becca seemed incapable of further speech. The look of loss and betrayal in her eyes was unbearable.

"She means your son could have killed us both last night." Jo spoke to Rachel with great restraint. "And he could have killed us two days ago when he cut the brakes of my car."

"Becca *wasn't supposed to be with you.*" Rachel's voice emerged as a sudden hiss and Jo almost recoiled. A wild denial crossed her withered face. "You were supposed to have breakfast with me that morning, Becca! You promised me you would!"

"Stop shouting at us. And sit down." Jo took three steps and touched Rachel's elbow with pragmatic detachment. She guided her to the side of the wide, raised bed and helped her sit. Becca stood frozen near the doorway.

Rachel brushed her finger across her lower lip, wiping away spittle with a wince of repugnance. Her face cleared, and she looked up at Jo calmly. "None of this had to come out, Joanne. We have you to thank for raising these old ghosts. And I don't know whether to hate you for it or thank you. Both, perhaps."

"I believe that." Jo stepped back from the bed and crouched on her heels slowly, making herself as unthreatening as possible.

She did believe Rachel, and that amazed her. Rachel's facial expressions had convinced Jo she wanted this study to succeed, for the truth to be known. Some part of her psyche had badly wanted confession, this very confrontation. And another part of her had arranged to have Becca burn to death last night. Both were Rachel's absolute truths, and Jo found this amoral dichotomy incomprehensible.

"You were afraid Becca and I would learn the truth about what happened to her parents. So you asked your son to come back to Seattle."

"I paid my son very well." Rachel folded her veined hands in her lap, and Becca stared at them. "Loren has been in and out of prison these past years. I've had to cut him out of my heart. I've learned he'll do anything to finance his habit. Anything at all." She wouldn't look at Becca.

"You paid him to break into my office," Jo continued. "And into the Bentley. To put that doll on the front porch. And to set fire to the house last night."

"Yes," Rachel said.

"And to plant a bottle of Scotch in my bedroom." Becca's voice was soft, and Rachel looked at her at last. "Rachel?"

"Do you have any idea how much I loved her?" Rachel's tone was equally tender. "Try to remember that, if you can. All of this tragedy was born in the purest love I've ever known. I would have given my life for her."

Rachel looked back at the window, and the stained glass threw a lattice of distorted color across her features. "If it matters, and I doubt it matters, I was out of my mind on prescription pills at the time. I had been for years." She smiled mirthlessly. "Like mother, like son, I suppose. Loren's addictions consumed him, but I conquered mine, finally. Well enough to help you tackle yours, Becca, when you needed me. But I was crazy that night. I wanted Maddie to leave Scott and run away with me, immediately. I would have left my son, my practice, everything. She refused, of course. I had hidden my feelings for her well until then, and I believe she was shocked by my proposal. Even repelled."

Rachel glanced at Becca. "Does any of this surprise you? It shouldn't. I fell in love with your mother, but she rejected me entirely. She wouldn't leave your father, wouldn't even discuss it. Maddie was devoted to Scott, despite all his faults. Not to Mitch. Not to me. She never loved me." She fell silent.

"So you returned to the house that night, after the birthday party." Jo was seeing it unfold, hearing Madelyn Healy whisper in her mind, telling her what happened. "You confronted Becca's mother in the kitchen. Scott Healy joined you there. You'd brought a gun with you?"

"In my delirium, I thought I would have to subdue Scott. When he interrupted Maddie and me in the kitchen, I raised the gun at him, and I fired. I didn't see Maddie lunge in front of him before I pressed the trigger. I didn't see her, Becca." Rachel swallowed, and Jo heard the dry crackling in her throat. "I caught your mother as she fell, and I cradled her on the floor in my arms as she died."

But then Rachel's face changed, and Jo realized she was looking at something much more atavistic, more alien even than her own strange distance from the world. Rachel looked serene; cruel and content. "I had to shoot Scott to keep him away from us. He had no business with us in those last moments. That was my time with Maddie. Finally, Mitch's infernal little brother was out of the picture. It was right, at last. I carry those moments in my heart, Becca."

Becca resembled a chained prisoner who had just inhaled poison gas. She knelt beside Jo and looked up at Rachel like a child hearing a particularly dreadful bedtime story. "My parents died on my fifth birthday. They gave me a birthday party that day, in our backyard. I remember the grass, music, other kids around, my uncle and aunt. You were there, Rachel. You gave me a present."

"Yes, I did. I gave you a doll."

"The doll was bloody that night, as I held it in the living room. And it wasn't my mother who handed it to me. Not at the party, and not that night. It was you."

Rachel nodded. "I wanted so badly to comfort you, Becca. You were so little. You were weeping, afraid, you looked so bereft and alone. I have always loved you, so much. I picked up your doll and gave it to you on my way out."

"There was blood on your hands," Becca said. "And on one of the doll's hands."

"Yes." Air seemed to leak out of Rachel slowly, and she sat slumped on the bed. Her eyes closed with a relief that struck Jo as entirely genuine.

"I can't ask for your forgiveness, Becca. But in honor of our many long years of friendship—in honor of the healing I've given you—can you find it in your heart, please, to leave me in peace? Let the horrors of my conscience be punishment enough, for the little time I have left. I promise you, they are horror indeed."

And again, Rachel was telling the absolute truth.

Becca sat motionless. "You paid Loren to kill me. To kill the woman I love."

"Yes," Rachel whispered.

Becca's fingers were ice-cold as they closed around Jo's, but her voice was low and steady. "You allowed the world to believe, for thirty years, that a woman you say you cherished was a murderer. You let her daughter believe it. I won't save you from paying the price, Rachel."

Becca rose to her feet, and rested her lips against the top of Rachel's bent head. She turned and went to the door, and Jo followed her. Becca didn't look back, but Jo did. Rachel was sitting quietly on the bed, watching a red flashing light turn through the colored panes.

Jo had no scathing last words for this particular murderer, but she found no pity in her heart. Rachel met her eyes one last time, and Jo left the room.

❖

Pam Emerson was leaning against her cruiser, her uniform smartly crisp in spite of her long night. Another cruiser sat next to hers, and Becca could see the silhouettes of two officers inside. Pam spoke into the mic clipped to her shoulder as they emerged through the doors of the hospice. The revolving red lights on the cruiser shut off. Pam took one look at them and cut straight to business.

"Mr. Perry is coming down off his high, and he's suddenly very talkative about his mama. He's got a long rap sheet and he'll face multiple charges, but we'll need your help making them stick."

"You'll have it." Becca felt the warmth of Jo's arm in hers and figured she could find strength for this on some future day.

"But Rachel Perry." Pam stepped closer to them, eyeing the doors of the hospice. "No promises, Becca. We'll charge her if she confesses today, but we won't take her in, given her illness. She's not exactly a flight risk. There's no statute of limitations on homicide, but I doubt she'll be prosecuted. If anything, they'll set it on the docket a year ahead. She'll be long gone, then."

"I know." Becca shivered, but Jo pressed her arm and that pleasant, detached peace descended on her again. "I don't need a bloodbath, Pam. I just want this investigation added to the official record."

"That'll be done," Pam promised her. "A damn thorough one. I take it I can get ahold of you guys by cell?"

"I'm afraid not." Jo spoke with the unquestioned authority of a goddess. "Neither of us will be available for the next three days. We're going to find the most beautiful vacation house on Cannon Beach, and we're going to rent it. We don't want to be disturbed."

"Yes, sir." Pam's eyebrows rose, but she smirked. "Guess I'm going to have to live with that. Sounds like an important trip."

"We're going to sleep." Becca spoke reverently. She appreciated Pam's innuendo, but she wanted no greater excitement than three solid nights of sleep, for them both. She was dizzy with relief at the prospect.

"Three days," Pam said sternly. "You call me when you get back. Travel safe." She pointed at the doors, and two other officers stepped out of the cruiser. "If you two don't want to be around for this, I'd make tracks now."

"We don't." Becca closed her eyes. "We're going."

Pam gripped Becca's arm, then moved past them with the other officers toward the hospice.

Becca turned to Jo and took her hands. "I love you," she said. "Just in case I haven't been clear on that until now."

"I love you back." Jo wet her lips, and Becca had to smile. Spontaneous displays of affection still made Jo a little nervous, but she was practicing, and their kiss was brief and sweet. "Now, let me take you away from here."

Becca nodded. "You can take me away, to the ocean. But there's a place I'd like to show you on the way."

CHAPTER TWENTY-TWO

Joanne. Dearest? I'm honestly not hungry."

"You will be. Any moment." Jo was reasonably certain of this as she pulled the BMW away from Top Pot Doughnuts. They had already stopped at Ezell's Chicken, and the lush interior of the car was filling with enticing fragrance.

She hoped Becca would be hungry soon; she craved that hint of returning normality, nature coming back into balance. The last twenty-four hours were a blur in Jo's mind, and she wasn't having to cope with the betrayal of a lifelong friend.

Becca had been silent since they left the hospice. She looked older in the harsh sunlight slanting through the window, but some animation was returning to her face at last. She still had tears to shed for Rachel Perry, and for old lies, old losses. Jo trusted she would be ready for them, whenever they came. "We're not in any hurry. The ocean isn't going anywhere, and neither is Mount Rainier."

"Neither are we," Becca pointed out.

"True."

Perhaps the morning of Gay Pride was not the wisest time to try to navigate Seattle streets. Jo braked at another intersection thronging with a rowdy crowd heading downtown.

"If I were driving, we'd be halfway to the mountain by now." Becca sighed. "I still can't believe they moved the march from Capitol Hill to Fourth Avenue."

Jo sighed too, in relief. Becca's remote melancholy seemed to be lifting. "Becca, that happened six years ago."

"It's still a sacrilege. An injustice most dire. Don't get Marty started on this subject."

Jo shrugged. "I never went to the march when it was on Broadway, and I don't go now. I've never felt it had anything to do with me."

"Yeah?" Becca studied her with an odd smile. "Look again. Tell me what you see."

Puzzled, Jo stared at the laughing men, women, and other genders passing in front of them. "Well. They all seem so young to me, these years. Still lots of white men. But…I like them. I like seeing all their children, their dogs. They look happy today."

"They're clan, Dr. Call." Becca brushed Jo's forearm with one finger. "Maybe distant kin, but still family, if you choose them. You're starting to let people into your life. You're seeing them with new eyes. Me, Marty, Khadijah, Pam. Mrs. Pam, when we meet her. You're building that clan you've always wanted, Jo. I'm happy for you."

Jo swallowed. "Thank you, Becca. I—"

"Now floor it," Becca suggested.

"Oh." Jo saw the cleared intersection and floored it.

Becca kept her hand on her arm as they drove out of the city.

❖

Jo tried not to tramp wildflowers flat with her boots, but missing them was all but impossible. They grew so thick in this mountain meadow it was like wading through a carpet of snarled color. She shifted, balancing the boxes of food in her arms and trying to keep Becca in sight ahead.

"You seem to know where we're going," Jo called hopefully.

"I do." Becca, carrying only a small satchel, gestured toward a copse of distant trees. "Just keep an eye out for the mountain Gestapo."

Jo took this warning seriously. She kept glancing over her shoulder toward the paved road far behind and above them, leading to the Paradise Inn. The leased BMW was parked just off a side path, reasonably hidden by brush.

The low fence Becca had stepped over so blithely was clearly posted, marking this field as off-limits. Apparently, her beloved was quite capable of felony. Jo understood why the officials who guarded Mount Rainier deemed these lush wildflowers too fragile for human traffic. Her attention was divided between stepping carefully and expecting arrest at any moment.

"This place wasn't cordoned off thirty years ago." Becca waited for her at the edge of the trees, panting lightly. "At least, I don't remember my parents smuggling me down here in their picnic basket, way back then. Come on. Through here."

That dimple appeared in Becca's cheek, and Jo would have followed her through the gates of hell. Or to prison, possibly, should any rangers find them in this field.

Jo recognized the tall young trees they wended through as white pine and maple, but she wasn't well versed in nature and couldn't be more specific than that. Their cool shade was welcome as the sun crested noon. The long box of doughnuts almost slid off her arm, but she pulled a quick save.

They emerged from the trees, and Jo's mouth fell open. She had always believed in an afterlife, but she'd never had a clear image in her mind of heaven. This came close.

Wildflowers exploded in wide swaths at their feet, cutting through the thick grass that layered the ground. But Jo's eyes were drawn immediately from their beauty to the stark glory of Mount Rainier above them, looming white and crystalline against the blue sky.

"Have mercy," Jo breathed.

Becca laughed. "That's what Khadijah said when she saw this place. Her exact words." She folded herself gracefully into the grass and Jo tried to follow suit, managing to set the boxes down without disaster.

"Those red, lacey cups over there are Indian Paintbrush." Becca nodded at a patch of scarlet blossoms dotting a small slope at their feet. "The little yellow claws are Glacier Lilies, and the ones that look like purple daisies are Alpine Asters."

"You know your wildflowers." Jo watched Becca's hair drift off her face with a breeze, grateful for the new peace in her eyes.

"I know the flowers here. Marty and Khadijah drove me up here when I was nineteen years old. Well. They drove me up here several times. We circled Rainier for an entire summer, looking for this meadow. We had a guide to go by."

Becca opened the satchel in the grass at her side. She drew out a small framed square, her hands gentle on its wooden corners. She studied it, then handed it to Jo.

It was a simple oil painting of Mount Rainier, well done, unsigned, less than a foot square. Its colors had faded slightly, but the perspective was unmistakable. Jo looked up and saw an exact image of the mountain reigning over the meadow.

"My mother drew Rainier during our picnics here when I was little. She made that painting from her sketches. I knew we'd found the right place when the mountain looked down at us from precisely that angle."

"You found the right place," Jo agreed. She imagined Madelyn Healy's fine hand holding a brush, stroking the craggy peaks to life. Becca's fingers were gentle in the grass between them.

"I could always picture my parents so clearly in this meadow. When I'd been clean for one year, I asked my friends to help me find it. Khadijah and Marty were with me when I scattered my parents' ashes here."

Jo could see them too, now. Scott Healy sitting at the base of this very tree, reading a newspaper. His lovely blond wife nestled in the grass nearby with a pad of creamy paper in her lap, sketching. And a very small girl dancing in the sunlight amid the riot of wildflowers.

Becca touched the frame of the painting and checked her heart. She was sure. "I brought this with us because I'd like you to have it, Jo."

Jo looked stunned. "This painting? Your mother made this. It has to be precious to you."

"It is, sure. I know you'll take good care of it." Becca sat back on her hands, the sun warm on her face. "Consider it a thank-you gift from my mom. And from me."

"But Becca, this is—"

"Joanne. You made it possible for me to bring peace to my dead mother." Becca smiled. "You'd be astonished how rarely this happens in relationships." She nudged her gently. "Honey. It's all right to accept a gift from a friend who loves you."

"A friend I love." Jo was quiet, cradling the frame in her hands. "Thank you, Becca. I'll treasure this."

Jo lifted the satchel and slid the painting carefully into it. "I wanted to give you a gift, too. I was going to wait for a moonlit night on the beach, but I like this place better."

Becca realized the gift Jo intended before she drew the music box out of her shirt, and her throat constricted. Aside from her beloved Spiricom, this was the only personal possession she had ever seen Jo touch with true affection. She accepted the box and rested it on her knees. Jo was content to let her sit quietly for a moment, which was a good thing, because she couldn't speak.

The square she held in her hands was soft, covered by worn purple cloth. The wood beneath it was strong, and it held music, like Jo. Finally, she lifted the lid, and soft, tinkling notes issued from the small speaker. Becca remembered hearing this light Spanish melody the first time she saw the music box in Jo's home.

"Tell me about her," she said.

"Her name was Consuelo, and she was my mother." Jo's low voice was tender, like the music. "My parents hired her as an au pair. She was with me for six years, until I was ten. She only left me because her younger sister was deported to Mexico. My parents were kind enough, but Consuelo was all I knew of real maternal love. She gave this to me the day she left."

"And you're giving it to me."

"You're all I know of real love, Becca."

It would have taken her breath away if she'd had any air to spare.

Jo kissed her, and there was nothing nervous or hesitant in her now. Becca was still aware of the sweet scent of the wildflowers and the sun on her face. She still heard music, but all of that pretty much faded in the warm blend of Jo's lips against her own.

"You're getting really good at that," she gasped finally.

"I know." Jo sounded proud. "You're a good teacher. Becca?"

"Joanne?"

"We don't have to spend the entire three days at the beach sleeping." The contours of Jo's side were quite close against her. "If you'd be willing to continue my lessons in Becca School."

"Hey." Becca brushed her finger beneath Jo's chin. "Please consider class in session."

The kiss lasted longer this time, and Jo's light touch on her breast was welcome, very welcome, too welcome, and Becca lifted her head quickly.

"Sorry. I'm sorry," she stammered. "But not here. I simply can't carry on like trash in this meadow, not with the possible ghosts of my parents looking on."

Becca bit her lip, but Jo just grinned down at her.

"All right. You'll find I'm a patient woman. Tell me what you need from me now, Becca."

Becca thought about this. It didn't take long.

"First, I want to honor your impulse to feed me. I wouldn't want to hurt your feelings by refusing this picnic. So now, we're going to eat a lot of junk food."

"Of course."

"Then we're going to drive to the nicest house on the beach, where we will enjoy three days of Becca School."

"That sounds delightful."

"And I'm going to drive."

"Of course."

The End

About the Author

Cate Culpepper has resided in Seattle for the past twenty years. She's the author of the *Tristaine* series, *Fireside*, and *River Walker*. Her books have won three Golden Crown Literary Society Awards, a Lambda Literary Award, a Lesbian Fiction Readers' Choice Award, and an Alice B. Medal for her body of work.

Books Available From Bold Strokes Books

Oath of Honor by Radclyffe. A First Responders novel. First do no harm…First Physician of the United States, Wes Masters, discovers that being the president's doctor demands more than brains and personal sacrifice—especially when politics is the order of the day. (978-1-60282-671-7)

A Question of Ghosts by Cate Culpepper. Becca Healy hopes Dr. Joanne Call can help her learn if her mother really committed suicide—but she's not sure she can handle her mother's ghost, a decades-old mystery, and lusting after the difficult Dr. Call without some serious chocolate consumption. (978-1-60282-672-4)

The Night Off by Meghan O'Brien. When Emily Parker pays for a taboo role-playing fantasy encounter from the Xtreme Encounters escort agency, she expects to surrender control—but never imagines losing her heart to dangerous butch, Nat Swayne. (978-1-60282-673-1)

Sara by Greg Herren. A mysterious and beautiful new student at Southern Heights High School stirs things up when students start dying. (978-1-60282-674-8)

Fontana by Joshua Martino. Fame, obsession, and vengeance collide in a novel that asks: What if America's greatest hero was gay? (978-1-60282-675-5)

Lemon Reef by Robin Silverman. What would you risk for the memory of your first love? When Jenna Ross learns her high school love Del Soto died on Lemon Reef, she refuses to accept the medical examiner's report of a death from natural causes and risks everything to find the truth. (978-1-60282-676-2)

The Dirty Diner: Gay Erotica on the Menu edited by Jerry Wheeler. Gay erotica set in restaurants, featuring food, sex, and men—could you really ask for anything more? (978-1-60282-677-9)

Slingshot by Carsen Taite. Bounty hunter Luca Bennett takes on a seemingly simple job for defense attorney Ronnie Moreno, but the job quickly turns complicated and dangerous, as does her attraction to the elusive Ronnie Moreno. (978-1-60282-666-3)

Touch Me Gently by D. Jackson Leigh. Secrets have always meant heartbreak and banishment to Salem Lacey until she meets the beautiful and mysterious Knox Bolander and learns some secrets are necessary. (978-1-60282-667-0)

Missing by P.J. Trebelhorn. FBI agent Olivia Andrews knows exactly what she wants out of life, but then she's forced to rethink everything when she meets fellow agent Sophie Kane while investigating a child abduction. (978-1-60282-668-7)

Sweat: Gay Jock Erotica edited by Todd Gregory. Sizzling tales of smoking-hot sex with the athletic studs everyone fantasizes about. (978-1-60282-669-4)

The Marrying Kind by Ken O'Neill. Just when successful wedding planner Adam More decides to protest inequality by quitting the business and boycotting marriage entirely, his only sibling announces her engagement. (978-1-60282-670-0)

Dark Wings Descending by Lesley Davis. What if the demons you face in life are real? Chicago detective Rafe Douglas is about to find out. (978-1-60282-660-1)

sunfall by Nell Stark and Trinity Tam. The final installment of the everafter series. Valentine Darrow and Alexa Newland work to rebuild their relationship even as they find themselves at the heart of the struggle that will determine a new world order for vampires and wereshifters. (978-1-60282-661-8)

Mission of Desire by Terri Richards. Nicole Kennedy finds herself in Africa at the center of an international conspiracy and being rescued by beautiful but arrogant government agent Kira Anthony, but is Kira someone Nicole can trust or is she blinded by desire? (978-1-60282-662-5)

Boys of Summer edited by Steve Berman. Stories of young love and adventure, when the sky's ceiling is a bright blue marvel, when another boy's laughter at the beach can distract from dull summer jobs. (978-1-60282-663-2)

The Locket and the Flintlock by Rebecca S. Buck. When Regency gentlewoman Lucia Foxe is robbed on the highway, will the masked outlaw who stole Lucia's precious locket also claim her heart? (978-1-60282-664-9)

Calendar Boys by Logan Zachary. A man a month will keep you excited year round. (978-1-60282-665-6)